The

the Prince

and the Pirate

Vanessa Hancock

Wild Blackberry Publishing

ISBN: 9798865985051

Image by kjpargeter on Freepik
Image by onfocus on Freepik

Wild Blackberry Publishing

DEDICATION

To my fabulous four! Life may not always be easy, but how beautiful that we share the songs of our hearts along the way.

ACKNOWLEDGEMENTS

Mrs. Patricia Martin for her endless encouragement and graciousness

Thank you Patsy Fowler and Patrick Patterson for helping me naming my pirate ship

Lynna, you give me honesty to help create worlds

CHAPTER

One

Mikal stood up and shouted, "Are you crazy? We can't kidnap the Prince!"

Jazier turned abruptly, "We can with Alahandra's help."

Mikal knew Jazier was growing tired of Alahandra's attitude. "You can't ask her to do this. I don't want her to be a part of any of this. She isn't like us."

Jazier laughed, "Isn't like us? You can't be serious. Where do you think the bread comes from that you so enjoy for breakfast? My friend, your daughter has the stickiest fingers I have ever seen in all my days of thievery. She is cunning and sly, and she could charm the clouds right out of the sky."

Mikal couldn't argue. He had taught his only daughter to steal from the market when she was little so they could have food to survive. Living with Jazier was purely out of necessity. He always found shelter. The woods they found just last year gave them safe haven, and being so near the village gave them convenience needed for basic survival. Together they built a small shack to keep them out of the rain and cold. Alahandra was older now and grew tired of taking orders from Jazier. They needed money and needed it fast.

"Alahandra will help with the Prince, or you both can leave." Jazier knelt down near the fire.

"I'll talk to her when she returns from the village," Mikal said with a heaviness. He was ready to be finished with stealing as a way to live but didn't know how to make that happen.

How he missed Soldra. She had been his only love, and when she died in childbirth, she took his heart with her. He was left to raise Alahandra on his own. He gave up on everything and had nothing left to share with his daughter. Little by little Mikal had to sell what they had to survive. It didn't take long until they were without a home. He and his little girl had to face the cruel world without any help and without any hope. How fast time had passed, and now his daughter was a young woman of age to marry but never wanting to.

"I'll not be a slave to some ignorant man when I can live under the open sky and go as I please," Alahandra said often.

Jazier dropped a plate at Mikal's feet. "You didn't hear a word I said, did you?"

Mikal shook his head.

Jazier spoke with a malicious look. "I said, you will tell her she has one week to get invited to that ball the King and Queen are throwing for the Prince's twenty-fifth birthday, or I will turn you both out. One week, Mikal."

Mikal nodded. He knew persuading Alahandra to do anything that Jazier wanted her to do was going to be a miracle in itself.

The smell of fresh bread coming from the baker's stone oven drifted through the morning air and made Alahandra stop to savor the aroma. How she loved fresh bread. The baker never noticed the loaf she took off the back corner of the stack he would make for the opening of the market. Oh, she had to be sly. Buying a little along the way, as if she lived alone and was buying her breakfast each morning.

The bag she carried had trinkets she would use to barter with the marketplace people, but if they dared take their eyes off her for even a second she could easily slip apples or potatoes in her bag. There was always a moment that eyes were off the money boxes and a coin could find its way into her bag. There was great skill in being cunning enough to fool the baker. His ever watchful eyes in the back of his head made Alahandra nervous, but she smiled tenderly at him, and he always blushed. Only as of late had she been able to use the fact that she was a woman to pull all the stupidity out of a man and cause his sanity to lapse just long enough for her to rob him blind. It was as if after her twenty-fourth birthday something had unlocked inside her. Other young women her age were settled into marriage and beginning a family, but no one ever mentioned her lack of those things in her life. Perhaps it was her skin being darkened by the sun that gave her a more youthful look that caused others to ignore her status, or perhaps no one really cared. Whatever the case, she had no intentions of having her heart snared.

"If a man can be so easily distracted by the smile of a woman he doesn't know, then why would I want one. I'll not fight for the affection of any man." She had told her father the night before. "You should see the mill worker down by the creek. Old enough to be my father and slammed the hammer onto his thumb when I stretched my arms above my head to help an elderly woman get a basket."

"It's just that your beauty far exceeds the women they are used to seeing, dear child," Mikal laughed. "But don't be fooled. A man sees a pretty face and forgets there's a brain in there too. Men will say whatever they can to convince you that you can't live without them."

"Well, unless he's got gold in his pockets, a boat to take me out onto the open sea away from here, then he best keep walking lest he should stumble upon my dagger," Alahandra smiled.

"Aye, I fear for the man that falls for you. He'll not only need a fortune, but be made of steel for the times he angers you."

"No worries, sweet father of mine. I have no intention of giving my heart to any man. Men only give back broken and useless hearts. My heart is forever pointed toward the open road, the open sea, and the open sky."

As she walked in the marketplace she wondered if there would be a time when she would want love. She wondered if a love existed that would last forever. The flour woman stood up quickly and slapped her husband, the egg cart man when his eyes were lingering too long on Alahandra. She laughed, shook her head, and went on her way taking little by little as she made her way to the end of the street.

A new sign was posted above the small building that had sat empty for some time now. "Haya's Dress Shop" and from the looks of it, the door was unlocked and ready for business. Intrigued and amused, Alahandra quietly moved through the door and closed it gently behind her.

As she looked around at all the finery she became aware of her appearance.

Her clothes were worn and tattered by the many washings by hand. Her shirt repaired many times over was big enough for almost two of her, and her pants were a pair of her father's she had taken in and hemmed. The dirt on her arms and face proved bathing for her was not always an option. Her dark hair was always frizzed around her face, not owning a brush, and she kept it pulled back and low with a leather piece that she found at the back of the tavern. Her hands she kept clean for eating when she had the chance. She knew others looked upon her as a pauper and a thief so she made as many friends as possible throughout the market to keep sympathy at a high.

Her biggest secret was that she wanted her own dress. She knew she could never own the finest cloth and ribbons, but to be able to walk down the street in an ordinary dress, be invisible among the villagers, and simply blend in with the world was her goal. Perhaps someday she could find a way to make her own money so she and her father could give up life on the run.

Alahandra touched the beautiful fabric filling the tables. It was as if the air itself flowed under her fingers. Nothing she had ever known had felt so fine.

"It's an exquisite piece isn't it, deary?" a voice behind her said softly.

Alahandra turned to see a short older woman with the greenest eyes. She moved quickly away from the cloth, startled and not wanting to appear in want of such an expensive thing.

"It is that, yes, and unlike anything I've ever seen. Where did it come from?" Alahandra tried to not sound shaken by the woman.

"Ah, I came to own that piece not so long ago. Bartered with a pirate for it, I did. Now, is there something I can help you with?" The old woman smiled.

"I didn't want anything. I just noticed your shop, and I've never seen it open. I hope you do well here." Alahandra felt a strange sense of belonging in the shop.

The old woman laughed. "Well, thank you, my dear. I'm hoping this shop will help keep me here. I've had my share of adventures, and I'm ready to settle, I am."

Alahandra was intrigued. "What kind of adventures?"

"How about you come back tomorrow, and we'll have some tea by the fire. I could use some company. I'm still getting things organized today, and can you believe I already have 5 dress orders? You come back tomorrow, and I'll tell you about my adventures." The old woman stepped closer to Alahandra. "I'm Haya, but I guess you must have figured that out by my sign outside."

Alahandra shook her hand. "I'm Alahandra, and I'm pleased to meet you."

Haya patted Alahandra on the arm as she walked her to the door. "Nice to have a friend in town. Tomorrow then?"

Alahandra smiled, "I'll be here." She turned and walked out of the store. Taking a deep breath of the morning air made Alahandra feel alive. Walking back through town she realized for the first time someone actually wanted to spend time with her. It made her stomach ache.

What would Haya think of her if she knew the truth? Haya had said something that sparked her interest. She already had five dress orders. Alahandra knew how to mend and would be willing to learn how to sew if Haya could teach her. She would ask her tomorrow if she needed help. A real job making real money, and in that shop she could learn how to sew her own dress. Alahandra walked happily thinking of all the possibilities that could come from a job.

Looking off in the distance she didn't see the man bent over in front of her. She stumbled into him and knocked him down. She lost her balance and fell across his legs.

"Madam, you will do well to watch where you are going!" the man snapped at her.

"You would do good not to bend down in the middle of the marketplace," Alahandra said loudly. "I was going to apologize, but you don't deserve it."

Two guards stepped forward and took Alahandra lifting her up, and then helped up the man. He dusted himself off.

The guards stepped back and took hold of Alahandra. She tried to break free. They held her tighter. One spoke to the man. "Shall we arrest her?"

"Arrest me, for what, daydreaming?" Alahandra tried to pull away.

"No, it was an accident. Let her go," the man said. He looked at Alahandra. "You will leave."

The guards let her go. Alahandra stood her ground and glared at him. "I'll leave when I get ready to leave. Who do you think you are?"

The flour lady was listening to the conversation. "That's the Prince, dear. Best be on your way."

Alahandra's eyes widened. How lowly she must look to royalty. It angered her. She bowed to him. "Excuse me, Princey. I wouldn't want you to have to be too near us common folk."

She turned to walk away as gasps and whispers surrounded her. She just wanted to disappear. Perhaps it would be best to stay clear of the market for a while and hunt for their food. She needed the people to forget her untamed mouth and feel sorry for her again or she might never be able to swipe anything from them. Then she thought of Haya. She didn't want to miss time with her and a chance to ask her about a job. Perhaps she could find a way through the woods that would lead her closer to Haya's shop without having to go directly through the marketplace.

Making her way to the end of town she turned to see if anyone was watching as she turned into the brush. She wanted to make sure no one followed her to the shack where they were staying.

Walking through the woods gave her a sense of freedom. The smell of the earth, the rustling of the leaves, and the path that felt like an old friend welcoming her for a walk. She had walked the path so many times that she didn't have to think about her footing.

She smiled when she saw her father sitting by the fire. "Hello," she announced. She didn't want to startle him. He turned and smiled at her.

"I brought us a good breakfast today," she said, giving half the bread from her bag.

Jazier came out of the shack. "Tell her, Mikal."

Alahandra moved to stand by her father. "Tell me what?"

"Jazier has a plan," Mikal said. "He wants to kidnap the Prince for ransom."

Alahandra laughed.

Jazier stepped forward. "You have to get invited to the ball the King and Queen are throwing for his birthday. Rumor has it he is coming to the marketplace daily this week to invite townspeople. Not on his own, mind you. The King is making a grand gesture to the town hoping to create stronger loyalties among his people. It's said to be the biggest event this kingdom has ever seen. You will go to the ball and woo the Prince to come outside with you. We will take him once he is outside without the guards."

Alahandra stood listening with her anger growing. She started to speak, but Jazier held up his hand. "You will do this, Alahandra, or you and your father can move on out of here. And, I'm sure the good people of this town would love to know how you steal from them."

Alahandra closed her eyes for a moment taking in what he had said. She was trapped. "I saw the Prince today. Woo him? That pompous brat!"

Mikal turned to her. "Did he see you?"

Alahandra laughed. "When I knocked him down, I was hard to miss," she laughed harder.

Jazier grabbed her by the arm. "At least when she's cleaned up and in a dress he won't know it was her."

Alahandra snatched her arm away from Jazier. "Since you mentioned it, where exactly do you expect me to obtain a dress to go to the ball in, and what exactly do you expect me to wear to get invited to this gala event?"

Mikal pulled a necklace from his pocket.

Alahandra took it quickly from his hand. "This is all that I have left of my mother. You said I never had to part with it."

Mikal looked to the ground. "It will buy you all you need to make this work."

Alahandra turned to walk away. She stopped knowing she had no choice. She said softly, "I'll do whatever I have to do. But, know that when this is done I will take my share, and I will leave." She took a deep breath. "I'm going to go back to the village. Leave me be, and I'll let you know when I get the invitation."

CHAPTER

Two

Alahandra made her way through the woods knowing she couldn't go through town for fear of seeing the Prince again. She didn't have time to make a new trail in hopes of finding a new route to the other end of town. She had to be clever and go around the edge without being seen. Owners of the stores and stands didn't like people going behind their establishments. It screamed thievery. She would dodge into the woods whenever she could find a chance, but she had to be quick. She needed every moment of this day.

After stepping in mud, being chased by a dog, tearing her pants in a briar patch, and catching her hair on a branch, she made it to the end of town and could see Haya's shop. Moving quickly, she entered and closed the door. The bell hanging on the door jingled.

"I'll be right there. Feel free to look around!" Haya yelled from the back.

Alahandra stood completely still not wanting to soil anything around her.

Haya walked around the wall and stopped. She looked at Alahandra, paused, and then started laughing. "Oh dear, what happened to you child?"

"It's a long story, but I need to ask you something. I couldn't wait for tomorrow." Alahandra produced the necklace from her pocket. "Would you be willing to make me two dresses for this? I need an everyday kind of dress and a ball gown."

Haya took the necklace from Alahandra and moved it through her fingers. "Such a fine piece. Old. Very old. Dear, this is a diamond. Why, even with what you ask of me I would still owe you money. Anyone else, I might not tell that too, but I don't want to cheat you. By the look on your face, you don't really want to part with it, do you?"

Alahandra breathed deep and sighed. "Like I said, it's a long story, but this is all I have that I can trade. Since you say that it's worth so much, is there any way it could buy me a place to sleep in the back of your shop? I'm willing to work if you have anything I can do. I can learn to sew. I can hem. I'll clean. Anything at all. I'll do anything at all."

Haya looked at Alahandra. "With this necklace you could go to any shop and buy your dresses."

Alahandra looked down at herself and laughed. "I don't think they would sell to me, and they would accuse me of stealing the necklace. It was my mother's."

Haya closed her hand around the exquisite piece of jewelry. "I don't know what it is about you, my dear, but I like you. And, since I usually don't like anyone, I say you must be something special. I think perhaps there might be space back in the back for you. I've turned the entire back of the store into a little place of my own, so company will be appreciated. I only have one bed, but we can make you a place until that pirate comes back around. He'll no doubt have something we can barter for that will make for a bed for you. But for now, let's get you cleaned up. I have some old dresses that were going to be thrown out by other customers in my last shop that I have kept in an old trunk in the back. I'll get one and we can get rid of those clothes."

Alahandra spoke quickly, "Please, if you will, give these back to me. I hunt in them, and I wouldn't want to go into the woods with a dress on."

Haya smiled and nodded, "I believe you have stories of your own to share."

Alahandra laughed, "We shall never lack for conversation."

Haya hung a sheet up for privacy and placed a basin of water on the table for Alahandra.

"Go ahead back there, dear, and get cleaned. If the dress I laid out for you doesn't fit, let me know, and I'll get another one for you." Haya said.

"Oh, I'm sure it will be fine." Alahandra said as she began to clean her face. The water was warmed and the cloth was soft against her skin. She took her time to remove all the mud and dirt from her body.

After Alahandra had cleaned herself up and changed clothes, she came from behind the sheet. Haya's eyes widened. "My dear, do you have any idea how beautiful you are?"

Alahandra's face reddened. "You are kind."

"No, I am honest. You would think that dress was made just for you. It's yours, and this one is on me. It will be a good start for your new look. Haya stood up and took a brush from her dresser. "Let me brush your hair. It's in frightful tangles. Can I braid it for you?"

"I would like that. I've never had anyone help me with my hair before." Alahandra paused, not wanting to give Haya too much information all at once.

She wanted to hear more about the pirate Haya had mentioned and thought it would be a good way to get the conversation off of her. "So how often does this pirate come to port?"

"As often as he can to see his mum, but not as often as I would like. I miss him so." Haya's comment drifted into a whisper as she brushed Alahandra's hair.

Alahandra turned around. "Your son is the pirate you spoke of?"

"Yes, I'm afraid so. His ship overtook a ship filled with great treasures. Much of this cloth being on board. I didn't barter with him to get things. I couldn't tell you the truth until I felt like I could trust you. Being the mother of said pirate, I told him to give all the cloth to me to open this fine store." The old woman laughed. "Now don't you go telling my secrets to these townspeople. Uppity refined and simply lost they are, those that have come to buy from me. Wanting to adorn

15

themselves with such finery and it all be stolen. I laugh when I think of sewing their fine gowns and wonder what they'd do if the owner of this cloth came and ripped it right from them. Oh, laugh I do, because to me it's just business. I care not for what they say. Calling me a witch and all. I'm not you know. I just like to act a bit more rustic than most of the townspeople. I'm actually born of noble blood you see, but I refused to become what I saw in me mum so long ago. So I left my brother, the only friend I ever had, and I ran away. Took to the sea, I did, and never looked back." The woman looked at Alahandra. "Let's get that hair fixed shall we?"

Alahandra nodded, and Haya led her to a chair near a full basin of water where she lathered the soap through Alahandra's hair. It felt cleaner than she had ever known.

She mulled over what Haya had said. Her son was a pirate. A real pirate. She wondered if when the ransom was paid for the Prince if she could convince Haya's son to take her away from here. She could start anew in a different land, and never have to think of stealing again.

"Your mind must be far away. I don't think you've heard a single word I've said," Haya laughed.

"I was just thinking about your son. I would like to meet him someday. I am fascinated by pirates. I know it's a vulgar thing for a woman to talk about, but it's true. I used to dream of stowing away on a pirate ship to see how much of the world I could see," Alahandra said.

"Well, a pirate ship is not the place for any woman. I can tell you that. I've gone out with my son before, traversed the seas, and I won't go again. He's not like the others on board, not like the crew. It is a dangerous way to live and not an honest one among the lot of them. He is different. If you meet him you will see what I mean. You wouldn't know he was a pirate. He's clean cut and beautiful. It's why he is so successful at thievery. A gentleman pirate is what they tease him to be, but he is a cutthroat just like the rest of them and will prove himself to gain respect if need be."

Haya sighed. "Funny thing. You would be perfect for him if he wasn't a pirate."

Alahandra turned and smiled at Haya. A quiet moment of understanding passed between them. A moment that gave Alahandra a feeling of comfort and peace. How hard it was going to be to lie to Haya, do all that had to be done, and leave. She hoped that in the time that she had with her, she could simply enjoy her only friend.

"Time to look at yourself." Haya stood and led Alahandra to a side area beyond the wall. "I call this the fitting room. It has a giant mirror from a load of treasure commandeered."

Alahandra moved in front of the full length mirror and gasped. "Oh Haya! Thank you!" Her raven hair captured the sunlight coming through the window, and her dark blue eyes matched the color of her dress.

"It was the Creator himself that gave all that to you my dear. I just helped straighten it all. You are stunning, even in that simple dress. I cannot imagine you in a finer gown fit for a ball. You'll steal the heart of the Prince right away along with every other man in the ballroom."

Alahandra laughed. "You do say the funniest things." She looked at herself over again, and would not have recognized herself. She wondered if the Prince would.

"One last thing." Haya stood behind Alahandra and put the necklace on her neck.

"Haya, no, I…"

"It's perfect on you, and your mother would be happy that you're wearing it."

Alahandra moved her fingers over the beautiful piece of jewelry. "I've put it on many times, but never felt like I do right now."

"Sometimes the right moment presents itself and everything just feels right." Haya patted her arm.

Alahandra looked at herself and smiled.

"Now my dear, I'm all but starving, and I need you to go out to the market to buy us lunch. There's an old woman in the middle of the marketplace that likes to roast meat. She's a sly one she is, but you give her one coin for two sticks of roasted meat. I dealt with her yesterday."

"I know her. She's not very nice, and I've wanted to try that meat," Alahandra laughed. "I just never have approached her."

Alahandra took the coin and made her way through the market. She came to the old woman selling meat and asked for two sticks. The aroma drifted through the air and made Alahandra's stomach tighten. She realized she had not eaten since lunch the day before.

The old woman looked her up and down. "This fine meat is one coin each."

Alahandra leaned closer. "This meat is two sticks for one coin, or I can go buy meat from the butcher to cook myself. Perhaps I can open a stand and sell three for one coin, or four."

The old woman looked at Alahandra and took four sticks from the roasting fire. She wrapped them in paper and handed them to her. Alahandra put her hand up. "I only wanted two. I don't want to cheat you."

The old woman laughed. "Deary, you are the only person in this market that has ever even spoken to me that way. I think I scare people here. Truth is, I make enough that I can sell you four for one coin. You come back anytime. Just don't tell anyone else, and I'll always give you a fair deal." The woman winked at Alahandra.

"Thank you…"

"Celia, my dear. You may call me Celia," the old woman smiled.

"Thank you, Celia," Alahandra said with a slight curtsy.

The old woman curtsied back, and slapped her leg laughing.

Alahandra turned to go and bumped into someone. "Pardon me."

The Prince bowed before her. "No, pardon me, miss." He looked at her and didn't move. He stood there staring at her. She lowered her gaze, and curtsied slightly.

"I forget myself, my lady. Your beauty hypnotized me. Forgive me."

Alahandra nodded, wanting to get away from him before he realized she was the same woman from the morning. She turned to go.

"Wait. I must ask you something," The Prince was following her.

She walked faster.

"I'm sorry, your highness, I must hurry on my way. I'll be late for work and lose my job. Forgive me," Alahandra lied.

The Prince stopped and watched Alahandra walk through the marketplace. He watched as she entered the dress shop. "A thousand times over I would forgive you," he whispered.

"Sire, we must return to the King. He will be expecting a report from your venture," a man said, walking past the guards.

"I know what my father expects of me, Beasley, old friend. If you weren't in his service to watch my every move, I do believe I would chase down that beautiful siren that has absconded with my heart and whisk her away on the next ship in port."

"I'm going to pretend I didn't hear that and get you back to the palace," the older gentleman said.

"I want to return here tomorrow and ask her to the ball," the Prince said quietly.

"Be careful, sire. She has her place here, and you have your place," Beasley said.

"With her at the ball, I might not dread it so much. Besides, Father told me to invite the peasants, right? I am merely doing as I am told," the Prince said. "Let's go before I forget the crown in my future."

Alahandra went inside the dress shop and shut the door quickly. Haya came to the front room.

"I've drawn the water and tea is on," Haya smiled.

Alahandra remained silent.

"Dear, is everything alright?" Haya asked.

"I bumped into the Prince this morning and again just now. He didn't even realize I was the same person." The thought of it all infuriated Alahandra.

"Well, my dear, when you are all cleaned up, that raven hair catches every ray of sunshine and your skin glistens. You are not fair skinned like other women. The sun has made your skin golden, and you look wild like you're from the jungles I have heard about in stories."

"I've always loved being in the sun and swimming in the lagoon. There's such freedom there. I know if I stayed indoors, I would look more fair-skinned and would be more like other women my age."

"And you would be as boring as they all are. Never feel like you have to be something different or change for anyone," Haya smiled.

"I appreciate that, Haya. I've never had to be around many people, and the Prince made me uncomfortable. I didn't like it," Alahandra admitted.

"He is a ravishing man to behold, I must say," Haya said. "But, don't let him make you uncomfortable. You just need more confidence."

"I am confident in my old clothes with a bow in my hand and a knife in my belt," Alahandra said.

Haya laughed. "Well, you can't help that you're beautiful, and you just learn to hold your head high knowing you can stand against anyone by just being you."

Alahandra nodded and opened the paper producing the four sticks of meat.

Haya laughed again. "Did you steal these?"

"No," Alahandra smiled, "I just told her to be fair and she gave me four. She said I can always have a deal from her because I actually talked to her. I'll be sure to get lunch from her often for us."

Haya sat down at the table and motioned to Alahandra to do the same. "You are full of mystery, you are. Now let us eat this fine lunch and get to work. We have your dress to make before I make any of the others."

Alahandra smiled. She felt welcome in the four walls, but knew her time here was limited. The Prince had shaken her, but she knew that catching his eye was key. Now all she had to do was get her courage up to talk to him. She had to get invited to the ball.

CHAPTER
Three

Alahandra woke to the smell of eggs cooking on the stove. She had not slept so sound in a very long time. Being with Haya made her feel at peace in a way she had never known. A lonely feeling crept in her heart and she knew the day she had to say goodbye would break her heart.

"Ready to eat?" Haya said, as Alahandra got up.

"My stomach seems to think so. You should have woken me to help," Alahandra said.

"My dear, you looked so peaceful I didn't want to wake you. It's been a long time since I have done for anyone, I was simply enjoying cooking. Plus, the sun has yet to greet the day."

Alahandra wanted to know more about the woman she was staying with and took her lead into the conversation.

"Thank you for the dressing gown. I have never had anything so soft in all my life," Alahandra said, hugging her arms.

"I'm glad I had not cut that one up to use for cleaning cloths. It fits you perfectly."

"I need to change quickly before I eat," she continued. "How long have you been alone?" Alahandra asked.

Haya sighed. "Nonsense, come eat first, and I've been alone for far too long. The man I loved was a man of the sea. He worked on merchant ships, sailed with great soldiers, and was a great explorer. One day he left, and his ship never returned. A village full of broken hearts there were. Many women lost their husbands that day. We were to be married. He didn't even know he was to be a father."

Alahandra came to the table and put her hand on Haya's. "I'm so sorry."

"I sailed with him for many years, and then I got a job helping in the dress shop in the little village where his ship made port. We were wanting to settle there and raise a family. A beautiful man he was until the sea took him. I see him in Rylic's eyes."

"That's your son?" Alahandra asked.

"Yes, Rylic is his name. When he turned to the sea it almost broke my heart all over again, but it's in his blood as true as the sunshine pours from the sky. I could no longer catch laughter in my hand than I could try to keep that boy on land. He is my joy, but he will never come here to stay."

A knock at the door startled them both.

Haya rose from the table. "Who could that be at this early hour?" She whispered low. " The sun is not even up."

She stopped and took a knife from the drawer.

Alahandra followed her to the front room.

Haya leaned to the door. "The sign says closed. We open later in the day. You'll have to come back."

"You mean I've come all this way and don't even get a hug from my mum?" a man said. His voice was deep, and he spoke with an accent similar to Haya's.

Haya's face brightened, and she quickly opened the door. A tall dark haired man stepped in and scooped up the older woman in his arms. She laughed. Alahandra smiled, and a warm feeling passed through her.

The man noticed Alahandra and put Haya down.

Haya smiled. "Rylic, this is Alahandra. She's staying with me, and I'm going to be teaching her to sew."

Alahandra had never seen a man like Rylic. His face was darkened by the sun, and his hair was as black as hers. He wore rings of great worth on his fingers. He also wore a pouch around his waist.

She noticed he was staring at her just as she was staring at him.

Haya laughed. "Well, are either of you going to speak?"

Rylic stepped forward and took Alahandra's hand, kissing it gently. "Forgive me. I am Rylic of The Lady Amore and The Silver Phoenix."

Alahandra felt the heat rise to her face. She had never had a man kiss her hand before. He still held her hand, and she became aware that she was only wearing her dressing gown. She cleared her throat. "I am Alahandra. So you're the pirate?"

Rylic laughed. "Oh, you know about me, do you?" he said, releasing her hand.

Haya nudged him. "Be nice."

"I am a pirate, so best not leave your purse strings open, fair maiden."

Alahandra felt challenged and couldn't contain herself. "Are you looking for ways to lose fingers or is it the entire hand you want removed?"

Rylic was silent. Haya was silent. Alahandra felt her heart begin to pound. She had overstepped in her anger, and Haya would probably send her on her way.

Rylic leaned his head back and laughed. "Oh, you are too wonderful, beautiful woman."

Haya took Alahandra's hand. "She's not one to go toe to toe with Rylic. She is a spirited one she is."

Alahandra decided to direct the conversation elsewhere. "Would you like to join us for breakfast?"

Rylic removed his sword and locked the door. "I would love to, my lady."

Haya clapped her hands. "Now this is going to be an amazing day."

The three made their way to the table. Alahandra took a plate and sat down on the floor where she had slept on bedding prepared by Haya.

"You'll not sit on the floor, dear child. I have a stool I can use. You take this chair." Haya said.

Alahandra noticed how Haya had changed with Rylic there. She was joyful and couldn't stop smiling.

"I'll take the stool, Mum." Rylic sat down and began to eat. "I do love when you cook. I have new spices for you, and some beautiful new trinkets you can sell here. Nothing like taking cargo from a Middle Eastern ship. There was so much in the haul that I need you to come see what you can use. You too, Alahandra."

Alahandra looked at Rylic. His gaze lingered on her, and she felt heat rise in her face. Never had she met such a man as this. Wild. Free. She knew she should have lowered her eyes from his, but she could not bring herself to look away. Staring at him as he stared at her made him smile.

Haya interrupted their silence. "We best be on our way before the town stirs. We can clean up from breakfast later. I can borrow a wagon from the blacksmith. He'll be up. He usually is by now."

Rylic raised an eyebrow. "And how would you know the rising and lending of the good blacksmith?"

Haya laughed. "Oh, you silly boy. He drools at the sight of gold. I gave him two gold pieces once and told him there might be a time I would need his wagon, and if he would allow me to use it, he could take the gold with no questions. Since then we share breakfast and stories on occasion. Mind you, he never spoke to me before the gold. He's just wondering if I have more. Men and money. If you have one you won't have the other."

Alahandra laughed. "Oh, it is the truest statement I have ever heard!"

Rylic looked at Alahandra. "So what if the man is the one with the money?"

Alahandra took his challenge. "My dear pirate, either you would take it from him, or he would lose it on frivolities by the end of the day. I have not seen a man yet that can keep his money lest he has a woman that knows how to hide it from him."

Rylic threw his head back in laughter. "I do believe there is much to know about you, Alahandra. Perhaps the day will give us chance to talk."

When Haya and Alhandra were dressed, the three made their way to the Lady Amore with the blacksmith's wagon, Alahandra drank in the view of the town before sunrise. How quiet and beautiful it all seemed. Such a lonely place for her. No one to ever believe she could be more.

She could hear the sound of the water as the port came into view. She gasped at the sight of Rylic's ship. It was a grand vessel with the crew up and about cleaning the decks.

As she and Haya made their way aboard, she noticed everyone stopped to stare at them. One younger boy shouted. "Mother Haya, how are you?" He ran to their side and hugged Haya.

"Joba, dear lad, I have missed your sweet face," Haya smiled. She held the young man and turned to Alahandra. "This is Joba. Joba, this is Alahandra, my new employee and friend. Joba is the newest member of the crew.

Alahandra couldn't believe how young Joba looked. "Nice to meet you."

Joba took Alahandra's hand and kissed it gently. "No fairer maiden have I seen in all my travels, my lady. It is an honor to meet you."

Rylic laughed. "He's a bit dramatic, but a good worker. Joba, you can help us when we are ready to return to Haya's."

"Yes, sir," Joba said and went back to cleaning.

Alahandra spoke quietly. "He's such a little boy."

Rylic turned to her. "His parents were killed right in front of him. Another pirate ship raided the town where he lived and destroyed everything and anyone who stood in their way. We made port to trade with the townspeople as we always had, and there wasn't anything left but burning buildings. He was sitting in the middle of the street crying as others ran around trying to save all they could. He had no other family so I told him perhaps he would like to take to the sea. He nodded, and I carried him back to my ship. He's the hardest worker on this ship, braver than ten of these men, and smarter than all of them put

25

together. I hope to find him a home someday, but I do believe he'd rather sail forever."

"I can understand that," Alahandra said.

Rylic looked at her but made no comment. Alahandra was thankful he didn't pry. She was lost in thought over Joba. How she wished she had a place of her own for children like him. A place to give him a home. It made her heart ache for him.

The three came to a locked door. Rylic took out a key. "I'll have to light the lamps. Come in, but stand still. There are a lot of things near the door."

He allowed them entrance, and locked the door behind them. As he lit the lamp Alahandra gasped. The room was lined with golden treasure and items she had never seen. Candlesticks sparkled in the lamplight. Ornate dishes and goblets shimmered before her. Stacks and stacks of cloth. Rows of boxes and crates. The table was filled with jewels and gold pieces. She felt a strange tug inside as thoughts tumbled in her head. How easily she could live on what she saw. No more stealing, and she could get her father a decent home away from Jazier.

"It's a lot, I know, and it seems overwhelming at first." Rylic said. "Go ahead, Alahandra, look around."

"You've made quite the haul this time, son," Haya said.

"I have a lot of things I want to do, and this will get it done. I want to make sure you are taken care of too. Go ahead and start searching for things you can use or sell in the shop. Then I want you to take this bag of gold. You'll have to find a safe place for it though," Rylic talked low.

"Alahandra, since you are helping my mother, I want to pay you in kind. I know it seems I have great wealth, but most of this is accounted for. I can't pirate the seas forever. But, for now we shall all enjoy a few of the finer things in life."

Haya began searching quickly through the grates and set some things aside. "Oh, Alahandra, look at these." Haya lifted a small hair comb covered in pearls. "This would be beautiful on you."

"I wouldn't even know how to make that fit in my hair."

"Allow me," Rylic smiled, stepping forward. He took the comb from Haya and moved behind Alahandra. Gently he lifted her hair on the sides and twisted it all together on the back of her head. He then slowly slid the comb into the gathered pieces of her hair to keep it up. He moved his hand down her neck and shoulders before stepping aside.

"It's perfect," Haya smiled.

"It's yours," Rylic said as he turned back to the crates.

"Thank you," Alahandra responded softly. The feel of Rylic's hands on her neck sent tingles all through her and she wondered what it would be like to have his hands move all over her. She had to shake those thoughts from her head and keep looking through the crates.

Alahandra lifted the lid to open a crate in the corner and gasped. It was filled with beautiful gowns adorned in exquisite beading. She had never seen anything quite so grand.

Rylic stepped up close to her. "It looks as if it was made just for you. It's yours if you'll take it. But, I suggest you take one of the necklaces from the table and perhaps one of the diamond head bands. You will look like a foreign princess in such finery."

Alahandra wanted to share her plot with them, but with such a perfect dress she didn't dare tell them. The secret of her having to help kidnap the Prince was almost more than she could stomach.

"How I wish I knew how to dance in such a fine gown. I think I would wear it to the marketplace just to twirl around," Alahandra laughed.

"You don't know how to dance?" Rylic asked. He stepped to a box, lifted the lid, and Alahandra listened as beautiful music surrounded them.

She had heard of music boxes before, but had never seen one. Rylic took her hand and pulled her to him.

She pushed him away.

He laughed and spoke quietly, "I should have asked properly. I want to show you how to dance. Just put your hand in mine, and step

27

closer."

Alahandra did as she was told and took a deep breath.

Rylic circled his arm behind her and straightened himself as he smiled. "Follow the lead of my hands. Step to the side, together, back, and together."

Alahandra realized she was having to think about breathing in the arms of the pirate. She had never been so close to a man before, and all of her insides seemed to be erupting with nervousness. With a deep breath, she tried to regain her confidence. She felt the music as she moved in time with Rylic and was surprised how easily she was learning.

Haya sighed, "Watching you two is like watching the wind sway the moors."

Rylic spoke quietly, "Try to keep your head up. Look at me, not your feet."

Alahandra locked her eyes with his and smiled. Her eyes drank him in for the first time. The dark skin, kissed by many days at sea. His black hair, longer than most gentlemen. His eyes, bluer than the depths of the ocean. His body was rugged and lean. There was strength in his shoulders, in his hands, and she tightened her grip to his hold onto him. He smiled and moved his hand along the small of her back, pulling her closer.

Rylic took a deep breath and exhaled slowly. He was stunned by the striking face staring at him. Her beauty was unmatched by any woman he had seen. Her face taunt with a healthy glow of being in the sun. Her hair was as raven black as the night cascaded down her back and shoulders. Her hands, calloused from work, and he wondered what she did in her day to have such strength in her grip. He moved his hand at the small of her back to pull her in tighter and he swung her around faster. For the first time he was aware of himself with a woman, and wanted to know everything about her. He knew the song was ending soon and didn't want to let her go. They moved faster and faster as the song came to its finale, and he stopped to lean her back at the end of the music. His heart beat wildly in his chest and all he wanted to do was know the feel of her lips to his.

Haya clapped loudly. "I do believe that was the most perfect dance I have ever seen. Is that music box mine?"

Rylic slowly raised her to standing, and Alahandra moved from his arms, regretfully so. The feelings that raced through her were unfamiliar, and she felt unsure of herself. No man had ever made her feel unsure, and she didn't like it. She did enjoy the feel of his arms about her, though she thought she must seem so plain and drab to a man who has seen so much of the world.

Rylic closed the lid of the box. "It's yours, Mother. Our collection is growing, and this is by far the grandest of them all."

Haya looked at Alahandra, "I have a collection of small music boxes in my store. I like to sell them, but I do love keeping the ones that make the music float through the air."

Rylic looked out the window of the ship. "We need to hurry and gather what you can sell, and enough money to keep you two out of trouble." He winked at Alahandra, and she felt her face reddened at his attention.

They worked quickly taking their find back to the wagon. Joba helped carry all he could.

"Thank you for your help, Joba. I do hope we see each other again soon," Alahandra said.

Joba hugged her. "I would like that beautiful lady."

Alahandra's throat tightened. How she wished she could carry Joba home with her. If she only had a home to call her own.

Alahandra was silent on the ride while Rylic told Haya of his latest adventure. Haya held her son's arm as they rode. "You'll have to take Alahandra with you the next time you come in and let her port with you in a different town. Just to show her someplace new."

Rylic looked back at Alahandra. "Would you like to go with me?"

Alahandra nodded. "I've always wanted to sail the seas."

"Then I promise to take you to my next port. I have trading to do, and then I shall return for the both of you." Rylic smiled at Haya.

Alahandra noticed the shop coming into view. They must hurry and get everything inside. The town would wake soon.

Rushing back and forth to the wagon made Alahandra's heart pound. Beads of sweat rolled down her face as they finished the last haul.

Rylic stood in the front room and smiled. He opened a small box on top of all the other crates. Dozens of pieces of jewelry sparkled. "This should be enough to keep you both for a while. I put two bags of gold in the back room. Both of you, enjoy yourselves. Alahandra, take care of my sweet mother, and, Mother, keep watch on this beautiful creature."

Haya hugged Rylic. "Let's deliver you back to the ship quickly. Alahandra, come with us."

The three rode with great speed back to the docked ship, and Rylic didn't hesitate to jump from the wagon once they arrived. He held out his hand to Alahandra. Placing her hand in his, she felt warmth flow through her.

"I shall see you soon, Alahandra," he said.

"You'll have to return soon and dance with me again," Alahandra said, without thinking. "Forgive me for being bold."

Rylic kissed her hand. "Returning to dance with you will captivate my mind until I hold you once again," he smiled softly.

"God's speed to you,my darling son. Safe journeys until you return," Haya said.

"Take care of you," Rylic said, glancing at Haya, still holding onto Alahandra.

Their hands slid apart as Haya pulled the wagon away. Alahandra couldn't take her eyes from Rylic. She watched him as the road curved and he was out of sight. He never moved, his gaze on her was the last thing she saw.

Alahandra sighed. She would see him again. He would take her out on the Lady Amore. She... she... she had a job to do. For a moment she had forgotten her real purpose. Her one purpose. To kidnap the Prince.

Haya nudged her. "He is smitten with you, my dear. I have never seen him behave as he did with you. What woman could keep her senses around him? I tell you, he is a man with a wild heart. I don't know if he can be tamed to keep a woman. I have never known him to love before, Alahandra, and I fear for your heart lest it be broken by him."

Alahandra looked at her hands clasped in her lap. "I have no desire to give my heart to anyone, Haya. Forgive me for my boldness with Rylic. I've never had a man even touch my hand before. I didn't know what to do or say."

Haya watched as the townspeople began to gather in the marketplace and whispered to Alahandra. "Sometimes, our heart leaps without our giving the consent, dear child. Let us get our new items out for display. Perhaps a stand outside on this beautiful day. You can help me decide what to bring out."

Alahandra listened, but didn't respond. Her mind wandered back to the Lady Amore and to a man as untamed as the sea.

As the morning began to busy itself and the streets filled with people, Alahandra found herself daydreaming about sailing off into the distant blue with Rylic's arms about her. She didn't notice the people in the street had parted for a group of men walking her way.

"Hello, fair ladies," came a familiar voice from the crowd.

Alahandra snapped back to reality. Standing in front of her was the Prince. She stood and curtsied properly as Haya had taught her.

"A good morning to you, your highness," Alahandra said.

"Good morning, Prince... um... Prince... " Haya stumbled.

Alahandra realized she didn't know his name either. She had never inquired about him to anyone, and the townspeople spoke little of the royal family.

A man with the Prince barked at Haya. "Prince Niklas, old woman. How can you not know Prince Niklas?"

"Young man, you won't speak to me with such disregard or you'll find a hot poker from the fire between your shoulder blades. I am new to these parts and the name of the Prince is not one I speak daily," Haya said.

Prince Niklas moved quickly between the man and Haya and took her hand. "I don't expect people to know me. I have kept to myself for far too long. That is a fact that is changing, Miss Haya," He said.

"How did you know my name?" Haya smiled. "Oh, the sign," she pointed above her.

"I have learned the names of all the merchants yesterday. I'm having a grand ball and inviting all the merchants in the town. I want you to join me if you will," Prince Niklas said as he released Haya's hand and moved closer to Alahandra.

Haya curtsied. "I would be delighted."

Prince Niklas took Alahandra's hand. "And do you work with Miss Haya?"

Alahandra nodded.

"I met you yesterday. Your name, fair maiden?"

"Alahandra, your Majesty," she said.

"Alahandra, I must admit, since yesterday, your face has haunted my every thought." Prince Niklas said. "Would you do me the honor of accompanying Miss Haya to the ball?" he asked.

Alahandra's heart began to pound. Everything was working out far better than she could have planned. "I would love to come."

The Prince continued to hold her hand. He stepped closer and brought her hand to his lips, kissing it gently.

Alahandra's eyes widened, and her heart raced. She noticed others' look of surprise that lingered near.

"Then I shall be honored once again if you shall save me a dance." Prince Niklas stared at her as if they were the only two people in that moment.

Alahandra looked into his eyes. "If I can do so without stepping all over your feet," she laughed. "I've only danced once, and I'm not very good."

Prince Niklas smiled. "I'll be right back." He disappeared into the crowd and his men followed, exchanging glances. They did not look pleased with Prince Niklas's behavior.

Haya hit the table laughing. "I say, dear child, it's not a man that can keep his wits about you today."

Alahandra shrugged. "Men are nothing to me, Haya. I've seen the worst of them, and the best of them become the worst. There's not much I haven't seen, but there is one thing I know for sure. No man will ever take control of my heart."

Prince Niklas came back with a small group of villagers carrying instruments behind him. "These men can play the most joyful music. I heard them yesterday. If you will allow me, I will help you learn how to dance for the ball."

Alahandra laughed, "Here? Here in the street?"

Prince Niklas bowed before her. "There's lots of room." He offered her his hand.

Alahandra curtsied to him, taking his hand, hoping she could look somewhat normal.

He held up her arm level with his. "Let the music flow around you. Think of yourself floating in the rhythm of the song. I'll count, and that's when you step. Follow my lead and step in the direction I step."

Alahandra nodded, her eyes locked with his. He leaned into the movements, and she followed. He stepped and counted.

"You are a natural dancer, Alahandra." His hand on the small of her back pulled her in closer. He nodded to the musicians and they upped their tempo.

Prince Niklas started moving faster. Alahandra looked down at her feet. He took his hand and put it beneath her chin. "Keep your eyes up," he whispered.

His hand moved back around her slowly and he pulled her near. She enjoyed having him so close. With a swift movement he twirled her around as they moved faster with the music. Alahandra started laughing. Niklas smiled.

"Now put your hand up and touch mine as we move around in a circle."

She touched his hand and fire seemed to move through her. He looked into her eyes as he took hold of her hand and twirled about unaware that the crowd was gathering around them.

Alahandra saw a familiar face and stiffened. Niklas twirled her out and then twirled her back in catching her and holding her close. The crowd erupted in clapping and cheering. For just a moment Alahandra didn't want to think. She only wanted to be held by Prince Niklas and forget the watchful eyes of Jazier staring at her. Prince Niklas released her and bowed. She curtsied to him and the crowd continued clapping.

"I believe they enjoyed the show," Prince Niklas said, smiling.

"Thank you, your highness, for the dance. I think the ball will be an amazing night." Alahandra stepped close as everyone began to depart. "I do hope we can dance more. I'm sure you'll have so many others wanting to dance with you, I'll be lucky to have one turn," Alahandra laughed.

Prince Niklas stepped close and took her hand. "Lady Alahandra, I will dance every dance I possibly can with you," he kissed her hand.

Alahandra looked into his deep green eyes. His skin was flawless. His hair a deep brown and face taunt and muscular.

"Until then," he said.

"Until then," Alahandra whispered.

Prince Niklas turned to go, and Jazier stood in the distance looking at Alahandra. She saw him wink and then he turned to walk away.

Alahandra watched the Prince as the crowd parted for him to walk through the village street. He stopped and turned to look at her. He nodded and smiled at her. She nodded back and smiled at him.

Haya walked up beside Alahandra. "Two men so taken with you, Alahandra. Two men who have no idea of the fire that burns in your eyes. Two men that don't know how good of a thief you really are."

Alahandra turned sharply to Haya with wide eyes.

Haya laughed. "I thought you looked familiar. I've seen you here and there as I scouted the town. I've seen you lift a thing or two unnoticed. I've also gotten to know you. That hateful man that nodded to you. I've seen him around and know he is a bad man, Alahandra. Promise me that he won't be coming to the shop."

Alahandra's eyes filled with tears. "I promise. There is so much about me that you don't know, Haya, but working for you, I don't have to steal anymore. I only want to live life in such a way that I can just be invisible and free." Alahandra turned to walk inside and looked to Haya. "That man will never come here. I won't allow it."

Haya patted Alahandra's arm. "Let's bring out a few more things, put on some tea, and you can tell me all about you. The real you that you don't want to share. You see dear, we all have secrets. Some just darker than others, and some just filled with more hurt. But, I'm your friend, and friends keep your secrets."

Alahandra felt the heat in her face and knew she couldn't share everything with Haya. Not yet. She did tell her about how her father had to raise her alone, and how he learned to take what he needed to keep her fed. She told her about Jazier and their dependence on him. The plan to kidnap Prince Niklas she kept locked in her heart. She feared Jazier and what he might do if she didn't follow through.

When Alahandra finished her story Haya spoke quietly, "You know dear, I can ask Rylic to give us more than we need to help take care of your father. He will help if he can."

Alahandra's stomach knotted. "I don't want to depend on another man for anything. I want to make it in this world without feeling like I owe someone. That's why I want to work with you. Learning from you will give me a skill I can use to make my way. Then I won't ever feel like I'm less than anyone else ever again."

Haya nodded. "I know exactly what you mean. It's why I got out of the life I was in too. There's just something about being able to say, this is mine. I may rely on Rylic for now, but it's our way. He knows he has a home if he ever wants to leave piracy, and I know I have a son that loves me. My business will grow, just as it has before, and I'll make enough to keep myself happy."

Alahandra's mind wrapped around the thought of Rylic. Being in his arms made her feel like a woman. She wanted to fight her attraction to him, but she enjoyed thinking about his beautiful smile.

Haya laughed, "Seems your mind drifted away again. Rylic does have you spellbound I'm afraid."

Alahandra's face reddened. "He overwhelmed me, I guess. His freedom is intoxicating."

Haya looked to the ground. "By no means is he free, child. A pirate has to keep stealing just to survive. I fear for his life, and I'm thankful every time I see his face."

Alahandra nodded, "I understand."

"Now the Prince, he seemed to have taken a fancy to you. Can you imagine if you fell in love with the Prince? What a story that would be!" Haya smiled at Alahandra.

"A bit unrealistic though. A prince and a thief? Hardly the kind of thing the King and Queen would approve of," Alahandra said as she busied herself with the items on the table.

"You're not a thief, remember. Not anymore," Haya said.

Alahandra smiled, but she thought silently. *Not until I help steal the Prince away.*

The afternoon went on and Alahandra watched as Haya bargained with others. She learned tricks of selling merchandise and ways to talk to people to make them feel welcome. As the sun began to set they moved everything back inside.

Haya stretched. "A good day's wages we have made and a good dinner ahead. Let's eat and we can see about fitting the dress Rylic gave to you."

Alahandra nodded. She couldn't wait to have the fine ball gown ready. The ball was a week away and she wanted everything perfect.

CHAPTER

As the days passed Alahandra learned the tricks of sewing from Haya. She worked hard from the time she rose from her spot on the floor until she lay her head down to rest. Haya would open one of her music boxes and Alahandra would twirl around the room. How she enjoyed being with Haya. The thought of having to leave her and do what must be done gripped her heart.

As the ball drew closer Alahandra grew more nervous about everything. She busied herself with organizing the shop and talked less to Haya.

"I think I'll go to the market and pick up a few things for dinner. You watch the shop for me dear." Haya said.

"I will," Alahandra smiled at her, but felt a strange sense of distance from her friend.

As Alahandra worked alone she opened her favorite music box. She imagined herself in Rylic's arms again and twirled around the room. As she hummed along she didn't hear the door open and close. Rylic stepped up as she twirled toward him. He quickly slid his arm around her. Startled, she stopped rigid in his grasp. He smiled, and she softened to his touch as he twirled her with him twice around the room before he stopped and stood still peering into her eyes. Neither spoke or moved as the music ended.

She wanted to say what she was feeling being near him but found no words in their silence. Her heart raced.

"Ready to sail away with me, beautiful lady?" Rylic whispered, stepping closer.

Alahandra stepped away from his grasp. "Of course. Where are we going?" she laughed.

Rylic sat on the table. "Why to forbidden islands where the morning dew drips sweet nectar from the leaves of the trees, and we can lie on white sandy beaches, drink the milk of the coconut with not a care in the world."

"Paradise," Alahandra sighed, folding fabric on the end of the table.

"Only if you are with me," Rylic winked. "We can swim in the bluest waters," he said, sliding off the table and moving closer, "and have the sun kiss our skin until the moon pulls the night across the sky."

"Your words are as thick as honey," she smiled at him, feeling heat rise to her face.

"You are beautiful when you blush," Rylic said, touching her cheek.

"I've never known a man that talks like you, pirate."

Rylic laughed. "I've never known a woman as beautiful and intriguing as you."

"I didn't expect you back here so soon," Alahandra said.

"I took care of my business and have come for you and Haya. I want you to sail the day with me," Rylic moved a strand of hair from her face.

Alahandra turned away from him, picking up a piece of cloth to fold. "Haya should be back soon."

Rylic took Alahandra's hand, and she turned to him. "I don't mind it just being us for a moment longer. I haven't been able to think about anything but you since the moment your hand slid from mine, Alahandra. Forgive me for being bold. I am not a man of social decencies. I say what I feel."

She allowed her hand to stay in his. He moved his fingers to intertwine with hers. Her heart began to pound as she squeezed his hand in hers. Her mind was screaming run away, but she wanted to enjoy being near him again.

Rylic touched her face, moving his thumb across her cheek. "I do believe you bewitch me with your beauty."

She sighed heavily.

Haya came in the door. "You two are a bunch of trouble brewing, I can tell you that."

Alahandra laughed, "I told you. I have no intention of giving my heart away."

Rylic smiled and kissed Alahandra's hand. "I take that as a challenge."

Alahandra closed her eyes and sighed softly. Rylic kept her hands near his face.

Haya pushed Rylic's arm from Alahandra as she passed between them. "You don't know who you're dealing with, son. I suggest you just keep on sailing away from here without a thought of this lioness. You are back so soon. Is there trouble?"

Rylic took Haya's hand and twirled her around. "My business finished quicker than expected and I thought I could take you two to port in Trobornia."

Haya turned quickly, and Alahandra noticed her face light up with joy.

"I haven't been there in ages," Haya said. "I would so love to go." She turned to Alahandra. "It's a day's sail but there's no finer food, no finer people, and no finer markets. It's as if time stands still there. You won't be disappointed, child."

"I have never heard of this Trobornia," Alahandra said.

"It's real enough," Rylic said. "Small and beautiful. One of my favorite places to go and just be. We can go and have the men sail the night while we rest. We take our midday meal there, enjoy the festivities, rest for a moment, and sail late tomorrow night. It's the Feast of the Three Rivers tomorrow. It's why I hurried so to return."

Haya clapped her hands. "Oh, Alahandra, you'll think you've stepped into a dream when you see how they celebrate. It's the town's founder's celebration. Three rivers come together at the point of the

39

town where the founders set foot and decided to call the land home. I say, we are all in for a treat."

"Let's be on our way quickly. The day is nearing end, and we want to get a good start. The men are ready to sail the night. Gather what you need to travel."

From the extra clothes trunk, Alahandra and Haya each took a dress that looked a bit brighter and finer than what they wore each day. Haya packed ribbon from the rack on the table.

"I'll braid these in our hair. It's going to be a grand time, Alahandra," Haya said.

Alahandra felt as if all that was happening was a dream. Invited to the ball. The Prince openly admiring her, a pirate wanting to whisk her away, and headed to a pirate ship to go to a town party with her only friend in the world. She wondered what her father was doing, but her life with him seemed so distant and unreal. Her life as a thief felt as if it never happened. But, she couldn't forget that in a few short days, all of this would come to an end and she would return to the shack in the woods with Prince Niklas bound in chains until ransom was paid for him. How cruel it all seemed. She felt as if her life was just beginning and soon the dream would end. Reality was an ominous shadow waiting impatiently for her to return.

As the three walked out of her shop, Haya waved to the blacksmith as he was getting into his wagon. She hurried to him, and after she said something to him, he nodded. Haya motioned for Rylic and Alahandra. "We have a ride to the docks," she said, smiling at the blacksmith.

The three got in quickly and they all rode quietly while lost in their own thoughts. Alahandra wanted to laugh with all the excitement building inside her, and at the same time she wanted to scream.

She could run away.

Leave and not care. Harden her heart toward her father and be free.

Looking at the three with her made her feel lost. They knew who they were. All she wanted to do was disappear and find a passage to a different life.

The docks came into view and Haya squeezed the blacksmith's hand. "Thank you for the use of your fine wagon once again."

He winked at her. "Anything for you Miss Haya. Anything for you." He rode away and for a moment, Alahandra watched as Haya paused to see him ride around the bend of the road.

"He fancies you, Haya. Why don't you ever spend time with him?" Alahandra asked.

"You won't give your heart away for your reasons, and I won't give away mine for my reasons," Haya nodded. Alahandra decided to ask later when Rylic wasn't within hearing range.

Rylic stood at the bottom of the boarding plank. "Ladies first."

Alahandra followed Haya on board and noticed the men all staring at her. She didn't like the way their eyes lingered on her, raking over her.

"Time to set sail, men. We port in Trobornia!" Rylic shouted.

All around the ship the men yelled out in approval as the anchor began to raise.

"Seems we aren't the only ones excited about the destination," Alahandra said.

"Aye, many a man has found a wife in Trobornia. It seems the fairest maidens of this world live there, and I have lost many a crew members to the fluttering of eyelashes and swaying of hips," Rylic laughed. He turned to Alahandra. "But wait until the men there see you. Why, I may have to fight them all just to get to stand by you. It's said that you can find your true love at The Feast of the Three Rivers because the magic from the fairies that inhabit the forests float in the air and bind the hearts of those meant to be together. A foolish notion, but the superstitious will wait for that particular day in hopes of realizing the one they were meant for."

Haya laughed, "Well, I better look my best."

Alahandra laughed, and Rylic smirked at her. Walking to the side of the ship, Alahandra looked down as the water began to move quickly by. She slid her hands along the side railing. It was smooth and worn with time. Raising her face to the sun she breathed in the moist air. Her hair blew around her and she laughed trying to catch it.

Rylic stepped up beside her laughing. "Let me help you or you'll have such a knot by the time we port you'll have to cut it out." He gathered her hair in his fingers and turned it over his hand. Taking a piece of leather from his pocket, he tied it around the hair bunched that he held, securing it tightly. His hand slid down her neck and then down her back. She allowed him to keep it there as they stared out over the water.

"It does mesmerize, doesn't it," Rylic whispered.

"It takes my breath away," she said, keeping her eyes on the horizon. She spoke low. "How is it that you know so much about how to fix a woman's hair?"

Rylic sighed and leaned closer to her. "When I was quite young, Mum fell from a tall ladder after she patched a hole in our roof. She tried to do everything herself," he paused and looked at Alahandra. Silence held him for a moment before he returned his gaze to the water. "When she fell, she broke her arm, and I did all I could to help her. I learned to cook and do all the cleaning. I helped her with her hair during that time, and I never forgot how to do it. She had a dress shop and taught me to sew so she wouldn't get behind. I was slow, but I was a perfectionist and she didn't lose business. We take care of each other, she and I. My mum," he paused, "one of the toughest women in the world. I would do anything to make sure she's happy."

"I love that you love her so much," Alahandra said, keeping her eyes locked on the water to hold back her tears.

"What of your family, Alahandra?"

She took a deep breath. "Let's just say, at this point, I do for me."

Rylic didn't press her, and they stood together enjoying the quiet of the sea.

As the day turned to night Rylic took them to his cabin. "The hour grows late, and we must rest," he said. "Haya, you take my bunk. Alahandra, you can rest here on the blankets on the floor."

"Where are you going to sleep?" Alahandra asked.

"I'll stay here but over by the door," Rylic said.

Haya didn't hesitate. She kissed them both on the cheek, and as soon as she laid down she was asleep. Alahandra could not settle her mind. Everything seemed to be happening too quickly. How she wished she could just sail away from her old life and never think about who she was again. Rylic fell asleep without effort. Alahandra lay awake for a while staring at the ceiling. She had her own demons to tame so she could rest.

Morning came too soon and Alahandra felt exhausted from the little sleep she had. Rylic and Haya were up and about, and she sat alone for a moment as she breathed deeply. As she emerged from the cabin the excitement of the day was all around her.

Haya came up to her smiling, "Time to get ready dear. We dock soon and the celebration will begin!"

Alahandra looked around for Rylic and spotted him at the other end of the ship. His eyes met hers and he smiled, nodding a good morning to her.

She felt heat rise in her face as she nodded back to him. He made her completely aware of herself. She didn't like it.

Following Haya into the cabin, they took their dresses and changed quickly, to have enough time to eat breakfast. Fruit and bread on the table made for a filling meal, but Alahandra could scarcely eat for the excitement coursing through her.

"Trobornia just ahead!" a man called from beyond the doors.

"It's going to be a grand day," Haya said, braiding ribbons through Alahandra's hair.

"The anticipation is overwhelming!" Alahandra laughed.

The sound of men rushing around filled the ship. Everyone was cleaned and changed into their finest. Alahandra and Haya made their way to the plank placed for leaving the ship and saw Rylic standing at the bottom. His clothes looked like that of royalty. He bowed as they came off the ramp.

"Ladies, you are breathtaking," Rylic said taking Alahandra's hand, kissing it gently.

"You, sir, are stunning," Alahandra said, trying not to react to his lips on her skin.

Haya nodded, "She's right. You will turn every head in Trobornia. Every woman here will think you arrived just for her."

Rylic looked to Alahandra. "I don't think I'll even notice them today."

Alahandra looked to the ground. Rylic's boldness in front of others made her uncomfortable.

Rylic offered his one arm to Haya and the other to Alahandra. She took it and breathed in deeply.

"Let's go have some fun," Rylic said.

Joab ran down the ramp. "I'm ready!"

"I wondered if you were coming." Rylic smiled and gave Joab a handful of coins.

"Thank you, Rylic." Joab looked up at him.

"You just go have fun, eat, play, and we'll find you when it's time to go. The children have a special play area just at the edge of town. It's like nothing you've ever seen."

Joab hugged him and ran into the crowd.

Haya smiled and watched Joab run from them. "It's a good thing you do with that child."

Rylic nodded.

Alahandra wondered if Rylic regretted having Joab around. It had to worry him, and his face told it all. He was starting to care deeply for the little boy.

As they all walked from the docks and entered the town, everything there was dreamy and unlike anything Alahandra had ever seen. Flowers adorned every post and every doorway. Booths were set up with all kinds of foods. Tents with chairs under them and tables for eating. Flowers and vines were wrapped around the ties of the tent. Ribbons of every color hung from everywhere. The sweet smell of jasmine filled the air. A stand was set up with a band playing. Music and laughter filled the air. Haya took Alahandra to buy flowers to weave into their hair and Trobornian ribbon to tie on their dresses.

"All the women wear the ribbon on their dresses and the men tie them around their waist," Haya said. "Oh, wait, I'll be right back!" Haya turned and moved quickly through the crowd. She returned with a paper filled with roasted nuts. "Try these. They are only grown here."

Alahandra laughed. "You're different here. I don't think you've stopped smiling."

"In all my travels, I do believe this is the happiest place I've ever known." She pointed to Rylic, surrounded by women. "Can you believe how overbearing some women are? They have no pride or respect in themselves falling all over Rylic like they do."

Rylic pointed to them and then made his way to them quickly. He put his arm around Alahandra and waved back to the crowd of women.

"What's all that about?" Alahandra asked.

"I had one of the women say she had found the man she was going to marry and clung to me. I told her I had already found the woman I am supposed to be with this morning. She will leech on to the next victim shortly I'm sure. They all seem to think I was the one. So now they assume you are the one for me."

The women dispersed and Rylic released Alahandra. "Sorry. I didn't mean to offend you. I just wanted so desperately to get away from them all."

"No need to apologize," Alahandra said.

A man came up beside Alahandra. He stumbled slightly, and then straightened his vest about him. "Would you do me the honors of dancing with me, beautiful lady?"

Alahandra took Rylic's hand. "I'm sorry. This is my only dance partner for the day." Alahandra said, leaning her head on Rylic's shoulder. He turned his face to hers and kissed her forehead. Alahandra gasped with the feel of Rylic's lips on her skin. Emotions were unbound and crashed all around her as she felt heat rising to her face.

The man bowed. "My apologies, sir."

"My apologies to you, good man," Rylic smiled, lifting

Alahandra's face to look into her eyes. "since I have the most beautiful woman here."

The man walked away and stumbled slightly running into a tree.

Alahandra stood motionless near Rylic. Haya clapped her hands. "You two put on a grand show. Seems like if we are going to have any fun today you two may have to stick together."

"I think that sounds like a great plan," Rylic spoke softly.

"If we must, then we can only make the best of it," Alahandra said, wondering what it would be like to have him kiss her in that moment. She didn't want to allow her mind to be filled with such thoughts, but being near Rylic scrambled reason, and she was left with only the joy of his hand sliding into hers.

Laughter filled the air as Rylic stayed close to Alahandra. Beautiful woodwinds began a tune that made Alahandra smile.

"I love the sound of this music," she said, closing her eyes. "It's unlike anything I've ever heard before."

"It's the Dance of the Maidens!" Haya clapped. "All the single women, young and old, dance in the center of town while men throw flowers in the air to them. It's quite fun!"

A little girl ran up to Alahandra. "Come with us!"

Alahandra followed the little girl, and she grabbed Haya's hand as they moved with the other women to the center of the cobblestone street. The music changed to a faster beat, and the women began to dance. Men formed an outer circle clapping and laughing as baskets of flower petals were passed along so that each man there could get two hands full. Alahandra found Rylic in the crowd. He smiled at her and nodded. She felt alive and free dancing with Haya and the others.

As the music grew louder and faster it stopped abruptly and the air was filled with flower petals. Haya clapped and hugged Alahandra. The crowd cheered and everyone was laughing. Rylic moved quickly to them.

"You two looked like you were having a lot of fun out here," he said.

"Oh, I haven't had that much fun in a long time. Thank you,

Alahandra," Haya said.

"Thank you both for making this day so wonderful," Alahandra said, trying to catch her breath.

"I can't imagine being here with anyone else," Rylic said.

A young man approached the three and cleared his throat. He looked at Alahandra.

"Excuse me, ma'am. Would you dance with me? I mean I want to dance with you, oh, I mean, would you care to dance?" he sighed.

Haya and Rylic smiled. Alahandra stepped forward.

"What's your name?" she asked.

"Alexander, ma'am. I know I'm a bit young, but my friends were all talking about how beautiful you are and said no one would have the nerve to ask you to dance. I told them, you're a woman and you're here to have fun like everyone else, meaning no disrespect. They told me I wasn't brave enough to ask a woman like you to dance, and I told them I would do it. I just wanted to prove that to them is all. You folks have a nice day," he said as he turned to go.

"Alexander," Alahandra said softly. "You didn't wait for my answer. I would be honored to dance with someone so brave."

Alexander turned and smiled at her as his face reddened. He extended his hand. She curtsied and put her hand in his. She noticed a group of young men on the side pointing at them with their mouths open.

Alexander led her to the middle of the dance area and put his arm around her gently. He gulped as she stepped closer. "You won't break me," she smiled at him. His face softened, and he smiled.

"Thank you for dancing with me," he said.

"Thank you for asking me. I've only been asked by one other man, and he was a bit, how should I say, rough around the edges," she laughed, nodding to a man drinking to the side of the crowd.

"That's old man Drake. He's asking every woman here to dance. I think he's already had a bit of a nip this morning," Alexander laughed, twirling Alahandra out from him.

"He's a lively character," Alahandra said.

"He is at that," Alexander said.

They danced through the crowd and laughed as the music ended. Alexander bowed and Alahandra curtsied. He took her hand and kissed it gently.

"My lady, you have made my day."

"Alexander, you have caught the eye of a lot of girls," Alahandra said, looking to the side. Several girls smiled at him and then looked away.

Alahandra leaned close to him and whispered. "Now is your chance to be brave once again. Go. Take the hand of a maiden that just might steal your heart today."

Alexander smiled at her. "Thank you, Alahandra. You are the fairest of all on this day."

Alahandra curtsied once again and they both turned to go. She watched as he bowed in front of a shy girl about his age. She took his offered hand and they moved out in the crowd to dance. The girl looked longingly at Alexander, and his face was once again red. As he turned to face Alahandra he smiled at her and nodded.

Rylic came up behind her. "Seems you two created quite the stir."

"That was such fun. He looks so happy," Alahandra said.

"What about you, Alahandra? Are you happy?" he said.

Alahandra turned to look at him. "I've never known happiness, but I like that I'm smiling. I like that I'm laughing and dancing. I like being here with you and Haya. This is a good day."

Rylic offered his hand and she took it gently. He led her out to the crowd to dance. He leaned his face next to hers. His lips grazed her earlobe as he whispered.

"I believe all that you say defines happiness. Enjoy your day, my beautiful Alahandra."

He spun her out from him as the song ended and the tempo changed. The upbeat music made her feel alive. She took Rylic's hands and danced around the crowd with him. They laughed and twirled through the others and people began to watch them. They didn't notice the crowd moving apart for them as Rylic spun, held her close, and spun her around. Their eyes locked together.

As the song ended many clapped for them and Alahandra looked down, breathless.

He lifted her face. "You captivate everyone around you."

Haya walked up with plates of food. "I'm starving. How about we picnic over there under the big oak tree? It's one of my favorite places. We can use the cloth we brought from the ship to sit upon."

"I think that's a splendid idea," Alahandra said.

The three ate quietly as they watched everyone around them. Haya finished her plate and lay back on the cloth.

"This is such a dreamy place. I could live here forever," she smiled.

"Then maybe someday you will. I could live here. Everyone is so kind," Alahandra said.

"This is a place where dreams come true," Rylic said. "What's your dream, Alahandra?"

Alahandra looked at him and smiled. "I've always wanted a little house of my own where I can sit outside and watch the sunset and not think about anything at all but being happy."

"That's nice," Haya said. "I can see that for you."

"Then there's the other side of me that wants to live in a far off land at the edge of a jungle and learn a different language. I could live in a hut in a village and learn the ways of a different people," she sighed.

Rylic laughed, "I have never heard a woman talk of such things. You are a rarity in this world, Alahandra. The soul of a wanderer in the body of a goddess. You easily bewitch me with your honesty and the depth of your eyes."

Alahandra looked at him as he spoke, and his eyes never left hers.

Haya had closed her eyes and didn't notice the exchanged glances. She laughed. "My dear son, you say a lot of words."

"I speak only the truth. Always," he smiled at Alahandra.

She smiled at him and felt frustrated with herself wanting to be closer to him.

49

"I hate to say that we must be on our way. The day grows late, and we must leave soon," Rylic said, looking up at the sky. "I want to be well on our way before the sun goes down."

Haya nodded, "Let's have a bite more to eat, and then we shall go. I want to try the fried pastries at that stand," she pointed. "I'll go get us all one, and then we can go."

Being left alone on the blanket with Rylic made Alahandra aware of herself. He moved closer.

"I never like leaving this celebration. It is quite magical, and this town is more welcoming than any land I've ever visited."

His hand rested close to hers. Before she thought she reached out and moved her hand over his.

She looked up quickly at him and moved her hand away. "Forgive my boldness," she said quietly. "I've never kept the company of a man for this long. It seemed right to touch you in that moment."

"You are a puzzle indeed," Rylic said, taking her hand in his. "You can have my hand anytime." He moved his thumb over the back of her hand and she closed her eyes, sighing.

As Haya approached, Rylic continued to hold her hand. He reached up for the dessert Haya offered him and then gently released her hand so she could do the same. Haya looked at him with raised eyebrows, and he looked down at the fried pastry.

"This smells wonderful," he said, sniffing his plate.

"I think I could make these," Alahandra said.

"Well, if you can make these, I'll visit more often," Rylic said. The three laughed.

"Then I guess I better figure it out so you can enjoy my company more," she smiled.

"Oh, I will definitely enjoy," he took a bite and paused, "your fried pastries." He winked at her.

She felt the heat rise in her face.

They consumed the dessert, and Rylic sighed.

"Time to go," he said.

Alahandra nodded. The stark reality grew ever present in her heart that the fun she was having was about to end. All of it. Not just the celebration, but her time with Haya. She would have to commit to kidnapping Prince Niklas and the ball was only a few days away.

As everyone boarded the ship once again, and it left the dock of Trobornia, there was a gleeful feeling among them all. The crew smiled to themselves. Many hummed as they worked. There were memories to be cherished from the events of the day.

Alahandra looked around. "It seems we have lost several men to Trobornia."

Rylic laughed. "As it should be. It happens each year. Many a man loses his fascination with the sea with the promise of a woman's heart," Rylic said, looking at Alahandra.

Alahandra looked down. Her mind raced. Could Rylic ever be so taken with her that he would give up a pirate's adventure? Why would he? She dismissed the foolish notion and enjoyed thinking of all the joy from the day.

Joab ran up to them. "I've eaten so much! I think I'll go below and go to bed." He ran to Rylic and hugged him. Rylic held him tightly and smiled. Joab ran to Haya and hugged her.

"I'm glad you had fun, Joab."

He then ran to Alahandra. "You had fun too. I saw you dancing with Rylic. My mom used to look at my dad like you look at him. I'm glad you're here with us."

Alahandra hugged him. "I'm glad too." She knew she couldn't look up at Haya and Rylic lest her eyes give away the secrets of her heart.

The ship moved along quickly, and a silence fell among them all as the sky turned to night. Half the crew went to bunk for a few hours while the other half was waking to sail under the starry night. Alahandra knew she couldn't sleep as she settled on the floor of Rylic's cabin once again. Haya fell asleep quickly, worn from the excitement of the day.

Across the room, Rylic lay on his back near the door, and stared out the window at the night sky.

Alahandra raised up on her elbow. Rylic sat up, turned to her and motioned for her to come sit by him. He motioned for her to be quiet. She got up quietly and tip-toed to him.

"I want you to see this sky," he whispered.

Alahandra looked up and gasped. The stars were bright and blanketed the night sky like she had never seen.

"It's breathtaking," she whispered.

"You are breathtaking," he whispered.

Alahandra looked at him. "I must go back and rest."

Rylic touched her arm. "Stay beside me for a while. I promise to be a gentleman," he smiled.

Alahandra looked to the floor.

He touched her chin and raised her head. "I only want you to sit with me."

Alahandra moved close beside him. He placed his arm around her. "You can lean on me if you want and rest. I want to know more about you, Alahandra."

"There isn't much to tell. I don't feel like I've lived much until this week," Alahandra said. She settled in close to him, and he secured his arms about her.

"If I could stop time I would choose this moment and hold onto it forever," Rylic said. He leaned his head back against the wall.

Alahandra heard his breathing slow and deepen. She knew he was asleep. She reached up and touched his face. "Beautiful man, I wish I could trust you with my heart." She placed her arm around him and allowed sleep to overtake her.

CHAPTER
Five

"Wake up, sweet beautiful lady." Rylic whispered close to Alahandra's ear. She woke quickly with the feel of his breath on her ear.

She realized her arm was draped over Rylic and her head was resting on his chest. As she started to move he held her close.

"The sun is coming up, and I wanted you to see it over the water. But I'm finding it hard to let you go," Rylic smiled.

Alahandra felt bold in his arms and tightened her grip around him. "Then let's stay here and never leave the sea."

Rylic lifted her face near his. "Had I but one wish, it would be to capture your heart, Alahandra." His lips brushed hers gently.

Alahandra felt fire explode through her veins. Never had she imagined the feel of a man's lips on hers would cause such a stir within her, and she pressed her lips to his in response. She knew she was on dangerous ground, and Rylic was no man to stay put. She released her hold on him and smiled.

"Had we more time I would continue from there and see where it takes us," Alahandra teased.

"Had we more time I would..." Rylic said.

"Good morning you two," Haya interrupted. "Back to reality we go."

"Ah, yes. Reality. The place where dreams are squelched as all strive for prosperity," Rylic laughed. "Unless you're a pirate." He nudged Alahandra.

"Yo ho, yo ho, a pirate's life for me," Alahandra sang. All three laughed and stood to walk out on deck. The beauty of the sunrise stopped their laughter, and each drank in the beauty.

Rylic stepped close to Alahandra. "Seeing your smile in this light overwhelms me." He led her over to the side of the ship. The smell of the sea air inundated her senses. She leaned back on him slightly and sighed. He wrapped his arms around her and held her for a moment.

One of the crew shouted from below and Rylic stepped back. "Time to get to work and get you two home." He turned to walk away. Haya moved closer to Alahandra.

"He's never been like this, but you know he won't stay. Just let him go, dear." Haya put her arm around Alahandra's shoulders.

"I have never known anyone like him, Haya. I know my heart will hold him close, but like I said, I give my heart to no one."

Haya hugged her, "Good girl."

When the ship docked, Haya hugged her son. "Take care of you, and come see me soon."

"That's a promise," Rylic said as he hugged her looking to Alahandra and smiling.

Rylic escorted them off the ship. He hugged Haya once again. "You two stay out of trouble."

He moved to hug Alahandra. She welcomed him into her arms. He pulled her close, pressing her to him. He whispered in her ear, "My every dream shall be of you."

Alahandra whispered to him. "Then I shall meet you in those dreams for adventures."

Rylic's lips brushed her cheek with a gentle kiss.

Haya pulled Alahandra's arm, and the two released each other. "That's enough, you two. There's enough heartbreak in this world without you two jumping in that hole."

"Oh, Mum, I'm just trying to prove that her heart may not be so easily concealed," Rylic smiled, kissing Alahandra's hand.

Alahandra touched his face and teased leaning toward him. "And I'm just trying to prove, I can't be won over."

Haya laughed, "And if you're not careful, you two will be in a mess of trouble. Now, I say good day to you, my son, lest you sell that ship of yours and find a market job to keep you here."

"To the sea with me, then. Farewell, my beauties," he said, bowing and making his way back aboard.

Haya and Alahandra turned to walk away. Alahandra was tempted to turn and wave one last time, but thought better of it. No need to encourage him further when she knew the reality of her fate.

Haya whispered. "One last wave before we make the bend in the road. It's like I get one more chance to look at the boy in the man that sails from me."

They both turned together and watched as the ship began to sail away. Haya and Alahandra waved, and then turned to continue walking.

"My heart breaks a little each time he leaves, but I can't imagine him staying. He would drive me to the end of myself, and I would come close to killing him. We are too much alike, he and I, but, nevertheless, I love him more than my own life. Such is a mother's love, and worst when you have to love a pirate son."

Rylic could not steal his eyes from Haya and Alahandra walking from the ship. He watched until they turned the bend of the road and disappeared around the trees. He knew he should not have been so open about wanting to hold Alahandra, but he knew with her beauty, her mind, and the wild in her, she would find a suiter soon that would take her away from the market. The sea was his home, but a small part of his heart longed to have a home filled with the love of a woman that adored him. Could Alahandra ever see him as anything but a pirate? He shook his head at the notion and turned his face to the sun. There was a merchant ship from the tip of Africa that was said to be sailing through familiar waters in a two days sail from here. Time to move on. There was treasure waiting, and for now he had to close his heart to thoughts of Alahandra.

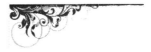

The days moved on and Alahandra found herself enjoying all her time with Haya. She was learning quickly about the business side of things, and the dress shop was thriving.

Alahandra sat down in a chair to eat her dinner. Haya locked the front door to end their day. Haya huffed as she was seated. "We still have a great deal of work to do tonight. So many orders to fill. That ball is bringing in so much money for us. Before we get into all that work though, how about we take a break after dinner. I want to get out and walk around a bit. The fresh air will do us both good."

"I like that idea. The sun is going down soon, and I love the night market. Not a lot of people, but night people are different," Alahandra said.

"Yes," Haya said, "as if they possess a secret."

"Intriguing," Alahandra whispered.

They both laughed.

Haya reached for her hand. "I see you staring off while you're working. He won't stop being a pirate until he's ready. Loving him is not an easy thing."

"I won't hold onto hope for him. I know better. I can't allow my mind to dwell on him. He's an amazing man, but I know my heart well enough to know that I can't give it to anyone."

Haya squeezed her hand. "Don't be so afraid to give your heart to the right man if he should come along. Love is something I wish for you to experience. The love a man that can't wait to hold you in his arms. The love of your children. The love of a life meant to be lived. Just promise me you will open your heart enough to let a little light in. You never know what might happen at that ball. The entire village will be there."

"I promise, only because you make it all sound so inviting," Alahandra said. "Now let's finish and go for a walk."

As the lights were being lit along the market road, and lamps illuminated each stand. The smell of roasted meat and onions filled the air.

"Ceilia must be out tonight," Alahandra smiled.

Haya breathed deeply and took Alahandra's hand. "Thank you for being my friend, Alahandra. I haven't known the company of friendship for many years."

Alahandra smiled and looked off into the distance of the castle. "You are my first friend."

Haya patted her on the arm. "Life is changing, my dear. Best to enjoy every moment."

"Indeed," Alahandra said. Those words sank into her heart and took root. Enjoy her life. She never thought about enjoying her life. Surviving had been the game she had played her entire existence. She wondered what her father was doing. She wanted to see him, but didn't want to be confronted by Jazier.

The blacksmith stepped from his shop and closed the lock around the handle. He stepped forward as the two women drew near. "Nice night for a walk," he said. He coughed and looked at his feet. "Miss Haya, I would be honored if you would walk with me for a while."

Alahandra elbowed her and nodded. Haya cleared her throat. "Yes, I would like that," she said.

He looked up and smiled, offering his arm to her. She took it gently and smiled to him. He cleared his throat and his voice cracked. "I know all the merchants have been invited to the ball. I wondered if you would like to ride with me there? You and Alahandra?"

"That would be delightful, but only if you'll save a few dances for me," Haya said.

"I'll save every dance for you," he said, clasping his hand over hers.

Haya looked back at Alahandra smiling. They waved to each other, and Alahandra watched them walk away whispering.

Alahandra breathed in the night air as the sun gave way to night. She had always loved the night. Darkness cloaked the road and she felt free from everyone's eyes. Music from the tavern began to fill the air. The street musicians played there at night while men filled their bellies with ale. Women found ways to entice the men to pay them well for a kiss or more. Alahandra shuddered at the thought.

She twirled in the street as she walked by the tavern windows. A man sitting at a table saw her pass by and came outside to talk to her.

"Hello, little lady. Want to come have a drink with me?" He said, grabbing her arm.

"You will release me, sir," she said low and without wavering.

He pulled her close to his face. His breath was thick and warm. "I'll release you when I'm ready."

A shadow from the distance saw Alahandra's struggle and started toward her.

The man from the tavern laughed in her face. "Maybe you and I need to have a little fun."

Alahandra lifted her foot and pulled a knife from a band around her ankle. She held it to his throat.

"Now, you can probably take this knife from me, and you can probably break my arm, but not before I slit your throat. You'll drown in your own blood before anyone hears your call for help."

The man shoved her back. "One day, missy. One day. I'll get you."

"And the next day, they'll bury you. Watch your words, sir, lest they be your last," Alahandra turned to go quickly away. She realized she was walking away from the shop but kept going. She didn't care where she went as long as it was far from the tavern.

She noticed the shadow running toward her. She paused and held the knife in front of her.

"Distance yourself," she yelled.

"Alahandra, it's me, Niklas," came a voice from the dark.

"You lie. The Prince would not be out in the dark unattended," she said, keeping her knife steady.

"It is I," Prince Niklas said, coming quickly from the shadows to move close to her. She lowered her knife. "I was going to come to your rescue, but I see you handled that nicely. You are a puzzle, Alahandra."

"Not like other maidens, I guess," Alahandra smiled.

"Unlike anyone I've ever known," Prince Niklas said.

"I've always taken care of myself. I didn't have a choice, and it has made me more calloused than most."

"I would like to know more of your story. Would you walk with me? Perhaps to the water? It isn't proper, and I know it's a long way. My horse is tied there, and I can give you a ride back to Haya's. I needed to get out and breathe a bit of freedom."

"I could use a good long walk, and I'm not one to adhere to social graces," Alahandra said, moving beside him as they began on their way. "Do you often come out alone?"

"Not often enough. If my family knew I snuck out, I would be confined to the grounds. The pressure of the throne weighs heavily on me. My father expects me to assume the role of King soon enough, and I feel like the world races by while I rot inside those walls," he said.

"I can't imagine being cooped up without freedom to go as I please," Alahandra said.

Niklas looked to the ground.

"I'm sorry. That was insensitive of me. I know your station is one of great importance," she said.

"I am not offended. I know the lands need me to rule, but I long for adventure," Niklas said.

"Then let's have an adventure," she said, taking his hand. "I know of a place where it feels like you can touch the sky. It's a bit of a trek, but well worth it."

"I'll go anywhere with you," Niklas said.

Alahandra stopped and looked at him. It was as if she saw him for the first time. Strong features, dark hair, green eyes that sparkled in the moonlight. He was different without the pageantry of the guards. Real. He moved his thumb across the back of her hand. She smiled at him and then turned to go down the road.

"The path is here somewhere." She led him along and stopped

abruptly, still holding his hand. "Here it is. I knew I had marked it. It's just hard to see in the dark."

Niklas followed along, tightening his clasp on her hand. She walked along until her dress caught on a briar bush.

They stopped and worked together to set her dress free. "Thank you," she whispered.

"You're welcome," he whispered back.

"We don't have to whisper," Alahandra laughed. "It felt like I should. Let me see. I got turned around getting my dress free. It's hard to hike in a dress." She reached down and pulled the side of her hem, raised it to her knees, and tied it in a knot. "Does this offend you, sire?"

"Not at all. The women at the palace tie their hems to clean all the time," he said.

They continued on as she looked for markers she had placed on trees and on the ground.

"Not much longer," she said. "Just ahead is the clearing. The climb gets a little steeper."

"It's so dark, I can barely see," Niklas said.

"Here we are. Just through the opening in the trees," she said.

They emerged into a clearing, and the moon welcomed them into the night. Stars blanketed the sky.

"This is the most beautiful thing I've ever seen," Niklas said, walking forward.

"Be careful," Alahandra said, grabbing his arm. She pointed down. They were standing not far from a cliff overlooking the docks. She continued to hold onto his arm as they stared up at the night sky.

"Seeing something so magnificent, so beautiful, makes me feel like I could cry," she whispered.

He placed his hand over her hand that held his arm. "I know exactly how you feel."

"There's more," she said, motioning him to follow. She climbed down the opposite side from where they had climbed up and came to another ledge. "Look there. That is my favorite place." She pointed down below. The water met the shoreline and stretched out before them. The moon cascaded through the water as it flowed upon the sands of the shore.

"Can we go down there?" Niklas asked.

"Yes, of course. Have you never been around the shoreline?" Alahandra asked, starting their dissent.

"No, I didn't even know this was here."

"It is beautifully secluded. There are only a handful of people that will make the trek. It's not easy. Others would rather go to the shore on the other side of the docks, but it can't compare to the beauty here."

Alahandra moved down the rocks with ease. She looked behind and Niklas was making his way easier than she had expected.

When they reached the bottom Alahandra took a deep breath and ran down to the water. She stopped to take her shoes off and took the knife from her ankle. Niklas followed her lead and took his shoes off too. They both ran to the water, splashing and laughing.

"You are wild, Alahandra," Niklas said.

"Not wild, just free," she laughed, kicking water at him. He kicked water at her and stumbled as the sand gave way under him. Unable to get his footing, he fell forward. Alahandra laughed, extending her hand to help him up. He snatched her quickly so that she fell beside him. He laughed and got up.

"You are no gentleman," she laughed.

He couldn't stop laughing. She leaned back in the water and looked up. "Do you swim?"

"I do love to swim. There is so much freedom in the water," he said, "I'm just not very good."

"No judgement here. Let's swim for a while. I have to take my dress off or I'll drown. Is that okay?" she asked.

"It's fine. I will stay a good distance from you to be proper," Niklas said.

Alahandra emerged from the water and unbuttoned the front of her dress. She tossed it further up on the sand so it would not wash away. As she walked toward Niklas she smiled. "No need to stay away from me, my undergarments are coverage enough. Like I said, I care not for social decencies. I like to have fun, and to most, I guess that would seem crass and crude."

She moved into the water and began to glide. Niklas took off his shirt and under shirt, tossed them to the shore, and moved close beside her. "I like not being formal with you, and doing whatever we want. The water is perfect."

"This night is perfect," she said.

They swam for a long time in the quiet.

"I'm going to have to go soon," Alahandra said. "I'm staying with Haya, and I don't want her to worry."

"I must return also before I am missed. How I wish I could freeze time and never leave this moment," Niklas said, as they made their way out of the water.

Alahandra picked up her dress. "I think I'll carry this up to the clearing. It will make climbing easier."

Niklas picked up his shirt but continued to look down.

"Is everything okay?" she asked.

"Your undergarment is clinging to you, and it leaves little to the imagination," Niklas said.

Alahandra walked closer to him. She felt bold in the night air, and the Prince had stirred within her an untamed desire. "I am not afraid to have your eyes on me. If you want to look at me, you may."

"It is improper," he said.

"It is part of your adventure. We have this moment, and none other like it," Alahandra whispered.

Niklas slowly raised his head, his gaze moving over her. "The want of you is too strong, and we must leave."

"Tell me what it is you want," she said.

He stepped closer to her so that his face was above hers. "You tempt me in a way no other woman dares, and I want nothing more than to pull you close and slide my hands over your body. I want my lips on yours and to taste the sweetness of your mouth."

He paused and breathed faster. They stared at one another, frozen in the moment. Alahandra's stomach knotted in excitement.

She took hold of his hand. "I have never been bold with a man before, but I have no reservations with you. I don't even really know how to talk to a man or what's proper. I wasn't raised knowing the graces of being social like others. I like saying what I'm thinking and what I'm feeling. How is it that you bring out such wildness in me?"

"I would like to see the wild in you unleashed, beautiful temptress," he smiled. "However, the night slips from us, and we must be on our way." He leaned his forehead to hers and breathed in deeply. They breathed in rhythm with the water lapping onto the shore. She touched his chest and he gasped. "Your touch makes my skin feel like it's on fire."

"Again, forgive my boldness. I wanted to touch you, and it felt like the right thing to do."

"You are welcome to touch me anytime you want," Niklas breathed deeply.

There were so many words she wanted to say to him, but she held her silence.

He stared at her as he pulled his shirt over his head. The wet fabric rolled up on his back, and he couldn't pull it free.

She moved her hands around him to release the rolled fabric and pulled it down his back. Her fingers grazed his back, and he moaned softly.

"I wish I could touch all of you," she whispered.

"I would let you, but then we would have to run away because I would never want to do anything other than enjoy all of you." Niklas breathed deeply.

They turned to walk away from the shore, holding their words, and slowly began their climb. When they reached the top, Alahandra donned her dress and buttoned the front.

"Back to reality," she said.

"You will be at the ball, yes?" he asked.

"Yes. I have acquired a dress, so I can come," she said pointing to the road through the trees up ahead. "We are almost out of the woods."

"When you arrive, I want your first dance, and then I have something to show you," Niklas said.

"I look forward to it," she said.

Just before she went through the last of the trees to step out onto the road, Niklas caught her hand. "Wait," he whispered. "My adventure is almost over. Will you allow me one kiss this night? It is quite bold of me to ask, but this is a night of adventure, yes?"

Alahandra turned and closed the space between them. "A perfect way to end our night," she said, moving her face closer to his. He bent down slightly, touching his lips to hers.

For the first time in her life she felt free. Free to feel, to enjoy, to explore. She placed her arms around his neck and whispered. "I've never really kissed a man before. I've had one other man kiss me."

"Then this night will be one that we both remember forever." Niklas pulled her close and caressed his lips to hers. "Kiss me," he said.

She pulled herself to him and her lips met his. She pressed herself to him and felt her body ignite. He held her close, losing himself in the feel of her. She leaned her head back to look at him. He stepped back slowly.

"My dear, Alahandra, you will fill my dreams. I must go," he said.

"Be off with you, lest I take you into the woods and never let you go," she laughed.

"I would not struggle, but the guards may hunt us down," he laughed.

They paused looking at one another and then stepped back together quickly as their lips met again and again. She playfully pushed him away. He laughed and held her arm bringing her close once again. Their laughter faded as she moved her lips over his softly before she stepped back.

He released her arm, ran to the edge of the trees, and looked back at her. "That was my first kiss too. I was to save it for the one I would call my princess, but you have opened the door for my soul. Goodnight, beautiful maiden."

"Goodnight, dear Prince. Until the ball."

"Until the ball."

Niklas went out onto the road and ran toward the docks. He found his stallion tied where he left him and paid the man more for watching the steed. The morning sun would be rising soon and he had to get back to the stables quickly. How tempted he was to go back down the road and give Alahandra a ride home. He breathed deeply at the thought of her arms holding around him. If anyone saw them together, word would spread to the King. He would go on his way and anticipate seeing Alahandra at the ball.

The wet of her dress slowed Alahandra down. She walked slowly, replaying each moment in her mind. Touching her lips she felt heat rise in her face. How could she let herself get involved with the Prince? She thought of Rylic. Would he care that another man's arms were around her? No, of course not. Rylic probably had women in every port. Rylic was wild and adventurous. He loved not being tied down. Prince Niklas wanted adventure, but she knew his adventurous days were numbered. A man in line for the throne would never want a common thief. He had given her his first kiss. She smiled thinking of his eyes moving over her body.

Alahandra was snatched by the arm, almost falling in between two shops. Jazier.

"Well, well, stayed out all night did we? I've been waiting here forever," he said.

Alahandra looked at him and glared. "What do you want, Jazier?"

"Midnight swim?" Jazier laughed, tugging at her dress.

"What do you want? I need to get back to the shop."

Jazier grabbed her face. "You work for me remember? Don't forget yourself or your precious father may wake up at the wrong end of a knife." The smell of strong drink from his mouth polluted the air around them.

Alahandra didn't respond. She breathed deeply wondering if she could get the knife from him and kill him.

He ran his hand down her side. "Well, papa isn't here right now. You and I could strike a deal. You have the body and the strength." He squeezed her hip. "There are many boats that find port here for trade. Many men needing company. We could make a lot of money."

His hands on her made her stomach knot in disgust.

"If you want to keep your hands, you will remove them from me," Alahandra seethed.

Jazier laughed. "If your kidnapping doesn't work, you will beg me to let you work the docks. If not, I'm moving on without you and your father. He no longer has worth." He pushed Alahandra away. She stumbled, fell hard onto the street, and scraped her hands.

She looked up at him. "You will pay for this, for your behavior, and your threats."

Jazier walked away laughing.

Alahandra stood up and looked at her hands. Small drops of blood dotted her palms. She wondered if she could get out of the kidnapping and start her life here in this village, but Jazier would kill her father in the woods and no one would ever know. All of the feelings she was having, she had to push down and do the job.

Walking up to the dress shop, she knew she would have to explain herself to Haya. She turned the doorknob quietly and pushed the door gently open. The bell rang softly to alert her entrance.

"I'm back here, dear. Lock the door," Haya said.

Alahandra walked to the back quietly. When she turned the corner, Haya stood up from the table. The blacksmith sat across from her.

"Miss," he said.

"Sir," Alahandra said, smiling.

Haya smiled. "We were walking and talking so much that we lost track of time. We came back here for hot tea. Alahandra, this is Bradford. I know you know each other but haven't been formerly introduced."

Bradford stood. "Nice to meet you, Alahandra. The way Haya

talks about you, I thought you were her daughter."

"She feels like family to me," Alahandra smiled. "Don't mind me. I'm going to go nap before we open. We'll be sewing all day, I'm sure."

"No doubt. I can't wait to hear what kept you out all night, dear," Haya laughed.

"There is always a story, my dear friend. Always a story," Alahandra smiled and winked.

She got another dress with more underclothes to change into and placed her wet clothes in a pile near her sleeping mat. Just a little rest until Haya's company leaves so she can survive all the work. Closing her eyes made her mind reel. The Prince. She kissed the Prince! How would she feel when she saw him again? Sleep overcame her quickly as she gave way to her imagination and allowed herself to enjoy each memory of Niklas.

CHAPTER
Six

Alahandra woke to the smell of coffee. Her dress had been repaired and was hanging on a line across the door. It had been cleaned and was drying. How long had she slept?

She walked into the kitchen. "I'm sorry I slept. What time is it? Is the shop open?"

"I kept it closed for the morning. I had to sleep too. Work will always be waiting on us. Come, sit. Let's talk."

Alahandra sat as Haya poured her coffee. She remained silent.

Haya's smile faded when she saw the scrapes on Alahandra's hands. "Dear, did something bad happen? Are you okay?"

Alahandra smiled and sighed, "So much happened that I'm having trouble processing it all." She proceeded to tell her about what transpired outside the tavern and the dark shadow that approached her.

"The Prince! That's intriguing. What else?"

"I took him on a hike through the woods. I thought he would give up and want to go back, but he enjoyed himself. It was beautiful up there with all the stars, and I took him to a secret place where the sands meet the water." She felt the heat rise to her face.

"And then he kissed you!" Haya clapped.

"What?" Alahandra said surprised.

"You are strong, Alahandra. A strong woman will blush when God moves in her life, a child touches her heart, or if she knows a man wants her body."

"Haya!" she laughed. "You are bold."

"I speak the truth. I have little time for social formalities. I kissed Bradford."

"You did?"

"I asked him in for tea, closed the door behind him and asked if he would like to kiss me. I think I shocked him. I told him there was no need to have anyone that might be out and about seeing us. People in this village need to see us as business owners, not objects of their conversations."

"Tell me what happened!" Alahandra leaned forward.

"He stepped closer and held my face in his hands. He kissed me so gently and so long that we were both breathless."

"Will you see him today?" Alahandra asked.

"Of course. I'll walk down the street and there he'll be," Haya laughed.

"You are quite terrible," Alahandra smiled.

"I told him we could walk again this evening after we finish our work. He said he would be in his shack behind his work building, and to come get him when I was ready. I wonder if we should walk or if I should suggest we stay in his shack for a while." Haya laughed loudly. "You must think me terrible, but I am not like normal women. You forget that I sailed the seas and my son is a pirate."

"Oh, I can't forget your son," Alahandra said and smiled. She felt the heat rise to her face again.

"Oh, no, you are conflicted aren't you? You know Rylic is not tame enough."

"Did I say I wanted tame? I did not say tame. I did not say I wanted either man," Alahandra said.

"You don't have to say so, my dear. I can see your heart through your eyes." Haya spoke softly.

"Prince Niklas and I kissed, and he said he would save dances for me. I just can't imagine being there in public with him. Why can't he just be normal? Why can't Rylic just be normal?"

"Dear," Haya patted her hand, "if they were normal, you wouldn't have even looked at them twice."

"Let's not talk about me anymore. Let's sew and talk about you. Will you tell me your stories? I would love to hear about you and all your adventures."

Haya clapped her hands. "I think I have some stories you would enjoy. I have seen many things in my time, and most you won't believe."

The two sat and worked all day and into the evening as Haya told stories of her youth and her time on the open ocean. Laughter filled the walls of the dress shop, and Alahandra felt that this was her life now, not the before or what was coming.

As the rest of the week passed, almost every woman from the village came through the dress shop doors to have a dress mended or made. Haya was a wizard with the fabric and could adorn the simplest dress with ribbon and pearls to create a gown worthy of any ball.

The day before the ball approached. Alahandra delivered many gowns to save time. The entire village was filled with frenzied excitement. She could hardly contain herself walking through the market. She nodded to the blacksmith.

"Bradford, sir, are you quite ready for the ball?"

He slapped his knees. "My dear, I'll not sleep a wink this night thinking about dancing with Haya. I am enthralled by her."

"She is excited too, just so you know. You have stolen her heart," she said.

He sighed, "I gave mine freely." he winked and walked back toward the fire.

Alahandra sighed. Love was beautiful.

"Hey," came a voice from beyond the shops. "Alahandra, come over here."

"Father!" Alahandra ran to him. "Did Jazier just let you leave? Can we go away? I have money saved that could buy us a way out of the port. Come with me."

"Alahandra," Mikal said, pulling her arm back, "I wanted to make sure you were still going through with the plan. The ransom we'll get will set us up for years. You won't have to work. We can travel away from here and enjoy a good life."

"But I have a job, Father. We could make this place our home. A real home."

Mikal laughed. "You sleep in a dress shop, my dear. That is not your home. We don't belong here." he pulled her closer. "Don't mess this up for us. Just say you're ready."

Alahandra looked down and felt her heart break. His only concern was the money. Not his welfare or his life. Not her feelings. He never once asked how she had been. She would get him the money. Jazier would have his share, and then she would deliver the Prince back to his world. She would go away forever and leave all the memories she made here behind.

She looked up at him with a stern expression. "Don't worry. I'll take care of it, and you won't have to worry about anything for as long as you live. Let me say though, if you are caught, I will show no loyalty."

"Agreed. We'll make our way to the castle tomorrow, and be waiting out in the gardens for you and the Prince. You've cleaned up nicely, and should have no problem enticing him to leave with you."

Alahandra's looked away. This was it. She was on her own. "Goodbye, Father, I must be on my way." She knew Jazier had gotten to him. In all their years together, he had never treated her this way and made her feel like a thief.

She walked on to the dress shop. There wasn't time to ponder the hurt trying to engulf her. She had to regain her focus and get ready for the rest of the day.

"I said, hey pretty lady, do you have a smile for this wandering soul?"

The familiar voice snapped her back to reality. Standing in the doorway of the dress shop was the one friend she needed today to take her mind off things. Rylic. The sun had bronzed his face and his eyes softened when she smiled.

"Back so soon?" Alahandra asked.

"Now, how could I stay away from such beauty," Rylic said, walking toward her. He picked her up and swung her around. "I swear on the Heart of the Ocean that you are even more beautiful since the last time I held you in my arms."

"Words drip from your lips like the morning dew, dear Rylic," she said, putting her arms around his neck.

"Words are easy when you are the topic," he teased, kissing her cheek and slowly putting her back down.

They stared at each other for a moment enjoying being close, and Haya came out of the door.

"You two stop before someone sees you," she laughed. "I can't decide which is worse, the girl smitten over the pirate, or the pirate taken by the strong willed maiden. Silly you both are."

Rylic took Alahandra's hand and kissed it. "What if I kissed her right here in the street?"

"What if I chased him around the market?" Alahandra laughed.

"Chase? Him?" Haya laughed. "I think you have that backwards dear. This hulagin does the skirt chasing. You just don't mind being caught. Now get in here you two, and let's have a bite to eat. It's good to have you back so soon son."

They entered the dress shop, and Rylic's eyes sparkled with excitement. "I was on my way to commandeer the ship from Africa. It's the one I've been waiting on. The biggest haul I could have ever made. We made port not far from the place I was told the ship would be to get more supplies, and I found out there was a ship from India in port with a grand supply of just about everything you could imagine. I know this is a busy day with the ball being tomorrow, but I want you to come see if there's anything you want from my take. I've never seen this much gold and gems in all my life."

"We still have a good bit of work to deliver, but we can do it later. Let me see if I can borrow the blacksmith's wagon," Haya said and offered Rylic tea.

He took it and drank it slowly. "I have more tea for you too. I know the ship from Africa would have been grand, but from what I made from this haul, I can travel and see what treasures I can find."

Haya got up from the table and motioned for the door. "I'll be right back."

Alahandra had so many words she wanted to say to him, but she kept them to herself.

Rylic breathed in deeply. "Are you excited about the ball?"

"I think I will feel out of place."

"I think you will be the envy of every woman there, and the desire of every man."

Alahandra would have looked away from him, but she wanted to see him smile after saying such words to her.

Rylic leaned back in his chair. "Want to come sail away with me?"

"Now what would I do on that ship?" Alahandra teased.

Rylic slowly raised from his chair and took her hand. She stood and he moved closer. "You and I could..."

"Do not finish that sentence, Rylic," Haya said entering the shop. "The wagon is outside. Let's get you covered a little so that you do not draw attention to us."

Alahandra and Rylic followed her out. Rylic, covered in a cloak, looked at Haya. "We must hurry. I don't want to port long."

"Wise to be on your way until you find a place for your wealth," Haya whispered.

They drove to the docks quickly, but quietly. When they arrived, one man was sitting on the edge of the ship. "Ahoy, Captain!" the man yelled.

"James, thank you good man for keeping guard," Rylic shouted.

The three boarded the ship and they made their way below. Haya stopped quickly as she walked through the door. She looked to Rylic. Alahandra put her hand over her mouth.

Rylic motioned for them to enter. "Look through it all. See what you would like to keep and what you think would sell."

Alahandra moved her hands over the fine cloth. Haya picked a few items up and put them by the door. She watched her sort through the cloth and take what she wanted.

A small intricate designed box was on the floor under the table. She picked it up and opened it to reveal items that would adorn a woman's dressing table. A brush with a pearl handle, a pearl colored comb to be worn in the hair, and a small hand mirror also with a pearl handle.

"It's yours," Rylic whispered with his face by her ear.

"I've never owned anything so fine."

Rylic walked across the room and brought a chest from under the table. He opened it slowly. "Ladies, come over here."

Alahandra couldn't believe what she was seeing. Jewels of all colors, diamonds, and gold coins. Rylic ran his fingers through it and picked up a handful.

"This chest is for you both."

Alahandra's eyes widened. "It's too much."

"It's never too much for you or my mum," Rylic said. "The men don't want the cloth, so let's load it all up on the wagon. I've got an old sail we can use to cover it all with in the back." he took out another huge chest and opened it.

"These are the teas, Mum. There's so many wonderful types. I know you'll find a favorite."

Haya patted his face. "I love it all, my son. I love it all. Thank you," Haya said.

The crew filled the wagon high with as much as they could.

"I'll ride back with you and help you unload. After that I'll have to be on my way."

Haya nodded.

The unloading was quick. Haya put as much as she could in her dwelling so as not to attract attention. Alahandra moved the mat she slept on out of the way to fill up her space too. So many containers were brought in. She wondered what could be in them all. She dared not ask. Not yet.

As the three finished, Haya wiped her brow. "I'll return the wagon to the blacksmith. Best you walk back quickly in the shadows."

Rylic nodded. Haya left the shop. Alahandra looked at Rylic, and he moved closer to her, extending his hand. "You won't see me for a while."

She laced her fingers through his and sighed. "I may be gone when you return."

She could see the shock on his face at her comment. Immediately she wished she had not said it.

"Haya doesn't know, and I'm not sure. I've been a thief for so long, and I'd like to move to a place I can make a fresh start. Perhaps open my own shop. Your mum has taught me well."

"If you go, take as much from the chest as you can carry. Never want or do without. You deserve a good life. Mum will miss you, and I…"

He paused, still holding her hand. The silence hung thick between them.

He pulled her to him, wrapping his arms around her. She looked up to him so their faces were inches apart. He started to speak, but Alahandra moved her lips to his. He welcomed the invitation. She allowed herself to feel all the passion of the moment and pressed her body to his. She knew their time together was brief.

His lips moved from hers kissing her cheek and moving to her neck. She gasped when his hands moved up her back. His touch sent a fire through her. The softness of his lips on her neck was a feeling she wasn't prepared for. It caused a want in her that she had never known. The desire to get lost in the feel of his arms was overwhelming and exciting.

Knowing Haya would return at any moment, she released her hands from around him and gently moved back. Rylic released his arms from her. They still stood close looking into each other's eyes. Neither spoke. Rylic stepped close then leaned his forehead to hers. She touched his cheek gently. Alahandra wanted him to ask her to leave with him. To take Haya and her away and never return.

Haya entered the shop. "I wish you could see yourselves. Caught up in the moment so that you don't even speak. Never have I seen two more taken with each other and neither want to talk about it." She paused when they still didn't move. "Rylic, come see us again soon."

Rylic turned to look at Haya. "I'll lay low for a while. This take was so big that I'll be hunted for some time. I'll make a way back to you soon." He looked back to Alahanadra and took her hand. "I will see you again." He kissed the back of her hand and then turned to go.

"Take care of each other." Rylic said, walking over to Haya. He hugged her and walked to the door.

Alahandra watched him and knew whatever she said in this moment would be the last words he carried with him from her. She dare not reveal her feelings to him or Haya. He turned and smiled at her. She returned the smile and watched him walk away.

Haya walked over to her and took her by the arm. "I don't know what was said between the two of you, but let's not dwell on it right now. We have treasure to look through and quite a few people coming in today to get their dresses for the ball. We need to fit ours one last time too. I want it to be a night we shall never forget."

Alahandra nodded. She should have said something to Rylic. Anything, but she let him walk out of her life.

The rest of the evening she helped Haya. Her thoughts were on the seas with Rylic and in the castle with Prince Niklas. She wanted to run away and not think about kidnapping Prince Niklas. He was going to hate her. Rylic and Haya would hate her when they found out what she had done. Haya had been so nice to her, and it was all about to go away. The wonderful way of life she was building was all about to be destroyed. Jazier would hurt her father, without doubt. Even though her father had said the things he had, she wondered if he was sent to say those things? She would find out the truth, and someday, Jazier would pay.

CHAPTER
Seven

The day of the ball arrived. Alahandra woke early, and busied herself around the shop. She could not shake the sorrow from her heart. A knock at the door startled her. Haya opened the door slowly, and in stepped a royal courier about Alahandra's age.

"A message for a Miss Alahandra," he presented a letter to her.

She stood to take the message, and curtsied to him. When she took the letter, the odd man turned to go.

"Your name, sir," Alahandra asked.

He turned to her and smiled. "My name is Landor. I usually do not deliver messages; however, I would do anything for Prince Niklas. I have served him since birth, and he is like a brother to me."

Alahandra held the letter up to open it, but hesitated. "Would you like some tea?" she asked. "We have bartered for some of the finest tea in India if you care to stay. A long evening awaits, and I can't think of anything I want more than a cup of tea."

"I would love a cup of tea. Thank you for your kindness," Landor said, bowing to Haya and Alahandra.

Haya clapped him on the back as she walked by. "No need for formalities within these walls, my good man. Have a seat and know you are welcome here to be yourself."

"I dare say, I have never heard a woman be so bold, but I appreciate your hospitality, and myself I shall try to be. Alahandra, would you like to read your letter? Prince Niklas did not say to wait for a reply, but I say, it would be fun to send one back. Don't you think?"

Alahandra laughed at the gentleman. "Mr. Landor, I'll do just that." She got up from the table and opened the letter. The letter started out abrupt.

"Dear Alahandra, I have thought of your lips and nothing more. Now, I have your attention. I wanted to say thank you for our adventure. I can't wait to share this evening with you. The surprise I want to show you will be worth your time here."

"Ah, she blushes," said Haya.

"Haya, you my friend, do you always say every thought in your head?" Alahandra said getting paper from the cabinet.

"Oh my, no, child. Someone might lock me in shackles if I spoke my mind."

Landor laughed. "You two are coming tonight, aren't you?"

"I wouldn't miss this grand affair for anything," Haya said.

"I'll send my reply, Landor, if you can stay but a little longer," Alahandra said.

"Of course. The palace does get quite dull, and this is the most fun I've had in a long while," he said.

Haya sipped her tea. "Tell us about yourself. Everyone has a story."

"I've led a small, but pleasant life. My parents served at the palace, and when I came along, they trained me to serve there as well. It's the only life I've ever known. The Prince and I actually were born just days from each other, and grew up best friends." Landor said, smiling. "I would do anything for his family," he said as he finished his tea.

"You are a good man, Landor. My letter is ready if you can take it to Prince Niklas, please. We shall see you this evening," Alahandra said, giving him the letter.

Haya walked him to the door. "You stop by anytime for a visit. There's always a spot at our table for a friend."

Landor nodded. "An odd pair, you two are, but I gladly call you friends. Until tonight," he said.

"Yes, tonight!" Haya said. She turned to look at Alahandra. "What was that all about?"

"He was telling me he would see me tonight," Alahandra said, looking at the floor. "I told him to save the first dance for me."

"He is taken with you. A prince. Can you imagine? You could be a princess? You could one day be queen!" Haya said.

Alahandra laughed and slapped the table. "Can you imagine? Oh, my sweet Haya, I will never be his princess. I'll not be caged. I want freedom."

"Plans change," Haya said.

"I don't even want to make plans," Alahandra thought about what she had to do. "Let's finish and get ready."

Deliveries were finished and the entire village grew in excitement. Merchants moved all their items in and pulled down tarps. Laughter could be heard throughout the market. The street musicians were wandering around playing merry tunes and singing throughout the village.

Women came by and picked up the few dresses that remained. Haya pulled the covering down over the shop door and bolted the lock. "Time for us to get ready, my dear."

"This will be a night we will never forget," Alahandra said.

Once they were dressed, Haya called her from the back. "Are you ready for me to fix your hair?"

"Yes, I'm ready," Alahandra said, coming from the back room.

"Oh, Alahandra, you look amazing! I have never seen a finer gown in all my days!"

"You really think it's okay? I feel so different," Alahandra said, touching the necklace Rylic had given her.

"It's called feeling beautiful, and you, my dear, will turn the head of every man in the court. Your prince will be captivated by you," Haya said.

"I want to dance all night," Alahandra said.

"Oh, me too. I can't wait to see Bradford."

A knock resounded at the door. Haya opened it quickly. Bradford stepped in. His eyes widened as he stepped closer to her.

"Haya, you are the most gorgeous creature. If I die today, I will know there will never be another more beautiful than you." He took her hand and kissed it gently.

"You scoundrel. Your words are meant to entice me. Well, it worked. I'm yours for the evening," Haya laughed.

"You two. Let's go," Alahandra laughed.

Bradford was quiet on the drive. Many other villagers were making their way. Some were riding in carriages, some were walking, and others on horseback.

The castle grounds were more exquisite than Alahandra could have imagined. Ornate statues lined the pathway entrance. Large pruned shrubbery decorated the grounds as far as she could see. Alahandra's stomach knotted in dread and fear. The castle grounds were huge. How could she get the Prince out without getting caught? She took a deep breath and decided not to think about the end of the evening yet. She wanted to enjoy the small moments and make memories she could carry with her when she left this place. Haya and Bradford had each other now. She wouldn't have to worry about her being lonely with him around. She could leave.

Once the three of them were walking up the stairs, Alahandra wanted to enjoy this beautiful moment. Haya looked to her and smiled. The excitement showed in her face also.

The formality of announcing each guest was put aside for the evening. Guards manned the entrance so that parties were ushered in little by little. As she entered the ballroom, her heart began to pound in her chest. The room was lined with familiar faces and royalty that must have come from far away to partake in the evening.

Alahandra scanned the room but could not find Prince Niklas.

Haya tapped her on the shoulder. "He'll be announced later."

Alahandra nudged her, and they both laughed.

The music softly played. She swayed gently, wishing she didn't have to be who she was and simply enjoy the night.

The trumpets sounded at the far end of the room. A man stepped to the balcony. "King Vaughn, Queen Anlita, and Prince Niklas." The three stepped to the balcony and waved to the crowd below. Prince Niklas looked around the room and found Alahandra. His smile broadened. She felt herself warm throughout her body when he looked at her.

Haya leaned to her and whispered, "You are blushing."

"You take care to mind your own business," Alahandra smiled and nudged her friend again.

King Vaughn raised his hand. "My loyal subjects, my friends, my kingdom, you are welcome here. May this night fill you with joy. Come, let the ball begin!"

The music began, and couples made their way to the middle of the floor. Haya and Bradford clasped hands and walked out on the floor. As they came together to begin dancing, Alahandra saw Haya a different way. She knew this would be a change in her relationship with Bradford. They looked longingly at one another.

Watching Haya, she didn't notice the Prince approaching.

"You appear lost in thought," Prince Niklas said.

"It is good to see Haya happy. She is a good woman and deserves much," Alahandra said.

Alahandra turned and looked at Niklas. He looked at her, and both stood motionless.

"You are stunning, Alahandra," Niklas said, stepping closer.

"And you, look as if you are ready to take the throne," she leaned over and whispered.

"The throne is the future. Tonight is made for fun, for dance, and for… adventure," Niklas said, bowing to her and extending his hand to her.

She placed her hand in his, and he led her out to the dance floor. Others parted and moved away to give the Prince room to dance.

"I don't like everyone watching," Alahandra whispered.

"Don't think about them," Niklas whispered, leaning close and tilted her head up. "Look at me, and feel the music. Pretend all those people aren't even here."

He twirled her out and spun her back in, keeping his hand firmly behind her. She followed his lead and allowed the music to fill her soul. She reeled in his arms moving and swaying with him. She didn't want the moment to end.

He whispered in her ear. "Do you know how amazing you are, Alahandra?"

She didn't respond. She wanted to be in the moment and not think about the reality of the night's end. She didn't want to think about saying goodbye to Rylic and how it had hurt. She didn't want to think about giving up on herself to save her father.

"You are lost in thought. Are you okay my dear?" Niklas asked.

"I'm overwhelmed by everything," Alahandra said. "Your life is magnificent."

"My life was a bore until I met you," he whispered.

The song ended. Niklas bowed and Alahandra curtsied, her hand still in his. He tightened his grip.

"Let's go to the buffet. I haven't had time to eat one morsel today," he said. "And then, we can dance all night."

"I think the other women in the ballroom have other plans for you," she said, following him as others watched.

"I have no obligations to anyone, so if you will allow me, I will be your dance partner all evening," Niklas said, turning to her.

She blushed and squeezed his hand. "I accept."

He took a small delicate plate and filled it with food. "Try this. It's my favorite." He handed her a small pastry filled with cream.

It seemed to melt in her mouth. "That's the most amazing thing I've ever eaten."

He motioned toward the table. "Our chef made all of my favorite dishes tonight."

The tempo of the music grew faster.

"Let's dance, shall we? Then let's take a picnic out to the garden where we can eat and talk in peace."

Alahandra started to respond when the Queen approached Nikals.

"Son, there is someone I want you to meet."

"Mother, this is Alahandra, she works in a dress shop in town," he said.

Alahandra curtsied deeply and bowed her head. "Majesty."

"Yes, child, it's nice to meet you. Come, Nikals," she said, moving through the crowd.

Niklas released her hand. "I shall return."

Alahandra watched him go across the room with the Queen to join a man and what she assumed was his daughter. Niklas bowed to her and extended his hand. The girl took his hand, and they moved to the center of the ballroom floor. He placed his hand on the side of the girl's arm and took her other hand in his, keeping his arms extended to create room between them. They began to move effortlessly across the floor.

Alahandra felt her stomach knot in jealousy. Jealous of the Prince? What was she thinking? This was not her world.

Niklas locked eyes with her each time he turned her direction. His smile was for her and not for the girl in his arms.

"May I have this dance?" came a voice beside her.

Alahandra turned to face a handsome man dressed in fine royal attire. His skin darkened by the sun and his face strong and beautiful. His eyes were dark brown and his hair blacker than the night sky.

"Yes, thank you," she responded, and took his extended hand.

What if she stumbled and made a fool of herself with this stranger?

"I am Prince Algoron, of the Bastik Hills," he said softly.

"I am Alahandra. I work in the village," she responded.

"Forgive my boldness, fair lady, but you are the most breathtaking creature I have ever seen. I saw you across the room and wanted nothing more than to hear you speak," he said.

"You are kind, Prince Algoron," she said, looking at him. "And I think you have intrigued every maiden in this room. Are you a friend of Prince Niklas?"

"If you would, simply call me Algoron, and yes, I've known

Niklas since we were children," he said. "We've been acquaintances more than friends I would say. Our families ruling neighboring kingdoms have thrown us together more than others."

The music ended and Alahandra looked for Niklas. He was standing with the girl he had just danced with, and as the music began again, he took her hand and continued to keep her as a partner. Alahandra looked at Algoron.

"Thank you for the dance," she curtsied.

"If you would indulge me, I would share the next one with you, or we could take a walk to talk," he said.

"Fresh air would be nice," Alahandra said.

Prince Algoron took her by the hand and twirled her out and then back to him. He pulled her close, and they both laughed. Nikals looked over to them and stopped smiling.

Algoron squeezed her hand. "Come, the garden is adorned with lights. It's almost as beautiful as you," he said, kissing her hand.

She laughed and followed him through a grand door to an outside patio.

He breathed deeply. "I do hate going to a ball. I had much rather be out of doors and enjoying the sunshine."

"That is why your skin looks as if it has been kissed by the sun," she said.

He turned to her. "Your words are different than other women."

"I could care less how I am supposed to talk to royalty or men for that matter. I have no time for social graces, but I do love to dance," she said, spinning around.

Prince Algoron moved quickly to her and took her in his arms. "Then let us dance under the stars, beautiful woman."

Alahandra breathed in and closed her eyes. "Yes, let's," she said softly, looking up at him.

He spun her around slowly and moved his hand across her back.

"I like being close to you, beautiful maiden," he said.

"I like being close to you, beautiful Prince," she said mockingly.

"Your words stir inside me," he said. "I like that you speak your mind. It makes me want to kiss you, though."

"You are bold," she laughed.

"Bold is what keeps my bed warm at night," he said, pulling her close. His lips were just above hers. She did not move, but then smiled and stepped away.

"A warm bed implies I might suffer by comparison. I do believe I'll save my kisses," she said, smiling at him.

"For Niklas," he said. "You know he has to marry a Princess. Give that dream up my dear. His mother wouldn't allow you within arms reach of that crown. She's a beast."

Alahandra didn't respond.

He stepped forward. "My mother and father have decided that my happiness is more important than titles and such. I," he touched her arm, "can have," he caressed her shoulder, "anyone," he slid his arm around her, "I so desire."

"Desire. Is that what this is?" she whispered.

"The want of you causes heat to course through me," he said. "What do you want, Alahandra?"

She looked up at him and stepped away. She had a job to do. He stepped close behind her.

"Let's leave," he said, putting his hands on her shoulders. "Let's walk down to the water, take off these restricting clothes, and enjoy each other in the moonlight." he kissed her neck. She sighed.

"You don't even know me," she said quietly.

"I don't have to know you to know your body wants mine," he moved his hands down her arms and across her stomach. "If you were a proper lady, you would have left me standing here long ago, but you are curious and bold."

She didn't move, but breathed deeply. "I'm not a proper lady, but not like you think. I have never known the touch of a man like you touch me. It is intriguing and a little frightening," she whispered, leaning against Algoron.

"Ah, you invite," he whispered. "If I get that dress off, you can wrap yourself around me, and we'll not sleep at all this night."

She turned to look at him. She could throw it all away, everything, everyone, and just leave with him. Someone wanted her, if only for a night.

A loud cracking sound startled her and Prince Algoron fell to the ground.

Jazier was behind him with a broken flower pot in his hand

"What is wrong with you?" Alahandra said. "That's not Prince Niklas."

"I've been waiting here forever, and I heard you call him Prince. He's out so I'm taking him to the wagon. Now go get the Prince out here. You with your swaying hips and firm breast, you could have the King follow you out with a promise of lifting your skirt tonight." Jazier laughed as he dragged Prince Algoron into the bushes.

Alahandra didn't respond. She looked around and made her way back inside. This wasn't going as planned. She wanted to leave.

Landor saw Alahandra enter the room and went to stand by her as she scanned the room.

"He's still caught up with the royals," Landor said.

Alahandra smiled at him.

"He does fancy you. You are all he has talked about since the first time he bumped into you in the market," he said. "Would you like to dance?"

"Yes, thank you," she said.

Alahandra looked at Niklas again, and saw that he was watching them instead of talking to the woman in front of him.

"He does care for you," Landor whispered.

"He is a wonderful man," Alahandra whispered.

"But do you have feelings for him?" Landor asked.

Alahandra was silent.

"I apologize. I'm protective of him," Landor said.

"No need to apologize, and yes, I do. I can't help but have feelings for him," she said, smiling. "He is kind and thoughtful. He makes me feel beautiful."

"So this isn't just about him being a prince?" Landor questioned.

"Your love for your friend is refreshing, but no, this has nothing to do with his being a prince. In fact, I wish he could have been a worker in the market. Then our lives wouldn't be so far apart."

Niklas moved quickly to them and tapped Landor on the shoulder. "May I?" he said.

"Of course. I tried to keep her busy so as not to have another steal her away," Landor said, smiling. "You two have fun, and you were right."

Niklas winked at Landor. "Told you so."

Landor smiled, bowed and moved on to ask a maiden to dance.

Niklas slid his arm slowly around Alahandra. "I apologize for leaving you. My mother is relentless. I'm free now," he said, twirling her around with him.

"He's protective and caring," Alahandra smiled.

"I told him you were not like other women. I told him you are…" Niklas stopped and looked at her. He held his words and smiled as he breathed in the moment with her.

"I want to remember this night forever," she whispered.

"Me too," he whispered. "I have something to show you."

Niklas took her by the hand and led her to the edge of the room. "There's something outside I want to share with you."

"Won't you be missed?" Alahandra asked.

"The party has started. No one will think of my whereabouts until the party is over. My father is surrounded by men who will hang on his every word, and my mother loves playing hostess to everyone. She will walk around the ballroom and meet as many people as possible before the night is over."

"Landor is on assignment to distract them if they do ask for me."

Alahandra took a deep breath. She knew what had to be done. She knew Jazier was somewhere in the garden waiting on them.

"Where are you taking me?" she asked.

"There is a secret passage through a cave that lies on the back wall. It's a short walk through the garden. The cave is a place I used to go to as a boy. Through the back gate, the cave is just out of sight. It's one of my favorite places, and I wanted to share it with you."

"Will you get in trouble for leaving the grounds?"

"How do you think I left when I saw you? I feel so confined here, and this is how I feel normal. I think you will like the cave," Niklas said, leading her through the royal gardens. "This is the South gate. All the guards are in the North towers at the entrance. We are completely alone," Prince Niklas said, opening the gate.

Alahandra stepped through the gate, and he closed it quietly behind them. It was all too perfect. Fear gripped her. She didn't want to go through with this.

"Niklas," she whispered.

"Wait before we speak. Follow me a little further," He motioned, leading her into the cave. He struck rocks together to create a spark. It ignited to light a torch and fed the small fire. Walking around he lit several torches on the wall. Alahandra looked around the modest dwelling with a place to sit and bedding near the wall. Books stacked in several places seemed as if they were old friends waiting on him to return. A small stack of clothing by the makeshift bed she guessed was for the endless hours he spent out here. A Prince in need of escaping the royals. In that moment, she felt sorry for him. How much time was he spending alone?

"You've made a wonderful place here."

He looked around. "It's the only place I feel like me right now. I wanted to share it with you because I knew you could appreciate it." He stepped closer and extended his hand.

"I always appreciate a place of refuge," she said, taking his hand. "I wish we could stay in here forever and forget the world outside."

Niklas took her other hand and stepped close so that his face was just above hers. "May I kiss you?"

Alahandra put her hands on his cheeks and moved her mouth closer to his.

"Now that's the way to lure him in, girl. You are a master," a voice came from the entrance.

Niklas and Alahandra both looked quickly. "Jazier."

"Who is this man, Alahandra?" Niklas asked.

"I am the man in charge," Jazier said, raising a sword.

Prince Niklas stepped in front of Alahandra. "Sir, you will stand down or you will perish."

Jazier laughed, "Alahandra, we have to hurry. The carriage is outside."

"Niklas, please, just do as he says," Alahandra said. "I'm sorry."

"You care for him?" Jazier asked. "Good, then you will be responsible for him, and I won't have to worry about keeping him alive."

"Keep me alive," Niklas said, looking to Alahandra. "What's he talking about?"

"We'll talk on the way. Let's go," Alahandra said, motioning for Niklas to move forward.

As the three made their way outside, Jazier kept the sword at Niklas.

"Get in the wagon, and keep quiet," Jazier said.

Mikal had the reins in hand. "Hello, child."

"Father."

"Father?" Niklas looked at her. "So it was all a trick?"

"No, Niklas," Alahandra said. "I'll explain it all later." Her stomach knotted with the heaviness of the moment. This was it. The beginning of the unraveling of the joy she had felt recently.

"I'll go with you, Alahandra. I'll do whatever he says," Niklas said, getting in the wagon.

"Let's go. They'll find out soon enough about their Prince," Jazier whispered.

"What are you going to do to me?" Niklas asked.

"Only going to keep you for a short while. Well, until your father pays for your return."

"A ransom. That's what this is about?" Niklas laughed. "You'll have your money soon enough."

Alahandra put her hand on his arm. He looked down at her touch and moved his arm away. He leaned close to her. "You know I will never trust you again."

She pulled her hand away.

They all rode in silence. The night sky was filled with stars. Alahandra knew that no matter what, she would never forget the way the sky looked in this moment, and she would never forget the hurt she felt or caused. Away. That's where she wanted to be. Away from all this.

CHAPTER
Eight

Once they were back in the village, Mikal drove the wagon back to the stables, and they all got out.

"We must hurry before others start returning. Mikal and Princey here can carry the other one." Jazier said, throwing back the blanket in the wagon. Prince Algoron lay unconscious.

"You brought him?" Alahandra said loudly.

"He's a prince, right? I thought they both would bring a good price. Two is better than one," Jazier said.

"I don't even want to know how he came to be here," Nikals said. "I saw you leave the room with him."

"Well, I can tell you," Jazier said. "His hands were having fun on that wild woman, and she was enjoying it too."

Niklas looked down. Alahandra glared at Jazier.

Jazier laughed walking toward the woods. "We must be careful returning to camp lest we get lost. Hurry with that other Prince. We have to get out of the street."

Alahandra heard the fabric rip on the hem of her gown as she made her way into the woods. She looked down and yanked her dress free. Her beautiful dress. She would never wear it again; she knew that now.

"Regretting are we?" Jazier laughed.

"You will not speak to me," Alahandra said.

Jazier moved quickly to her and grabbed her face. The others stopped abruptly. Niklas started to protest, but Jazier held his hand up to quiet him. "You forget your place, girl."

She pulled a knife from her gown and held it to his throat. "You'll not touch me again, or I'll spill your blood from here to the docks."

"You won't, but it's good to see your fire. It means this will work, and you won't go soft," Jazier laughed and pushed her away.

They walked slowly through the dark woods for quite some time. No one spoke. Alahandra slowly took off the necklace from Rylic. It had to have worth as beautiful as it was. She would hide it when they arrived at camp so Jazier wouldn't get his hands on it. They came to the clearing and Jazier threw out his arms wide and laughed. "Welcome home, Alahandra. Prince Niklas, welcome to your new dwelling for the time being. Make yourself at home."

Mikal and Niklas placed Algoron on the ground. Jazier shackled him to a tree. He turned to Niklas with another shackle.

"I don't need a shackle. I won't leave until you get your money. I won't put Alahandra in danger," he said.

A tear rolled down her cheek, and she turned to her father.

"Once Prince Niklas and Prince Algoron are returned safely, I'm going away," she said.

"Alahandra..." Niklas said.

"Don't." She looked at him. "Don't say anything. You may go in the shack. There are other clothes if you wish to change. If not, you may go to sleep."

"Sleep? This is my first night to spend in the woods. I'm too excited to sleep."

Mikal laughed. "Excited? I don't think you understand."

"I understand perfectly. You want money. I want to enjoy my freedom. Why cause trouble? Tell me what I can do, and I will help," Niklas said.

Mikal raised his eyebrows and nodded. "Let's try to wake up that man there. He's going to be quite angry, but he'll be better awakened now than to wake up on his own," Mikal said, passing a cup of water to Niklas. "Pour it on him."

Niklas smiled. "With pleasure." He poured the water on Algoron who startled awake. He raised up slowly and held his head.

"What are you doing, Niklas? What happened? Where are we?" Algoron asked.

"We have been kidnapped, old chum," he said.

"Wait, I was with a maiden in the garden," Algoron said.

"Oh, yes, she's here too," Niklas pointed to Alahandra.

"Did they hurt you?" Algoron asked.

Jazier laughed. "Hurt her? She's one of us."

Alahandra walked into the makeshift shack to change. She put on her old clothes and held her dress up in the light of the lamp. Her beautiful gown, now nothing more than rags to be burned. She walked quickly out to the fire Mikal had made. Tossing her gown in the fire, she stood there watching it burn. Fire ate it quickly as the hate inside her consumed her. Hate for Jazier. Hate for the life that she had to live. Hate for money and the love of it that caused so much sorrow.

She walked into the woods and sat down on her favorite rock as she began to replay all that happened. It was then that she realized she had sealed her fate. She had to cut her ties with Haya. Haya. Her only friend. She would say goodbye to her when the time is right. She owed her that much. Quickly she took the necklace from her under her shirt and buried it at the base of the rock.

As the night went on, Alahandra didn't move. The moon and stars made their shift in the night sky as she sat motionless. How very small her life seemed. She had wanted nothing more than to dance and forget with Niklas. Now, he was here. All was lost with him. She wanted to sail away with Rylic, but now she would leave this place and never see him again. With the rising of the sun, she would make this day the last she had in these woods. Niklas would be fine without her. She rose to go back to their camp. She would gather her things and go. There was nothing to hold her here now. Walking back into camp, she stopped abruptly.

Niklas sat by the fire with Mikal talking low. Algoron was propped against the tree asleep.

"I told you she would come back," Niklas said.

"I came to get my things. Father, you can take care of Niklas and Algoron. I have no need to stay."

"Alahandra, the money we will make. You will get your cut," Mikal said.

Alahandra laughed. "Money. It's always about money with you. All I wanted was to make a good life for us. I have been working, and I could have made a life for us here. But, you, you wretched man, you made sure I understood completely that it was my duty as your daughter to get the Prince for you. Well, now you have two. And, Father dear, Jazier came to me and let me know he would kill you if I didn't help kidnap Niklas. That's right. Oh, he propositioned me first, and I should have killed him in the streets. But, I tell you this, you will not own me. I'm free, and I am leaving."

Jazier came out of his tent with a sword and held it to Niklas. "If you leave, I will run him through. You will do as I say until the ransom is paid. Oh, don't look so surprised, dear. You would serve my head on a platter to the royal guards if I let you leave. So, my pet, you will do exactly as I say or I kill him. Now sit."

Alahandra sat down across the fire from Niklas. She looked to the ground. There had to be a way to get them all out of here.

Jazier came to sit near the fire. "This is the story that will be told. Alahandra, come over here."

She did as he said. He rose from his seat and punched her hard in the face. She fell to the ground. Niklas moved quickly to her on the ground.

"What is wrong with you?" Mikal yelled, jumping to his feet.

"She was the last person seen with the Princes. Don't you think they'll be hunting her down?" he said, squatting near Alahandra and offering her a piece of cloth.

"Wipe your mouth dear," he said.

She spat on his boot, and he laughed.

He got up and walked back near the fire. "A band of men came riding in on horses while Niklas was showing the maiden and his dear friend his cave. They beat her and took both Princes out of the South gate. I'm going to leave a note saying to bring the money in an old bag and drop it in an old barrel near the end of the market at the edge of town by the well. The barrel backs up the door of that old abandoned building where a lot of people store things. I've gone inside and cut a small hole in the door and the barrel. When the bag is dropped in, I can go through the back door and get the money from the hole in the front. While the kingsmen wait in hiding to see who will come get the loot, I'll take the money, put it in my grocery pouch, and carry it right through town under my turnips and cabbage."

"Alahandra, you will go back to the dress shop today and tell your old woman friend that you made your way back to your father and he treated your wounds. You will tell her nothing more. Work for the day, and when the kingsmen come to question you, do all you can to cry. Then, as the night approaches, tell the old woman you need to take food to your father and you might stay the night with him. If you bring anyone back with you, your Prince dies."

"Go ahead and kill them," Alahandra said.

Niklas jumped to his feet in defense.

"Settle down," Alahandra said. "He won't kill you. No Prince, no ransom. I can say whatever I want. I'm calling his bluff." She looked at Jazier. "I'll go to the shop because I don't want Haya to worry. She's a good friend, and I want to tell her goodbye."

Jazier laughed at her, and walked back into the shack.

Mikal came to sit by Alahandra. "Everything I said to you was all because I had to say it. Jazier threatened to kill you and Haya. Please don't leave."

Alahandra took a stick and poked the fire. "I don't want this life anymore. I want a home. I want to sleep with my mind at rest. This is your life, not mine. I will make my own path now, and we will part ways. I won't take the money from the Kings. I've saved money that will take me to a village where no one knows me." She looked at Niklas. "I know you said you could never trust me again, but all I ask is for your forgiveness."

Mikal got up from the fire and went inside the shack.

Niklas took hold of her hands. "Beautiful maiden, you don't need to ask my forgiveness. I know why you did what you did. I would have done the same for mine." He motioned around him, "Teach me how to do this."

Alahandra wiped her mouth and looked at the blood on her hand. "This? This is what happens when life doesn't make sense."

Niklas knelt in front of her. "I'm sorry that this is your life. I'm sorry that the men in there do not care that you are bleeding out here. I'm sorry that my life requires me to live in a palace and we can't just run off to the next village. I'm sorry that I'm promised to join with a princess from a neighboring kingdom in order to save their people from starvation, because in this moment all I want to do is pledge myself to you forever."

Alahandra felt her stomach tie in knots. She brushed his hair from his forehead. "Sweet Prince, you are crazier than I am." She smiled at him, and she took his hand. "You will live a peaceful life after this and forget all about me."

Niklas pulled her close. "When this is over, return to the palace with me."

Alahandra pushed him away smiling. "I'm going to the dress shop after we make breakfast. Do you want to learn to cook over the fire?"

He nodded.

"We can wake, Algoron when it's ready," she said.

She didn't want to hurt him, but she didn't want to give him false hope. There was a new life for her out there somewhere. She would walk forever to find it.

She went into the shack and brought out eggs and bread.

He looked at the bounty of food and raised an eyebrow when she took out an egg.

"You've never broken an egg, I see," said Alahandra.

"Show me, and I shall never forget," Niklas said.

Alahandra laughed. She took the egg and broke it gently onto the side of the bowl. The egg cracked neatly in her hand. She opened the egg and out dropped the inside. Niklas watched intently.

"Your turn," she said.

He took the egg and banged it on the inside of the bowl. The egg shattered in his hand and shell fell in the bowl.

"You're going to have to pick that out," she said.

"This is an unpleasant undertaking," Niklas winced, raking a finger through the egg.

She had him stir the eggs and stoke the fire. He cut the bread and put it on plates.

Niklas looked up at her. "It's you. The woman from the market that tripped over me. It was you."

Alahandra nodded, "That seems like forever ago."

"I do believe we've changed a little since then," he smiled.

"You are less pompous," she smiled back at him, "and I'm not quite as rude."

"Funny how a little time spent with a person can change your focus. I'm glad I'm here with you."

"You are quite delusional, dear Prince. Here is nothing, a farce of life."

He gave her a plate of food. "Here is with you."

Alahandra saw kindness in his eyes and wondered how he could have such a good heart. She had to keep her head about her and get away from them all.

"Wake Algoron," she said.

Niklas nudged Algoron. His eyes slowly opened. "Something smells wonderful," he whispered.

"I made breakfast," Niklas said.

"You? What do you know of making breakfast?" Algoron laughed.

"I have a good teacher," he said, looking at Alahandra.

Niklas sat back and looked at his accomplishment. He began eating and stopped to look at his plate. He looked to Alahandra. "This food. Did you steal it?"

She nodded, "Yes, it's either steal or go hungry. I don't steal anymore. I have no desire to have my heart blackened with thievery and lies."

"Stolen or not, I say I made a pretty good breakfast," Niklas said, finishing his eggs.

"Indeed," she said. "Now, let's go get water to wash everything."

"Go get?" Niklas asked.

"Yes. We have to take buckets and walk a mile or so to a creek. The water there is fresh. We'll each take two buckets to get enough for washing the dishes and for drinking. We take a bag of clean clothes to wash ourselves while we're there. You two are about the same size as my father, so you can borrow a shirt and pants from him. I know those ball clothes must be frightfully uncomfortable by now."

"I am a bit weary of wearing them," Niklas said.

"I could just strip down and wear nothing," Algoron laughed.

"Spare us," Niklas said. "Thank you, Alahandra, for helping me."

She nodded. He was so kind to her even after all that had happened. A true gentleman. His offer to come back to the palace with him shook her to the core of her heart. Their lives could never coincide. His royalty would never accept her for who she was, and she would change for no one.

"Algoron, do you need to stay in shackles or can we trust you to not run away?" Alahandra said. "I don't want a palace guard showing up here and killing me in my sleep."

"There is no need for shackles. I'll stay. I want to see this through. It's quite the adventure, eh, Niklas?" he said.

"Quite true. It beats having to go out and greet everyone," Niklas laughed.

They stood up. Alahandra released the shackles, they took clothing offered by Mikal, gathered the buckets, and the two followed her into the woods.

When they arrived at the water source, Alahandra showed them how to dip the buckets in and bring them out clean. The last bucket contained soap and a cleaning rag. She showed them how to lather the soap and wash their skin in the creek.

"Your turn. Get good and clean. This is not a daily activity in the woods," she said.

They each stepped into the water and lathered the soap. She stepped up behind Niklas and pushed him causing him to fall. He screamed out as he fell. Grabbing her legs he pulled her down into the water. She yelled out and started laughing as they both sat in the water. Algoron laughed at them. They looked at each other, got up quickly and pushed Algoron down. They all sat there soaked.

"It is good to see you smile, Alahandra," Niklas said.

She leaned to him teasing, with her face near his. "And you are all wet!" She laughed pushing him backward into the water.

He came up soaked and tried to grab her again. She got up and moved away quickly. Algoron jumped up to chase her. He picked her up causing her to scream again. He carried her to the middle of the creek and put her in the water.

"Now we are even," Algoron laughed.

"Even? We are never even," She said, picking up a handful of mud and throwing it at him and hitting him in the chest.

"Aw, now you're in trouble!" he said, reaching down for mud and throwing it at her. It hit her in the side of her head. Her hair dripped of muck. Niklas scoop up two handfuls of mud and hit both of the others in the head.

They all started throwing mud and laughing. When they were out of breath they stopped and sat down in the water.

She looked at her soiled clothes. "At least we have clean drinking water. We'll have to wash our clothes and let them dry in the sun. We'll have to do it here for I do not like Jazier's eyes on me."

"If he touches you, I will kill him," Niklas said, looking up at the sky.

"Thank you for your gallantry, but I can take care of him." She said, touching her bruised face. "And, one day he will pay for what he's done."

"No more talk of him. Let's get cleaned up," Algoron said.

She unbuttoned her shirt and pulled it from her wet skin. Each of the men followed suit, and began to undress down to their undergarments. Taking their clothes, they sat in the creek to scrub the cloth on the rocks and knelt down farther into the water to wash the muck from their hair.

"I know you don't care what I think, and you don't care what is appropriate, but I'm going to tell you that you are a beautiful creature, Alahandra. Forgive me for looking at you," Algoron said.

"Our bodies are beautiful, and I am not ashamed of mine. I should cover myself from you both, but I do not feel that I have to. I have never had a man look at me the way you both do. Your eyes on me make my stomach tighten, and it warms me all over. It is a foreign feeling," she said softly.

"It is desire. The want inside you," Niklas said, looking at her.

"Algoron talked of desire," Alahandra said.

Niklas looked at Algoron and smirked. Algoron smiled and winked at Niklas.

"Algoron is driven by desire. He has known many women," Niklas said.

"I have known many, I must confess, for I love the feel of a woman's skin next to mine," Algoron said.

"Desire is enjoyable and confusing. My body has an aching feeling. It makes me want to kiss you and touch you," she said.

"Yes, I know," Niklas said, looking down. "The want to touch you overwhelms me, but I will sit here and continue washing my clothes," he laughed. "How is it that you and I always end up soaked?"

"Because we are fun, and we enjoy life," she laughed, splashing him.

He splashed her back smiling. "I do enjoy these moments with you," he said, sitting back in the water. "May I kiss you again. My thoughts have been haunted by our first kiss in the moonlight, and we were interrupted before I could kiss you last night."

"I think of it also. The night is a temptress, creating a blanket of darkness where we are bolder than we are in the light. I would very much like to kiss you again," she said, standing to move closer to him.

"And what of me? Do I get to enjoy your kisses too?" Algoron said, laughing.

"Be quiet, Algoron," Niklas said.

"You two are quite the bore. I'm going to rest my eyes." He lay down on the bank in the warm sunshine.

Niklas's eyes moved over her body in her wet undergarment.

"I like when you look at me," she whispered as she knelt beside him.

He moved to his knees in the water in front of her. They gazed at one another without speaking. Her breathing quickened.

His hand moved up her arm and traced her neck. He touched her face, and she sighed.

She placed her hands on his chest and moved them down the front of him. His breath caught as she moved her hands around his hips and up his back.

He pulled her closer. "Your touch creates a fire in me."

His fingers traced the top of her undergarment and stopped at the ties. "May I?"

She nodded.

The ties slid through his fingers and the cloth opened slightly to reveal more of her chest.

She gasped.

He leaned his face to hers brushing his lips to hers. She moaned and moved her hands up his back. She dare not allow the kiss to continue lest her heart get lost. She leaned away from him, and he continued to hold her.

"Let me run away with you," he whispered.

"You talk of fairy tales. Your place is your throne," she teased, touching his face.

"Your place could be beside me," he said.

"I have no need for pageantry and rules," she whispered. "All I need is a wide open sky, enough food and water to keep me alive, and a few kisses every now and then to help me remember I'm alive." she said, kissing him quickly and moving away from him.

"You can always come to me for all the kisses you need," he teased.

"Can you see me showing up at the front gate and telling the guards I need the Prince to come kiss me, and I'll be on my way?" she laughed.

"I think they would agree to anything you ask if you came dressed like this," he said standing.

She gasped at the sight of him. His undergarments clung to his body. His chest glistened in the sunlight filtered by the trees.

"Your body is stunning, Niklas. So unlike any other man in the market or that I've seen anywhere." She said, extending her hand so he would help her up.

He pulled her from the water. Her undergarment slipped from her shoulder exposing more of her skin. He moved his hand over her shoulder. "How can I ever take the throne knowing you are somewhere playing in the water without me?"

"I fear you must suffer without me, or join me when no one is paying attention," she laughed. "For now, let us dry in the sun on the bank there where the light shines through. Our clothes can hang from the branches. I'll have to go soon to talk to Haya. She'll be worried."

"I understand," Niklas said, stretching out in the sun. "Is there anything you need me to do while you are gone?"

"You and Algoron enjoy the forest. Build something or make something from the thousands of sticks around camp. You can always cook more."

Niklas propped up on his elbow and moved his fingers from her neck down to her stomach. She arched slightly responding to his touch. She released a deep breath and closed her eyes.

"You are going to have to keep your hands to yourself," she said.

He lay back down closer to her and reached for her hand. She clasped hold of his and they lay quietly together for a while without speaking.

After a short while, she noticed Niklas's breath slow, and she knew he was sleeping. She raised up and leaned over him, draping her arm across him. Holding him for a moment was all she wanted. She knew her time with him was limited. She closed her eyes and breathed deeply. Leaving Niklas was going to be harder than she thought.

The sun dried them quickly, and she woke up with Algoron pressed to her back asleep. He must have rolled over near her while he was sleeping. His arm was across her with his hand resting on her stomach. She moved slightly and he tightened his arm around her pressing himself to her. His body was warm against her. She wondered what it would be like to have both men kissing her. Touching her.

She moved her hand over Niklas slightly. He turned in his sleep to her. His face close. She moved her hand down his chest and moved her leg between Algoron's. His hand alarmingly moved around her hip and pulled her close. Quietly he kissed her neck. He was awake. She touched his hip, and he pressed closer as he kissed the side of her ear. She took a deep breath and moved her hand along Niklas's side. His eyes fluttered open slowly and he smiled.

He leaned in slightly and kissed her lips softly. She smiled and turned to her back.

Both men propped on their shoulders and didn't say anything.

"Perhaps we should go," Alahandra said.

"Perhaps we should all have some fun," Algoron said, moving his hand across the edge of Alahandra's undergarments.

"I don't like to share," Niklas said, raising up.

Algoron pulled Alahandra to sitting and moved behind her.

"Niklas, have some fun," Algoron said. "You kiss her, and I'll explore her. Wouldn't that be fun, Alahandra?"

Alahandra remained silent.

Niklas stood, "Time to go back to camp."

Algoron kissed her neck. "Your skin is soft and sweet," he said, getting up and pulling her to standing.

Alahandra remained silent. How terrible was she that she enjoyed both men with her?

"Your body is wanting, yes?" Algoron asked.

"Yes." she whispered. "I did not know it could want like this. Am

103

I wrong to want both your hands on me? I have never known that could happen."

"It doesn't happen," Niklas said. "It only happens for Algoron."

Algoron laughed, taking Alahandra's hand and moving close to Niklas.

"We could pleasure her. Her body is not satisfied." Algoron said, taking Niklas's hand and putting it on Alahandra's hip.

Niklas sighed and embraced Alahandra once again, kissing her deeply, allowing passion to consume them.

Alahandra moved her hands along Niklas's back, wanting him. Wanting him to say that he wanted her body, wanted to love her, wanted to give up everything to be with her.

Algoron got dressed and stood by a tree waiting. When the two parted he clapped his hands. "You two should give in to that fire within you."

Alahandra got dressed quickly feeling unsure of herself.

As they started back through the woods carrying the water, Niklas looked around. "How long have you lived like this?"

"For as long as I can remember. We've moved from village to village, but we've lived in the woods or in an abandoned barn all of my life."

"You deserve so much more," Niklas said.

"I'll have more," she said. They walked back into camp.

Mikal saw them. "I thought you three had run off."

"If I was going to run, I would have stolen all your money first, Father." She laughed and looked at Niklas. "I'll be back later."

Niklas took her hand. "Be careful."

She smiled and nodded.

CHAPTER
Nine

Leaving the camp and being alone felt real. She enjoyed Niklas, but reality was that he would someday be King, and she wanted to live in another town to forget. Algoron would be King and would never be satisfied.

Alahandra entered the dress shop. Haya met her at the door and noticed her face.

"What happened to you? Who did this to you?" she asked.

"The men who took the Prince," Alahandra said.

Haya examined her face. "The Kingsmen were by here this morning asking for you. I told them I had not seen you since last night. I was so worried about you."

"After Niklas was taken, I went to see my father. I was so scared," she said.

"The men who took the Prince, did you recognize any of them? Did they say anything that might let the Kingsmen know where to look for him?"

"It all happened so fast. When I got him I was too afraid to do anything, and they took him away," Alahndra looked down as she touched her face."

"Well, I'm glad you're here. Go in the back and change. There's hot tea on the stove," Haya said and hugged her.

Alahandra felt her heart break lying to her only friend. More of a reason to leave. Haya would hate her when she found out the truth.

When she was changed out of the ragged clothes she felt more like herself. She was not who she used to be.

"My father wanted me to come back to see him when I'm finished here for the day," Alahandra said.

"We don't have a lot of work today, if you want to return to him. We do have a bit of treasure to enjoy. I didn't start looking through everything until you could be here," Haya said.

"Oh, that would be such fun. Thank you, Haya. I need this today," she said.

"Well, there is so much to look through we may have to close the store and simply enjoy ourselves today," Haya said.

"A day to ourselves does sound wonderful," Alahandra said.

Haya walked over and locked the door and pinned the curtain over the front so that no one could see in. "Now, let's go see what we have in the back room."

Alahandra was thankful to have a distraction. She helped Haya move the chest to the table. They stared at each other. Haya smiled, "It contains so much wealth that I fear if we open it, it may disappear."

They both laughed. Haya lifted the lid slowly. They both gasped.

"It's more than I remembered!" Alahandra said.

"We'll never have to worry about money again. I may even buy a little cottage outside of town," Haya said, smiling.

"With a little fence and a gate. Flowers lining the walk up to the door." Alahandra said.

"I may even buy a few chickens. I don't know what to do with them, but I guess I can figure it out," Haya said.

"Or maybe I'll leave this town," Alahandra said.

Haya stopped laughing. "Leave? Why would you leave?"

"Haya, I've stolen from everyone in this town. No matter how hard I try here I will never feel like I belong."

"I'll come with you. We can go to Trobornia and make a fresh start," Haya said excitedly.

"You have something wonderful with Bradford. Why would you leave?"

"I never said I would leave Bradford. I would ask him if he would like to go with us. What man can resist a woman that asks him to run away with her? Oh, and a woman that has the money to make sure we have a good life," she laughed. "He doesn't have family here. They've all moved away."

"Oh, Haya, do you honestly think we could do it? We could go to Trobornia and start a new life? We could open a dress shop there together, and no one would know what we have in that chest."

"Yes, and Bradford could do the things he dreams of. He's always wanted to open a cafe, but never could save enough. We could all start anew. Rylic would take us there."

Alahandra looked down.

"Let's not think on those things at the moment. Let's look at our treasure," Haya said. She took a handful of the jewels and let them sift through her hands. "My dear, we will never want again."

Alahandra nodded. "I like the sound of that."

They spent the day sorting the treasure and decided where to trade it. They looked through the cloth and talked about what they could sew and sell. They talked about the houses they would own and the gardens they would tend.

Alahandra sighed. "My own piece of land. My very own. I've always wanted to own a piece of land that I could put my sweat into and make beautiful. Like the gardens of fairies. I will be the crazy garden lady in town."

Haya laughed. "I'm going to be the crazy dress lady. Wearing bright colors and ruffles. We'll be a site to see, no doubt."

"The dream of something new makes my heart beat wild. Thank you, Haya."

"No need to thank me, dear. You are more than a friend to me. You are family," Haya said.

Alahandra wondered if she could keep the Prince a secret and leave. She reached into the chest and took out a handful of jewels. "What kind of rock is this? It seems to glow?"

"You can have it. Legend has it that rocks glow on the bottom of the ocean where the mermaids live. Consider it your lucky rock," Haya laughed and patted her on the arm.

"I'll take it," Alahandra smiled.

When darkness filled the night sky Alahandra yawned. "I think I need to check on my father."

"It's so late. Are you sure?" Haya asked.

"I'm sure. I'll be back tomorrow morning," Alahandra said and hugged her.

Walking through the woods was quiet. She didn't want to go back to the camp. As she neared she heard Niklas yell out. What was Jazier doing to him? She held up her dress and ran quickly to their camp.

Mikal and Algoron were laughing, and Niklas was waving his hand. "I told you to watch that thumb." Mikal laughed and slapped his leg. "In all my born days, boy, I've never seen anyone who didn't know how to do things, but I'll tell you this. I've never seen anyone so eager to learn."

Niklas nodded. "Yes, sir, I'll not stop trying until I get this right."

Alahandra walked into the open space. "What is it that you are learning?"

"I've been working on something." He produced a small seat made from limbs bound together. "I gathered the vines and all the wood."

"Niklas, I'm impressed. I take it you're not used to sitting without something to do," she said.

"In my world, I am never without something to do. This was so enjoyable. I would like to make something else, but I have no idea what to make. It's strange though, working with the knife and cutting tools. I think I could make things out of the wood. Like this piece here." he bent over and picked up a larger limb. "Can you see the face of a rabbit?"

Alahandra took the limb and studied it. "I do see what looks like the shape of the rabbit."

Niklas took it from her hand. "You see, if I use this cutting tool, I think I can carve out the face I'm seeing."

"Oh, do try. I would love to see that," Alahandra said.

Mikal got up from the fire and patted Niklas on the back. "Best company I've had in a long time. Glad to get to know you, son," he said. "And Algoron here has some of the best stories I've ever heard. I'm turning in. Goodnight, you three."

"Goodnight, sir, and thank you for taking time with me today," Niklas said.

"Goodnight, Mikal. Perhaps some ale tomorrow," Algoron laughed.

"Now that's something to look forward to," Mikal said.

"Where's Jazier?" Alahandra asked.

"He said he was going to go leave the note about the money for my ransom," Niklas said.

Alahandra walked over to him and put her arms around him. He did the same, and they held each other for a moment in the firelight.

He whispered. "How can I go back?"

"Who wants to go back?" Algoron said.

"Looks like you won't be going back for a while," Jazier said, stepping into the clearing. Alahandra stepped away from Niklas. "I couldn't leave the note. Everything was too heavily guarded."

Niklas laughed. "Well then, I'll make myself at home and see what else I can learn."

"We'll need a bit of ale for tomorrow," Algoron said, leaning against the tree.

Jazier looked surprised. "Neither of you are worried or upset?"

Niklas cleared his throat. "Sir, my father, the King, will be fine without me. When it concerns me, he moves even slower, so even when he has the note you intend to leave, it will take a while to get your money. Oh, he'll follow through, but I'm sure he's trying to teach me a lesson about something. If you want your money, have the note delivered to my mother."

"And my father," Algoron said, "does not even consider me missing yet. I often go off unannounced, so he's only angry at this point that I didn't come back from the ball."

Jazier kicked dirt into the fire and walked toward the shack. "Perhaps the Kings will act faster if he knows you'll be killed unless they pay."

"You won't harm them in any way, or I will kill you in your sleep," Alahandra whispered.

"Threaten me again, and I'll kill you in front of everyone," Jazier laughed. He walked into the dwelling.

Niklas moved close to Alahandra. "He isn't one to trifle with Alahandra. When a man doesn't care about anything, he becomes dangerous."

"Well, when a woman cares for her friends, she'll do whatever it takes to defend them," Alahandra said.

"So we are friends, are we?" Algoron said, smiling.

"Of course, we are. I wouldn't let just anyone haul water with me," she teased.

"Any other… chores you need help with?" he teased.

"If you want to build more and maybe carve tomorrow, we could get up and go gather pieces of wood deeper in the forest or down by the shore. We can start out early tomorrow, and then I'm going to go work in the dress shop for the day," she said to Niklas.

"That's a wonderful idea. I've got some ideas I want to try. Plus, I will have stolen moments with you," Niklas said.

She pushed him away.

"We could always hike down to the shore one day," Niklas said.

"We could find driftwood there. Beautiful pieces of wood tossed up from the water. Quite good for carving, I would think," she said. "However, we could go to my secret swimming place. It's near the shore but more secluded. A lagoon with water so blue that it mocks the sky. I always go there when I want to be alone. Jazier and my father have never found me there."

"Yes, let's go there and pick up wood along the way back. I could use some time to relax and enjoy myself without the worries of the kingdom, and without Jazier," he said.

"If we go to a lagoon, promise me there will be mermaids to

enjoy," Algoron said.

"I can take you there at the week's end if you are not gone by then," Alahandra said.

"My father will have paid the ransom by then. If not, it means he's planning something. We should go the next day or so," Niklas said.

"Tomorrow then. Let's get some rest," Alahandra said, yawning.

Alahandra went into the shack to get blankets.

Mikal grabbed her arm and leaned close. "If the money doesn't come soon, you are going to have to get them out of here. Jazier is serious, Alahandra."

"If we leave, Jazier will hurt you to punish me," she said.

"Not if I leave with you," Mikal said.

"I know Niklas will have you protected if you are willing to leave. You'll have to find work and take care of yourself. No more stealing, because I'm leaving, Father. I'm leaving for good with Haya. We'll be moving on and starting fresh in another village."

Mikal didn't say anything. He nodded and gave her his pillow.

"Thank you," she whispered.

Niklas helped her spread the blankets out by the fire. Algoron lay down and looked up at the sky.

"You take the pillow," she said to Niklas

"What kind of gentleman would I be if I took the only pillow from a lady?"

"The kind with a pillow. Now take it," she laughed.

"We could share," he whispered.

"Share. Do you think I can trust you," she said softly, walking over to him, "to stay," she lifted her face to his, "on your side?" she teased with her mouth close to his.

"No, fair maiden, I cannot be trusted. You stir fire in me," he laughed quietly.

"Exactly. You take the pillow so you can sleep. We have a long hike in the morning," Alahandra said, lying down beside Algoron.

Niklas moved his blanket a little closer to her, and lay down looking up at the sky. "He'll make me take the throne in the Spring.

My birthday is tomorrow. I should have taken the throne several years ago, but I have never actually wanted to rule. Until now, that is. The thought of ruling intrigues me if I could do it with you, Alahandra."

"Your birthday is tomorrow? Why didn't you tell me?" Alahandra smiled at him.

"The announcement would have been at the conclusion of the ball. It would have been a grand celebration as the cake was rolled out. We missed a good cake, but that's about all. I do hate the grandeur of that type of celebration."

"I am sorry," Alahandra whispered.

"Please don't ever apologize again for this," Niklas waved his hand around. "Being here feels real."

"Um, is anyone going to acknowledge that Niklas all but proposed that you be with him and rule with him?" Algoron sat up.

Alahandra looked at Algoron and then to Niklas.

"Can you imagine me as the Queen?" She laughed and looked from Niklas to Algoron.

Neither laughed.

Alahandra looked up at the sky. "We'll celebrate tomorrow. A birthday breakfast fit for a king." She nudged him, and he smiled.

"My coronation is at the end of the week," Algoron yawned, settling beside Alahandra and looking up at the sky. "My father demands that I take it whether a queen warms my bed or not."

"You'll both make fine kings," she said, yawning. She reached out her hand to Niklas. He clasped hers and pulled her close. She extended her other hand to Algoron. He intertwined his fingers with hers and moved close behind her. Niklas kissed her forehead and fell asleep quickly. Algoron kissed her neck gently. She didn't respond. He released her hand and moved his fingers slowly up her arm. She lay still enjoying his touch. He kissed her neck again, and she sighed. His hand moved around her and came to rest on her stomach. She placed her hand over his. He caressed her with his thumb and kissed her neck gently again. Breathing deeply she laced her fingers through his and pulled his hand up to her chest and held it close. He squeezed her hand in response, kissed the side of her neck near her ear, and then nuzzled his head behind hers. Once they were still, they allowed sleep to overtake them.

Alahandra woke with a hint of light in the woods. She moved her hand across Algoron's arm. She touched Niklas's face. "Happy birthday. Time to go. We'll make breakfast away from camp."

They both opened their eyes slowly. Niklas smiled and nodded. Algoron got up quietly and stretched.

They folded their blankets quietly and Alahandra gave him a satchel to carry. "For whatever we might find along the way."

They were silent for a long while, not wanting to attract the attention of Jazier or Mikal. Alahandra enjoyed the silence of the woods. It had been her refuge for so long. It was strange to share it with others.

Niklas spoke softly. "There is peace here like I have never known."

Alahandra nodded. "It's as if the trees sway with an ancient secret." She pointed ahead. "We can follow the creek up ahead. The brush gets thick through here. Watch your footing."

"I'm already lost," Algoron whispered.

Niklas stumbled slightly, but never fell. "I could never find my way back if you left me out here. How do you remember which way to go?"

"I've walked this way many times, and I recognize the trees as if they were old friends stationed here to greet me along the way."

"I wish I had your freedom," Niklas said.

Alahandra didn't respond. Her freedom. She wasn't free. Not yet.

They could hear the creek and hurried toward the rushing water.

"It's not too much farther downstream. The lagoon is beautiful this time of day." she said, picking up her pace.

The waters of the creek made a bend in the forest. Alahandra climbed up on a group of rocks on the banks. Algoron clapped his hands.

Niklas gasped at the site. "This must be a dream. Never have I seen such beauty."

They made their way down the rocks, and Alahandra found a flat rock to put all their things.

She built a small fire and took a small pan and bowl from her satchel. Quickly she mixed a dough from what she brought with her and made hot cakes in the pan.

"Algoron, do you see the berries on that bush where we came out of the forest? Can you please pick some?"

"Anything for you, beautiful," he smiled.

"Niklas, if you could carefully take the eggs from my satchel that I have wrapped in cloth, I can cook those next."

"I am intrigued that you can do all of this. You are a true wonder," he said, kissing her on the cheek.

After their meal was complete and everything was put away, Alahandra stood and stretched. She pointed to the water. "See how the rocks form the banks and the waters circle around? Just beyond the bend there the waters move into the sea not far from where we were that night. But this water," she said, taking off her dress and standing in the sun in her undergarment, "this is mine."

She got in the water and began to swim. She looked at the two men still on the rocks. "Get in. We don't have a great deal of time."

"Let's pretend we don't care of time and enjoy this moment," Niklas said, laying his outer clothing on the rocks. He moved into the water carefully and began to paddle around.

Algoron undressed quickly and splashed in.

"Niklas, you looked frightened of the water. You weren't scared the other night. You swam." she said.

"The other night we splashed around, and I never took my feet off the bottom. I do not swim regularly at home, if at all," he said.

She swam to him and stood in front of him. "I'm here with you, you don't have to be afraid of anything."

Niklas stepped closer to her.

"Swim," she teased, splashing him.

He laughed and tried to paddle around again. The movement

became easier the more he tried, and before long he wasn't thinking about the movements.

Algoron swam effortlessly.

"How is it that you swim so well? Your kingdom is not near water," Niklas asked.

"Way back in the woods, there is a widow woman with a large pond. I go there sometimes to keep her company and we swim late at night after we pleasure each other," Algoron said.

"You talk too much," Niklas said.

"I lie too. My father taught me in a pond just beyond my castle," he said.

Niklas started moving his arms to swim.

"I knew you would learn quickly if you wanted it bad enough," she said.

"There are other things I want." Niklas said, looking at her and smiling.

"You are bolder in the water," she said.

He swam close to her. "And you, beautiful siren, make me forget who I am," he said.

Alahandra laughed. "Who are you, kind sir?"

Niklas stood beside her in the chest deep water. "I'm a man," he paused, touching her face, "needing to kiss you."

"If you are in need," she said, brushing her lips to his. Her arms moved up around his shoulders. He placed his hands on her hips and pulled her to him. They both gasped and Niklas kissed her deeply, moving his mouth over hers with a passionate urge that surprised her.

The taste of his mouth was sweet with berries from their breakfast, and she wanted more of him. Lost in the moment neither saw the watchful eyes from the brush near their clothes.

Two of the kingsmen hid in the bushes that were sent to find him. They kept their silence and continued to watch. They nodded to each other. One whispered. "We'll take them over when they come out of the water. Draw your sword quietly."

"All right, that's enough of that unless you want me to join in,"

Algoron said.

Niklas laughed.

Alahandra released her grip from around Niklas and stood in the water. She took both their hands and led them to the flat rocks. She lay back on the warm rocks and looked at them. "We can dry here."

The three lay there silently. Algoron quickly fell asleep. Niklas moved to lay beside her, and could not stop staring at her. She closed her eyes and stretched her arms above her head. Niklas moved his hand to the top of her undergarment tracing the fabric. Alahandra breathed deeply. He slowly untied the top of her garment and moved the fabric to the side exposing her skin. She arched slightly, inviting his hands to move over her. Niklas moved closer and leaned in to kiss her softly. She sighed, opening her lips to invite him.

Niklas raised above her and smiled. "This feels like a dream," he whispered.

"Then let's make it a dream you'll never forget," she said, pulling him down to her.

His lips met hers passionately as her hands moved down his back. She pressed herself to him, inviting him.

Niklas whispered to her. "I want to kiss every inch of you."

"We have complete privacy. We can do anything we want," she whispered the words on Niklas's lips. She slowly opened the top of her undergarment. He moved his hand over her skin as she closed her eyes.

A rustle from the brush startled them as the kingsmen emerged. "Now, this is quite the site. The Prince, the Prince, and the dressmaker. So did you kidnap them both?" he laughed. Algoron woke with a start.

"No," she said, trying to fix the top of her undergarment.

One of the guards nudged the other. "I think they came willingly."

"And you, your highness, it seems you have been treated well during your stay with your captor," the other man laughed.

"You will remember your place," Niklas said.

"Sir, it appears you have forgotten yours. Now, let's go. We are taking you all back to the castle," the man said, producing his sword.

"How did you find me?" Niklas asked.

"A note was delivered to your mother about a ransom, and she sent the royal guard out in droves. We had strict instructions to not come back until we found you. So here we are, tromping through the forest until we came across you three."

Alahandra continued to tie her undergarment quickly.

"Oh, you don't have to even get dressed if you want to come with us like you are, my dear." the other man said.

"Dare you speak to a lady that way?" Niklas said.

"Lady?" he laughed. "No lady would be here doing what you three were doing."

Alahandra got her dress and donned it quickly. She could not look at the men. They had watched. What a fool she was to allow herself to get lost in Niklas's touch.

Niklas took her by the arm. "You will not be harmed," he said, getting dressed.

"That is not your decision," said the first man. "The King has ordered your captors returned and then hanged by the end of the week."

Alahandra tried not to show the fear that reached from within and choked her.

"She is not responsible for the actions of others. She can take you to their camp," Niklas said.

Alahandra looked at him and glared. He would see her father hanged to save her. She couldn't let it happen. Perhaps she could persuade the King to spare her life, but he would not spare her father.

"I acted on my own. There were no others."

"What are you doing?" Niklas said.

Alahandra remained silent.

"Well, she turned on you quickly, sire. But, she is but a bit of trash from the streets in need of elimination," the other man said, stepping close to Alahandra. "Perhaps the Prince wasn't man enough for you."

Niklas swung his fist at the man and connected with his mouth and knocked him to the ground. The second man unsheathed his sword

117

and moved it quickly to Niklas's neck. Algoron moved toward him. The sword nicked Niklas's neck. "If you try anything else, they will find your bodies in such a way that all will suspect she killed you and then killed herself."

The other man pointed his sword at Alahandra.

Niklas clenched his fists. "We will leave with you, but know this, when we arrive and stand in front of my father, your services will no longer be needed."

The men laughed. "The price on your head for your return will be more than enough to keep us both for years to come. You need to think about that, Sire, because I don't care about you or your precious imp."

Niklas took Alahandra's hand and walked behind the kingsmen. "I'll take care of this, you have my word."

"I don't know that I can trust you, Niklas. You would see my father hanged," she said.

"I spoke before I thought, and I apologize. I would not wish your father harm," he said.

"The throne will be in jeopardy if you cannot think before you speak. Let us be silent on our walk with them. I need to think about what I'm going to say to the King. I have to get out of this," she whispered.

"Fear not what my father might say. He will listen to my petition, and you will be free by the end of this day."

Alahandra nodded, but in her heart she knew only a miracle would save her now.

They made their way back to the street where a carriage was waiting with a hooded driver looking forward. Niklas helped her in and the kingsmen took the front. Algoron got in last. None of them spoke the entire ride to the castle, but the kingsmen laughed at how the three were found, and talked of Alahandra's body.

A trumpet sounded from the gate. The King and Queen came from the front and stood on the entrance steps.

Niklas, Algoron, and Alahandra walked up the stairs in front of the kingsmen.

One of the men spoke. "The reward, my King. And we will be on our way."

Niklas stepped forward. "These men threatened me, and they are no longer welcome here."

"You threatened my son?" King Vaughn asked.

"He was resisting coming back," one of the men said.

The other man laughed. "They weren't resisting each other, mind you," he laughed.

The Queen looked to the ground.

"Take your gold and leave lest you find yourselves in shackles." King Vaughn tossed the bag of coins to the men. They laughed and walked away.

Alahandra noticed the driver of the carriage unhooking the horses. An odd thing to do with the stables so far away.

King Vaughn stepped close to Niklas and took his arm. "You will go inside. And you," he looked to Alahandra, "you will be put in the dungeon until we can deal with you."

"Set her free, Father; this is not her doing," Niklas said.

"She was the last person seen with you on the night of your disappearance, and she was found with you today. I say she is to be questioned at my disposal. If you are found guilty of kidnapping the Prince, you will be hanged."

Algoron laughed, "Pardon me, King Vaughn, may I leave. I'm sure my father will be glad to know I'm safe."

"Yes, of course. Take a steed from the stables and be on your way," King Vaughn said.

Algoron stepped to Alahandra, took her hand, and kissed it. "Thank you for everything."

Alahandra nodded and didn't speak. She had to think about what she would say and do.

Algoron walked away.

Niklas looked at her and took her hands. "You will be free. I will see to it."

"Not if I see to it first!" The hooded driver ascended the stairs quickly.. He drew a sword and held it out. "Alahandra, come with me!" he yelled.

She gasped, took his hand, and followed him down the stairs.. He mounted the horse and pulled her up behind him.

"This girl is innocent. You have your prince, let her be," he said.

"She is our prisoner, you will release her or you will be hunted with her," King Vaughn said.

"She is a girl. You will not hunt me or your kingsmen will diminish one by one. Now, go inside, and we will all carry on with our lives."

The Queen touched her husband's arm. "Our son is returned. We have nothing more to do here." She nodded to the man, and he smiled at her.

He turned to the horse and galloped away.

"Rylic. You have a story to tell, yes?" Alahandra said, wrapping her arms around his waist to hold on.

"A tale to share when we are safe on my ship," he said, leaning into the horse. The ground beneath them moved quickly.

Her mind reeled. She was ready to give herself to Niklas. Was she in love with Niklas? How could she fall in love with a prince?

CHAPTER
Ten

The smell of the water filled the air. She knew the docks were close. Rounding the bend she saw Rylic's ships. The Silver Phoenix and the Lady Amore both were in port. She wondered in that moment if she would not see her father again.

Rylic whistled and crewmen appeared from the shadows. They ushered the horse onboard. Rylic motioned for one of the men to help Alahandra down. He jumped down after her.

"Go to the room where you and Haya slept. Stay there until I call you out. We have to make sure we are safe."

Alahandra ran the length of the ship and into the room she was familiar with. She noticed Haya's things from her shop. The furniture, cloth, things from her kitchen. It was all here. The ship began moving through the water at great speed. She sat down on the floor trying to process all that happened.

Rylic walked in and looked around. When he saw her he ran to her, sat down beside her, and engulfed her in a hug.

"I know you have a lot of questions, but let me tell you what happened first, then ask all the questions you want," Rylic said. He held her hands and began.

"I wanted to see you again so I came back to Mum's. She told me of the ball and the Prince's disappearance, and how you went to see your father. She said you were not staying at her place, and she was worried. I walked around the market to see if I could find out what was going on since you were the last person to see the Prince.

"I heard news of the kingsmen being sent to the village to question everyone and go through every home. Once they were finished, they were to go through the woods. Men stationed from one end of this town to the other, and two by two they were to enter and search the woods.

"I talked with Haya and asked if she thought you could be in on the kidnapping. She said she wasn't sure since you came in with the story of being beat up and the Prince taken. Two of the kingsmen came into her shop and all but destroyed the place looking for answers.

"Haya started packing as soon as they left. She went to the blacksmith and asked if he would want to come along with her. He said he wouldn't stay without her, and began packing his shop and home. We hauled all that fills this room in the middle of the night. My mum told me of your plans to move to Trobornia, and that is where I will take you. I know you have feelings for the Prince, but the King was angry. He would have killed you just to end whatever was going on between you and his son. I heard the kingsmen discussing how they found you with the two men. Do you have any questions?"

Alahandra shook her head. "I want you to know I appreciate your help."

Rylic released her hands and stood. "You are dear to my mother." He turned to walk away. "Stay in here, and rest when you can."

Alahandra pulled her knees to her chest and looked at Rylic. "Thank you."

He walked out the door.

She got up and looked around the room. All her belongings were thrown into a crate and tossed under the table. She saw the chest of treasure under the table. The one thing she could trust in right now was the money that would make her life more bearable. She was going to finally be able to buy food and know that the next day she would not starve. She was going to have a home and have a room of her own. No more sharing small spaces or sleeping on the ground.

Alahandra leaned against the wall and slid down to the floor. She wondered what Niklas was doing and if he got in trouble. They were from different worlds with different futures. How could she have allowed herself to feel and be distracted so easily? She closed her eyes and thought of Niklas's hands on her. She breathed deeply, replaying his touch, his kiss.

None of that mattered now. She would lock up her heart and stay focused on starting a new life. A life all her own.

When night fell, Rylic came in quietly. Alahandra was asleep on the floor. Rylic walked over to her and sat down beside her. He moved the hair from her face and smiled. Her eyes fluttered open.

"I'm sorry I woke you. I felt like I should guard you and your things. This crew is loyal to me, but they are still pirates."

"I welcome the company," she yawned.

"Go back to sleep. I'll sleep by the door," he said.

She touched his arm. "Stay by me. I feel unsure of myself tonight."

He settled back down on the floor close to her.

"The Queen released me to you. Why?"

"About a year or so ago, my ship raided a royal vessel the Queen was traveling on, and we took all the treasure onboard. At the end, I walked up to the Queen with sword in hand and demanded her jewels. One of her guards charged me, and I nicked his face with the tip of my sword. She called for everyone to stand down as she began removing her jewelry. She struggled with the clasp so I walked around behind her and unhooked her necklace. When my hands touched her neck, I remember that she sighed heavily, so I moved my hand around her neck to collect the necklace, grazing my fingertips along her skin. I leaned close and whispered 'thank you,' near her ear, and a smile played across her mouth. I think she enjoyed that moment. As we were leaving her ship I turned to smile at her, and she nodded to me. We left their ship and went on our way."

Alahandra didn't respond. Jealousy rose up within her. She sighed heavily wondering how she could be jealous of the Queen enjoying his touch when she was just found with Niklas.

Rylic took a deep breath and whispered. "Do you love him?"

"I don't know what I was feeling. I know love like I love my father and Haya, but I have never been in love with a man."

"What of the other?" he asked.

"He was a friend of the Prince that was accidently captured," she said.

"Are you going to see him again?" he asked.

"I hope not. He's a tiresome man who thinks of nothing but himself," she said, remembering the feel of Algoron's lips on her neck.

"Have you ever been in love before?" she whispered.

"Only once," he said.

"What happened to her?" she asked, yawning and closing her eyes.

"We could never seem to make it work, but I know I'll love her forever." he said and looked at her laying there with her eyes closed. "I'll love her forever."

Alahandra sighed. She was asleep once more. He moved to lay beside her.

The ship rocked through the night. Alahandra woke only once to see Rylic staring blankly at the ceiling. He seemed lost in thought and she didn't interrupt him. She closed her eyes and felt completely alone.

"Sir, sir, we are near the port of Trobornia." Joab whispered from the door.

Rylic opened his eyes and nodded. He was holding Alahandra as they slept. Joab left quietly, seeing Alahandra still asleep. Rylic didn't move, but tightened his grip around her. In her sleep she moved closer to the warmth of him and put her arm around him. He kissed her forehead softly and lay still.

Alahandra stirred, and her body responded to his being near. She moved closer and moved her hand down his side. He moved his hand and laced his finger into hers. She sighed and lifted her face so that her lips came to rest just in front of his. He closed his eyes, breathing in the moment.

Alahandra's eyes fluttered open slowly, and she tightened her hand in his. She smiled at his being close and whispered his name, "Rylic?"

He opened his eyes and smiled. "Good morning, beautiful."

She didn't move away from him. "I sleep so deep when you are beside me. It's as if the world melts away when you are near."

"You just know my sword can save us," he laughed.

Alahandra propped her head with her hand. "I'm safe in here, and the cruel world is kept at bay."

"You never have to see the world as cruel again. With Haya, your riches exceed anyone in the town you will be in. You won't have to worry ever again," Rylic said.

"Money doesn't solve everything," Alahandra said, sitting up.

Rylic sat up and leaned in close to her face. "At least you won't need a castle to be happy."

She started to protest, but he held up his hand.

"Forgive me. I shouldn't have said that. Let's not argue today about you and the Prince. You get to have a new life away from all your worries. Let's make it a day of celebration for you, Haya, and Bradford. This needs to be a day you will never forget."

He got to his feet quickly and extended his hand to help her up. The ship lurched slightly to the side and she stumbled. Rylic caught her, holding onto her.

She looked up at him and smiled. "A new life. A new me. I think you're right. It's time to enjoy every moment." She moved her hand across his face and touched his lips. She twirled away laughing.

He moved quickly to her and caught her in her twirl. "Every moment." he said, moving his face close to hers. She leaned her face to his and he let her go.

"Sorry, dear. Perhaps another time," he said smiling.

"Wicked man," she teased, enjoying their banter after all that had happened.

"Temptress," he smiled and held the door for her.

She curtsied and walked out as the sun was bursting from the horizon. She breathed in the salt air. "I love this," she said, closing her eyes.

"Perhaps one day you can journey with me on a long trip. A non-pirating trip, of course. I would love to show you tropical beaches and lands where animals of all kinds roam free," Rylic said.

"I will go anywhere with you. I've always wanted to be free on the open sea. For as long as I can remember, it's been a dream of mine. Once we are settled, perhaps we can go," Alahandra said.

"When you are settled, all the men in this town will try to win your heart. You may never leave port again," Rylic said, taking a plate of food and giving it to her.

"Never leave port. You know I won't be in shackles," Alahandra said, eating her bread.

"So being in love to you is the same as being in shackles," Rylic teased.

Alahandra put down her bread and looked to the sea. "I simply can't imagine someone wanting me or loving me."

"Wanting you is easy, wild siren. Loving you will be hard for most men. And you, my dear, better learn the difference when a man comes to call. Men can spout words of love only to serve their desires. Words drip from their lips to get your dress up to your hips."

Alahandra's eyes widened. "You are crass and disrespectful."

"You are a tease and temptress. It's no wonder the Prince fell all over himself for you in your undergarments," Rylic said, tossing his plate on a table and walking away.

Alahandra tossed her plate on the table and went after him. Some of the crew stopped to watch.

"I am no tease. I tempt no man. I do what I want, when I want," she said behind him.

Rylic turned to her and leaned in close. "And exactly what is it that you want?"

Alahandra stared at him, not knowing what to say.

He took her by the hand and led her back to the room they had slept in. He shut the door behind them and pulled her to the side so that no one could see them. He held onto her arms and pulled her close.

She looked up at him in anger.

"Tell me what it is you want," he said angrily.

"I want it all because all I've ever had is nothing," she said with her teeth clenched. "I'm tired of people. I'm tired of men. I'm tired of fear and worry. All I want is freedom. All I want is…" she paused and felt the fight drift out of her. Tears welled in her eyes but she refused to cry in front of Rylic.

They held their silence as he moved his arms around her.

The ship slowed, and she could hear the anchor being lowered.

"Looks like it's time to go," she said.

"Time to go," he whispered. He took her face in his hands quickly and kissed her. Their lips met again and again in an urgency that exploded passion in both of them. Rylic's hands gripped the back of her garment pressing her to him. She moved her mouth with his enjoying the feel of his lips on hers.

"Sir," Joab said, clearing his throat at the door.

Alahandra moved away from Rylic.

"Yes, Joab." Rylic said, straightening his shirt.

"I called you several times. We've made port. We're in Trobornia," Joab said excitedly.

"Thank you, Joab." Rylic said and moved out the door, not looking back at Alahandra.

She stood there in shock with the feel of Rylic's hands still on her. She had to shrug off any intentions and advances by him. She wondered if she would just be another face in another port to him. Smoothing her dress and taking a deep breath, she walked through the doorway and saw the landing on the dock of Trobornia. This was to be her new home and she would make today beautiful no matter what Rylic was doing. She didn't want to think about the feel of Niklas or Rylic. She only wanted to feel at home with Haya.

"Your eyes are filled with a depth that would frighten most people, dear child. Are you okay? Having second thoughts about Trobornia?" Haya asked.

"Not at all. Think about it. When we step off this ship, we are making this our home. I've never had a home before, and I guess I'm nervous."

"I can understand that. It's been a long time that I have wanted to put down roots and be at home. Things have had to move fast with Bradford, and here we all are, ready for our new adventure. It will be an adventure, Alahandra. I promise," Haya hugged her.

"Then let's go make this home," Alahandra said, hugging her back. She could see Rylic watching from the end of the ship. She offered him a soft smile, and he nodded back. She would watch him sail away and that would be that until he returned to see Haya. Perhaps being in his arms was all she really needed. He could see her and then leave. She wouldn't have to share her life with anyone, and she could still feel wanted. He would never love her, though, and she wondered if love would even matter.

Haya, Bradford, Alahandra, and Rylic made their way down from the ship. All four stopped and looked around from the docks. Bradford took Haya's hand and knelt in front of her.

"You are all I will ever need, and I love you. Will you make me the happiest man alive, and be my wife?"

Haya covered her mouth, and tears spilled down her cheeks. She nodded, and Bradford stood up quickly, picked her up, and spun around. When he lowered her to the ground, she hugged him, and everyone watching clapped.

"I love you, my sweet Bradford," Haya said, touching his face.

"I'm sorry I didn't ask you first, Rylic. I was so overwhelmed with love for this woman that I had to ask her right now," Bradford said, extending his hand to Rylic.

"Sir, it is an honor to have you love my mum so much, and it will be a joy having you in our family," Rylic said, shaking his hand and then hugging them both.

Alahandra hugged Haya but couldn't say anything. She had never witnessed anyone proposing before.

Haya whispered in her ear as they hugged. "Someday, you'll have to say yes to a man that you overwhelm."

Alahandra laughed and shook her head.

Haya patted her on the arm and took Bradford's hand. She looked at Rylic and Alahandra. "Let's go find a place for us. There has to be two houses next door to each other that we can buy."

"If not, you do know you could have two cottages built side by side." Rylic said.

Alahandra's mind was in a whirl. Her own home. She was going to look for her own home. She clasped her hands in front of her and looked down at the ground trying to hold in all the emotions tumbling inside.

Rylic put his arm around her. "It's going to be fine, and it's okay to feel all that you're feeling."

As much as she wanted to move away from him, she stayed in the comfort of his arm. She needed a friend today, and the three people beside her were all she had.

"Let's eat breakfast and perhaps inquire about a homestead," Haya said.

"A good meal sounds like a good idea," Rylic agreed.

They found a quaint little restaurant in the middle of town and went inside. A bell rang on the door as they entered and saw they were the only people there with it being early.

"Good morning!" yelled a voice from the kitchen. "I'll be right out! Make yourselves at home, and take a seat."

Haya pointed at a table near the kitchen. "No need to make someone run around the room to serve us."

"Something sure smells amazing," said Bradford.

An older gentleman came out of the kitchen. "Hello, folks. I'm Sero, the owner. What can I get for you today?"

"Sero? It is you, you old sea dog. How have you been?" Rylic said, standing and hugging the older man.

"I wouldn't have believed it was you if I hadn't seen it with me own eyes. Rylic the pirate. King of the seas. I'm doing well." Sero said motioning to the room. "I took a bride, and we bought this place."

"I haven't seen you anytime I've made port," Rylic said.

"No need for dancing in the streets during the times you are here. That's some of our busiest days." Sero said. "Your meal is on the house." he looked to Alahandra. "He had to put up with me cooking on the ship of his for years, but I promise this food will be better."

Rylic laughed, "Best cook I ever had aboard the Silver Phoenix. I look forward to this breakfast."

Sero laughed, "Looks like someone finally took hold of that heart of yours," he said pointing to Alahandra.

"Oh no, she…" Rylic started.

"She suits you," Sero smiled. "Now, what'll you have?"

Rylic didn't say anything else about him and Alahandra. She looked at him and smiled. Took hold of his heart. Could she ever take hold of any man's heart, and would she ever allow any man to take hold of hers?

When Sero went to the kitchen, Alahandra whispered to Rylic. "King of the Seas? Did I miss something?"

Rylic laughed loudly, and Haya held up her hand. "Oh, let me. You see, dear, the pirates that know him would die for him, those that don't know him fear his sword, and all the women want to love him. He's called that because among those with sea salt in their veins, he is known from top of the world to the bottom."

"She exaggerates," Rylic said, rolling his eyes at Haya.

"She doesn't tell the half of it," Sero said, bringing their water to the table.

Alahandra laughed and felt disconnected from Rylic. He had lived lifetimes at sea, and all she had done was try to survive.

When Sero brought out the food, Rylic asked him about any available homesteads outside of town.

"There are always places for sale here. It's like Trobornia is a jumping off place. Men port here and never want to leave. They take a wife, stay a couple of years, and then move on inland to other towns and villages. There is beautiful country over the hills. Trobornia is a magical little town, but those hills call out to be explored."

Sero gave them the name of the man in charge of the land all around town and where to find him.

"He should be around soon. You'll have no problem finding a place here. Two good homes for two good couples. You'll enjoy living here. Like I said, this place is magical."

Alahandra was eating quickly. She realized she had not had a good meal in a while. Eating with Haya in the dress shop was her only real meals at a real table. The food was exceptional. She was the first one finished, and Haya took the bread from her plate to put on Alahandra's while they were all talking. Alahandra didn't protest. Haya must have guessed she was starving. The meager meal she had prepared for Algron and Niklas wasn't enough.

She was silent and took in all Sero was saying. She looked around the table and knew these were the people she would spend her time with in the days to come. What of life over the hills? Perhaps one day soon she would venture there herself to find out why they called others away so often. Perhaps there was a new life for her there one day.

After their meal was over, Sero decided to walk them to the man they needed to see. The office they entered was small and the man behind the old wooden desk wore an old suit and small round glasses. His face was pleasant but serious. He stood upon their entering.

Sero extended his hand to the gentleman. "Good morning Gustav. I have friends who have just arrived here and are in need of a homestead."

Gustav extended his hand to Bradford and to Rylic. "Hello, gentlemen. Let's get you some land."

He produced papers from a file and a map from another table. He laid it out in front of them. "About two miles or so down the road, there's the perfect homestead for all of you if you want to stay all together on the same property. It was built by two brothers who came here, married two sisters. Two houses, one barn, one shed, nice farm land, and a creek runs along the backside of the property. It's close enough to town that you don't have to plan a trip for supplies, but far enough out that it still feels secluded. If I didn't live over this office and love it here so much, I would buy this one myself. It just came available last month. Those four up and left for the hills."

"See," Sero said, "those hills call people in."

Gustav laughed. "It is true enough, but for me and mine, we love Trobornia."

"I'm sold." Haya said. "How about you two?" she said to Bradford and Alahandra.

"I think it's perfect," said Bradford.

"Perfect," said Alahandra quietly.

Rylic paid Gustav in gold pieces, and Gustav gave them the directions to their new homes.

"It's really happening," Haya said to Alahandra. Her face radiated happiness.

Alahandra could not contain her excitement. "I'm going to have a home!"

As they looked around, Rylic suggested that he go purchase more horses and a wagon since they sold Bradford's at the docks. As he came to the pier with new transportation, the crew was unloading the ship.

James stood before him. "This is a good thing you do for your mum."

"She's happier than I ever saw her. A fresh start is exactly what she needed," Rylic said.

As the four of them rode to their new land, Haya laughed, "I'm so nervous. Isn't that silly?"

"I'm nervous too. Our new home. The home we'll make together," Bradford said, squeezing her hand.

Alahandra looked at Rylic and smiled. He nodded. She didn't say anything, but her stomach was tied in knots at the thought of having a real home and not being on the run any longer.

As they rounded the bend Haya gasped. The two small houses were not far from each other, and the land that surrounded them brought tears to her eyes.

"Do you think this will work?" Rylic asked, smiling.

"It's the most beautiful thing I've ever seen," Haya said. She looked at Bradford. "We'll have a wonderful life here. I promise."

"As long as I'm with you, dear Haya, my life is wonderful."

Rylic brought the wagon to a halt. Haya turned to Alahandra.

"Dear, the house on the right is yours, if that's okay?"

Alahandra nodded, but couldn't speak. She jumped from the wagon and ran to the house. She opened the door and stood in the doorway with her hand over her mouth. It was more than she could have hoped for. She walked in slowly admiring the craftsmanship of the room. It was empty, but she would do what she could to make it work. The fireplace was clean and there was a small room off to the left of the main room. Her room. Her very own bedroom. She twirled around the room and stopped abruptly as Rylic appeared in the doorway.

"I see that you like your new place," he said, walking in and looking around.

Alahandra ran to him and threw her arms around him. "Thank you for doing this for us all."

Before he thought, he circled his arms around her and held her tight. "Thank you for being such a dear friend to my mother. She's never had a real friend that she can trust, and she loves you like a daughter. With Bradford here, you three will be able to look out for each other and really make this homestead a wonderful place to call home."

Alahandra stepped back. She knew he would leave soon. She wanted to savor the moment with him here. "Look! I can sew curtains with the cloth we brought. I can build a table and a bed. Oh, and chairs. I'll have to have at least four chairs."

Rylic laughed. "Instead of you building everything, and I have no doubt that you could. How about I go to the mercantile and have two sets of tables, chairs, and beds sent here? That would save everyone some time."

Haya and Bradford came into the house. "I think that's a wonderful idea, son. We all could go together, but I don't want to cause a stir. We'll need the basics for food too."

Rylic hugged his mother. "I think a trip to the mercantile is exactly what we all need to do. I have boxes of food and supplies that I've been storing, but you'll need a few things that I don't have. Let's unpack the boxes and go get supplies. This will be quite the adventure!"

Alahandra looked around the room as everyone was talking. Her heart swelled with happiness until she thought it would burst. Shopping. She could go shopping for supplies. She had never done that before. She wiped a tear that escaped her eye.

"My dear, what's wrong?" Haya asked.

"Oh, it's nothing. I'm being emotional about everything."

"You can tell us," Haya said, putting her arm around Alahandra's shoulder.

"I've never gone shopping for supplies for a home. I don't even know what I'll need, or what I need from the boxes that Rylic brought in. I've never lived in a real house before. I won't even know what to do with this much space."

Rylic took her hand and kissed it gently. "You do whatever you want. That's the joy in this place. It belongs to you, and no one can ever take it from you."

They all stood together and silent for a moment. Enjoying the peace of their friendships.

Rylic nodded to Bradford. "Let's go open these trunks and crates and see what all is inside. I've been saving these for so long that I've forgotten what's in there! Each time I raided a merchant ship, I would take whatever I thought you could use, Mum, and stash it away."

The four went to Haya's house where the boxes took up most of the room on the floor.

Beautiful oil lamps and dishes. Tea cups, and utensils. Candles and beautiful lace. Kettles and blankets.

Alahandra couldn't believe her eyes. There were so many things. So many beautiful things that she had seen in display windows in villages where she had been a thief. Things she had admired and told herself she would never have.

She ran her fingers over a fragile tea cup with pink flowers.

"It's yours." Rylic said. "Please, take what you think you would want or need. This is about you two having all that you want. Nothing is too grand for the women in my life."

Alahandra looked up at him and for the first time, his face reddened and he bent down to open another box. It was filled with pots and pans for cooking over the fire. There were towels and seeds of every kind.

"We could plant a garden!" Alahandra shouted. "I've always wanted to have a garden!"

"Like I said, beautiful woman. You can have whatever you desire."

Haya laughed. "Be careful what you promise."

Rylic laughed along with her. Alahandra turned a bright shade of red this time.

Rylic diverted the attention back to the boxes. "I hope you can find a use for it all."

"I think all we'll really need are the table, chairs, and beds." Haya said.

"How about a stove? I would love to learn to cook on a stove. I've only cooked over an open fire, and that's the only thing I can think of that I really want," Alahandra said quietly.

Rylic took her by the hand and helped her up. "Do you know how happy it makes me that you want something? The luxury of a stove is something that most people take for granted, and to you, that would make your home complete. My dear, I can't wait to get you a stove. And how about a big bathtub you can heat water for? For both houses. I know a hot bath now and again is something that I enjoy."

Alahandra laughed. "I'll feel like a queen for sure with a hot bath and a hot meal cooked on my stove."

They all laughed. Haya looked at Rylic smiling at Alahandra.

"Let's go quickly into town and order the things we need before the mercantile closes for the day," Rylic said.

The four got back in the wagon and rode into town, each lost in their own thoughts.

They stopped in front of the mercantile, and a woman passed by nodding to Alahandra. She nodded back and smiled. She didn't have to wonder if someone noticed her or remembered her. She was new, she was innocent, and she was happy.

Rylic jumped from the wagon and helped Alahandra down slowly. "The joy in your eyes makes your face even more beautiful."

"Your words send tingles down to my toes, silly man," Alahndra said, shoving him away.

"You should know how beautiful you are, so that when other men tell you, it won't shock you or impress you."

"Would the attention of other men make you jealous?" She said, touching Rylic's face and laughing.

"Jealous, of course. Who would look at me so longingly if your heart was won by another?" he said, walking away before she could comment.

Haya elbowed her. "He is sure full of himself today around you. Happiest I've seen him."

"He's just excited to spend that money," Alahandra said.

Bradford walked by and leaned into the conversation. "On you."

Haya clapped him on the back and laughed. "Let's go order our things. Both of you see if there is anything else you want while we're here."

Once the items were ordered from the catalogs, the four wandered around looking at things on the shelves.

Rylic talked quietly to the couple that owned the store. They nodded and the gentleman shook his hand.

Haya pointed to the flour on the shelf behind the counter. "We'll need flour, sugar, butter, and coffee. How about we find some chickens. We could build a coop for them couldn't we Bradford?"

"Of course, my dear. My good man, do you know anyone with chickens for sale?"

"We have chickens for sale out back. The doctor gets paid in chickens some of the time so he trades for store credit and we sell them. It's a nice trade off, and we always have fresh eggs."

"We'll take a dozen chickens for now if you can spare them." Bradford said.

Rylic hugged his shoulders. "I'm so glad you're here."

"Let's go back home. I think we have everything we need for today." Haya said.

Alahandra ran her hand along the counter and looked at the woman working there and smiled. "I'm Alahandra." she smiled.

"I'm Dedria, dear. It's nice to have you all in our little town. I hope you like it here," she said. "You come back anytime."

Alahandra nodded and walked out with the others. She sighed.

Dedria's husband, Morris, carried the crates of chickens to the wagon. Life was developing in front of her, and Alahandra could barely contain her excitement.

"We have chickens!" she laughed. "I've stolen chickens to cook, but I've never owned a chicken!"

Rylic drove the wagon back to the homestead in silence. He realized tonight more than ever how hard Alahandra's life must have been. She had done without even the simplest things in life, and now he wanted to give her everything just to see her smile.

As Rylic helped Haya and Bradford settle in and put things away, Haya touched his arm. "I'm only going to say this one time son. Go to her."

"I think she would want to do this on her own. Make it hers. Without my suggestion. Alone."

Bradford laughed.

Haya pointed to the door. "We're fine."

Rylic stood and put his hands on his hips. "Well, if she kicks me out, I'm going to sleep in the barn."

Bradford laughed again, and nodded to Rylic.

Rylic walked out of Haya's house and saw the oil lamp burning in Alahandra's house.

"Alahandra," Rylic said at the door.

"Come in!" she said excitedly. "Isn't all this absolutely

wonderful?" She took him by the hand.

"I've made a small fire and made coffee. Would you like a cup?" she asked.

"I would love some," Rylic smiled, sitting on the floor.

"I can't wait to cook a real meal. This feels like a dream," she said, sitting in front of him.

"You look happy, Alahandra. I can't wait to see what you do with the place by the time I return again," Rylic said.

Alahandra felt a pang of regret with his words, but she would never tell him. His life was the sea, and who was she to turn his head from such a temptress?

"I think we could use a few cattle. We would have to check the fence to make sure there are no open places."

"Let's walk the perimeter. It isn't too big and the moon is out now," Rylic said, standing up and offering his hand to help her up.

"That sounds like a great idea. There are so many boxes to unpack and I have no idea what to do with some of this stuff."

"Remember you can go buy anything you want, anytime you want. If there is something you need, you can always ask the Millers at the mercantile. You can always go to Sero too. He'll be discreet about anything you want."

"Thank you again, Rylic, for giving me a chance at life. A life away from Jazier. Away from my being a thief. Away from my father." Alahandra looked up at the sky. She hadn't thought about her father. She felt betrayed by him and had no one to call family.

"It's okay to miss him. He's your father," Rylic said quietly and shook a post in the ground to check its stability.

"I don't know how to feel about him, but I'm glad I'm not in that shack in the woods." Alahandra said, taking a deep breath. She turned to Rylic. "When are you leaving?"

He looked up at the moon. "First light. We can ride into town and have a hearty breakfast at Sero's before I go. I'll pay him handsomely before I go so you three can go eat every meal there until you have all the supplies you need."

"Three meals a day. That sounds lovely."

Rylic turned to her. "You will never do without again. I'm so sorry you have had to suffer with your father and Jazier. I know how that feels. I know the want of food. The want of shelter. The two chests in your room, in the corner, are full of gold. I gave you more than Haya so you can take care of her and Bradford. The money is yours, and you never have to ask how to spend it."

Alahandra hugged him tightly. "Thank you. Thank you for everything."

Rylic slid his arms around her and held her in the moonlight. If she would ask him to stay, he would sell his ship and never return to the sea. But, he knew she would never utter such to him. She was free.

She released him and looked out over the land. "Cattle will do nicely here. Cattle tomorrow."

"Cattle it is." Rylic said.

"And a dog. I need a dog. I'll be terribly lonely here, and a dog will do just fine."

"Let's go get Mum and Bradford. When we're at Sero's we can ask him if he knows where you can get a dog." Rylic said.

"And an ax. I need to chop some firewood."

Rylic smiled. "I saw stacks of firewood out back at the Mercantile. Seems people pay with firewood too and not just chickens. We'll get some and an ax before we head back after dinner."

They hitched the wagon back up to the horses and rode quietly in the moonlight. Bradford reached out and took Haya's hand.

"Let's get married soon," Bradford said. "I don't want the townspeople saying anything about us."

"Tomorrow," said Haya. "We can find the pastor of the town church tomorrow morning."

"I'll be leaving straight away after the ceremony," Rylic said. "My ship in port will raise too many questions if I stay too long."

"I sure hate that you have to leave. Don't you think you could stay for a while?" Haya asked.

"Perhaps someday I can return and stay. For now, the sea is my mistress, and she has yet to be tamed," Rylic laughed.

"You are a pirate, through and through," Haya laughed. "For now. Let's just be a family." She turned to Alahandra. "A real family."

Once inside Sero's Bradford looked around while he was eating. "This place is quite remarkable."

Sero laughed. "A few gold pieces can make all the difference when decorating."

"Would you be needing any help?" Bradford asked.

"You want a job?" Sero asked. "I could use an extra hand. We have another little one on the way and my wife needs to be home now."

"I'd love the work and experience. I want to open a bakery and cafe here one day," Bradford said.

Sero clapped his hands together. "We could use more businesses here. How about I show you how things work, and you can start tomorrow."

He looked at Haya. "Perhaps in a few days. Tomorrow is our wedding day."

"A wedding! Oh I can have my wife make you a cake! She loves weddings," Sero said.

"Let's take a look around," Bradford said. He went with Sero to the back. They were laughing together, and Haya sighed.

"I do love that man," Haya smiled, sipping her coffee.

"I'm so happy for you, Haya," Alahandra said, squeezing her hand.

"You'll find that love one day," Haya said.

"Perhaps, or maybe I'll just hike up in those hills one day and see what adventure I can find," Alahnadra said.

"I can't wait to see what the future holds for all of us. There is much to do, and it will all be such fun," Haya said. She yawned. "We have had a full day, and I would love nothing more than to lay my head down to sleep. I want to be rested for tomorrow. My wedding day. Can you believe it? My wedding day."

"I look forward to sleeping too," Alahandra said.

"I'm going to walk to the ship. I need to tell my men we'll be leaving after the wedding," Rylic said. As he walked to the door he turned to Haya. "I'm so happy for you. I'll see you all in the morning." He looked at Alahandra. "The firewood will be in the wagon. Enjoy your rest."

Alahandra nodded. "You too."

She was silent after he left. Her mind wandered to thoughts of Rylic coming back in and begging to stay with her. She smiled.

"He would stay if you but ask," Haya whispered.

Alahandra laughed, "Haya, you are absolutely wicked. I would never ask him to stay with me. We are too different."

"You have the same wild hearts. You have the same adventurous spirits. You are perfect for each other."

"I am perfect alone," Alahandra said.

"There will be a time when love finds your heart, Alahandra. Don't deny yourself the joy of falling in love when it happens. It may not be Rylic. He is untamed, and he may never settle. Your life is moving on. Embrace who you are, dear one. Wait on no man."

Alahandra nodded. The thought of having someone love her was something she never considered.

The wagon ride to their houses was quiet. The day had been so full of adjustment. So full of change. Alahandra couldn't imagine sleeping.

She tossed and turned on the blanket on the floor. There was so much to do. So much to think about. So much to enjoy.

A faint knock at the door startled her. Rylic. She rose quickly and opened the door.

"Well, look at what we have here," Algoron said.

Alahandra hugged him. "Come in. Come in. How did you find me?"

"Before I left that day, I was down by the docks. There's always adventure by the docks. I overheard your pirate friend talk of Trobornia to his crew and mentioned your name. I went home, checked in with my family to make sure they knew I was alive, and came for a visit before my coronation," he said.

"I'm so glad to see you, your Majesty." She curtsied, and he laughed. "King Algoron. That has such a magnificent royal sound to it. Would you like some coffee?" she asked.

"Okay, that's enough of that. I didn't come for coffee, beautiful woman," he said, moving closer.

Alahandra remembered that look from the creek. She stepped back.

"I do believe you were left unsatisfied. We can fix that right now if you wish," he whispered, closing the space between them.

"You came all this way just to satisfy me?" she said, whispering.

"Well, I thought, if we enjoy each other, you might consider coming back with me and being my queen," he said.

Alahandra laughed. "You could never settle for one woman."

"You would have your freedom with me to continue to see your pirate if you wish," Algoron reached out for her hand.

"If I ever do marry it will be for love, not status," she said.

"Forget status. Do you know," he said, pulling her to him, "how much pleasure," he kissed her neck, "we could give each other," he slid his arms around her, "every day?" His face was above hers.

She enjoyed his hands on her, and didn't move. She became aware of the thin dressing gown between them.

His lips brushed hers gently. "Let me show you all the things your body can enjoy. All the places I can kiss you that will arouse you." His hands began to gather the hem of her nightgown. It moved slowly up her legs. His hands moved over her bare skin. She moaned.

"No undergarments. How enticing," he said, moving his hand around her thigh. She gasped and moved to the side away from his touch.

"Am I going too fast? We can take this slow. I know it's your first time, and you should enjoy every moment," he said, pulling her tight against him.

"I don't think I can do this," she whispered.

"Of course you can, and I can always come by for a visit. My kingdom is not far from here, just beyond the hill country," he said, taking her hand and leading her to the blanket. He moved to the floor and pulled her down to him. She sat beside him, and her thoughts were filled with Rylic.

He took the ribbon from the top of her gown and pulled it gently. The garment fell open just enough that she was slightly exposed to him.

"I have thought about the sweet taste of your skin and the softness of your body pressed to mine," he whispered, touching her shoulder, "when you let me kiss your neck."

He removed his shirt quickly and tossed it aside and untied his trousers, slipping them from his body, leaving only his undergarments. "You can touch me if you want."

Alahandra didn't move. Her face blushed.

"I can see you are reserved about this tonight. How about you kiss me," he said.

Alahandra nodded and leaned to him. He pulled her close and his lips met hers with urgency. She moaned, and with one swift movement laid her on the blanket as their kiss continued.

Waves of pleasure moved through her as he kissed her deeply. She knew she should stop, but he wanted her and she enjoyed him.

She didn't stop him so he moved his hands down her side and pulled up the hem of her gown again. She lifted her thigh to meet his hand and he pulled her tight against him sending a wave of pleasure through her.

Her mind screamed no, but her body was hungry for him. She moved her hand down his back. The feel of his skin was warm and soft. She pulled him tight against her. His mouth moved over hers and then down her neck.

Thoughts of Rylic invaded the moment. "I can't do this."

"Yes you can. Don't think about anything," he whispered.

She raised to sitting and looked at his body stretched out beside her. They both breathed deeply.

He held her hand. "Just kiss me."

She leaned toward him again, pressing her lips to his. He rolled to his back and pulled her down to him, moving her body to rest on top of his. She kissed him deeply enjoying the feel of him beneath her.

With his knee he moved her legs slightly apart so they would naturally drape over each side of him. Taking her hips in his hands he pressed himself to her, and she sighed heavily. Her body craved him.

She raised up over him. "This is wrong."

He gripped her hips tightly and pressed to her. "Are you sure?"

Alahandra gasped. "How is it that my body wants you, but my heart won't allow it?"

"Your words are not like other women, Alahandra," he said, raising up so that his face was near hers.

"I've never known what's appropriate or what should be said. I don't know anything about my body or what all it can do. I say what I please, and I do as I please. I know you must see me as wild."

He kissed her gently. "I want to be the one to unleash the wild in you." He pulled her tight across his lap. He kissed her chest along the top of her undergarment and moved his hands down her back. She leaned her head back inviting his mouth on her.

The reality of the moment crashed through her. She knew this was not what she wanted. She held his face in her hands and kissed him gently. He took her hand in his and helped her to her feet. "Beautiful woman. Your body is begging for release. Had you but given in, I would have shown you great pleasure," he said, kissing her gently.

She sighed heavily and enjoyed his kiss. "I can't give myself freely."

"Perhaps someday," he said, moving his hands down her back.

"I do enjoy your hands on me." she whispered.

"I've learned a lot about a woman's body," he said, turning her around. He moved his hands down the front of her gown. She leaned to him and closed her eyes.

"You could just stand here," he said, kissing her cheek, "and let me pleasure you." His hands moved to her hip and pulled her close to him. "You could take off the dressing gown so that my mouth and my hands could explore you."

Alahandra allowed his hands to move over her for a moment. "I know that if my gown is removed, I will not want to stop any of your advances."

"That's what I'm counting on," Algoron whispered in her ear. His hands moved hard across her stomach and down to her thigh.

"How is it that you can make my body respond to you?" she whispered.

"The want in you is great, and I know how to satisfy," he said. "Let me show you." he kissed her neck. "I know what you need," he said. "And I know you are curious about my body. Your hands are free to explore all that you want," he said, moving in front of her and untying his undergarments. They slid to his hips and exposed the taunt muscles in his lower abdomen.

Without hesitation, Alahandra moved her fingers along the top of his undergarment.

His breath caught.

"Your body is fascinating," she whispered. "I do want to touch you." She stopped and pulled her hand away.

He stepped closer, and she once again moved her hands along his hips. He kissed her deeply and moaned as her hands pulled his body close to hers.

"We could go to your bed, Alahandra, and I can give you all that you want from me," he whispered.

His words brought her back to her reality. Rylic had ordered her bed. She stopped kissing him and brought her hands from his hips to his face as she leaned her head to his.

"My body wants you, Algoron, but I must stop. I…" she didn't know what to say about Rylic.

"You love your pirate," he whispered, kissing her neck.

She was silent.

"Say no more. When a woman's heart truly belongs to another, even I can't satisfy the longing in her," he laughed. "I shall go beautiful woman." He kissed her softly. "Perhaps someday you'll seek me out and warm my bed." He took his shirt and trousers and donned them quickly.

She walked him to the door. He pulled her close one last time. "Goodbye, wild woman."

"Goodbye, Algoron. Go rule your kingdom." She kissed him gently.

He laughed and released her. She watched him walk into the dark and disappear down the road. *You love your pirate.* That's what he had said to her. Love. She wanted nothing more.

CHAPTER
Eleven

The sun rose and Alahandra got up to get started on her day. She dressed quickly trying to put all thoughts of Algoron's hands on her away in her mind. She went outside to feed the chickens and looked around at her home. The water pump at the back of her house was easy to use. She wanted to wash off and change clothes for the wedding. Perhaps she should check on Haya to see if she needed any help getting ready.

She knocked on the door and waited. Haya opened the door with excitement. "It's my wedding day!" she shouted.

Bradford was cooking eggs over the fire in the fireplace. "Come in and have breakfast with us. We're going to eat quickly and get ready. Biscuits are ready."

They ate quickly and Haya brought her dress out. "How about this one?"

The dress shimmered in the firelight. Alahandra gasped. "Oh, it's beautiful. I'm going to go get ready. Would you like me to put flowers in your hair?"

"Oh, I would like that!" Haya said. "Let's hurry!"

Once she was finished helping Haya, she ran to her house to change into one of the dresses she had gotten from Rylic. The fabric was soft and flowy around her legs. The top was just off the shoulders, and the color was a light blue. She twirled with her hands out and felt as if she was floating.

Haya and Bradford pulled the wagon to Alahandra's door. "Ready to go?"

Alahandra came out of her house. Bradford nodded to Alahandra. "You're going to turn a lot of heads today, my dear."

Haya laughed. "You are breathtaking, Alahandra."

As they arrived at the church, Rylic was there waiting with the pastor. Haya and Bradford walked into the church holding hands. Alahandra stood beside Haya and Rylic stood with Bradford as the minister began the ceremony.

Haya and Bradford had so much love in their eyes. Alahandra shifted on her feet and locked eyes with Rylic. His smile sent tingles through her. She wished he could love her.

"You may kiss the bride," the minister said.

Bradford put his arms around Haya. "My bride. My life. I will love you forever." He kissed her gently. He turned to Rylic and shook his hand. Haya turned to Alahandra and hugged her.

The four made their way to Sero's for cake. His wife Jilla opened the door.

"Welcome, new friends! Time for cake!" Jilla said.

They walked in and Haya gasped. The cake was on the middle table. There were flowers and greenery to decorate the table. "I hope you like it."

"Oh, we love it!" Haya said. "And, with Bradford working here soon, I hope you and I will become fast friends."

"I would like that," Jilla said. "Oh, and Alahandra. I have something for you. There is a basket in the back room for you."

"Thank you," Alahandra said, wondering what Jilla would give her. When she entered the back room, a basket was in the corner with two small puppies sleeping on each other. She picked up the basket and went quickly back to the front room.

"Puppies!" Alahandra said. "I have puppies!"

Rylic laughed. "I thought you could use two and they could keep each other company. These will be good guard dogs too."

Jilla laughed. "They'll be good housemates for you. Living alone can be quite lonely, but with these two, you'll never be lonely again."

"I can't thank you enough," Alahandra said.

"Now about that cow you wanted. I know a farmer just outside of town that has quite a few for sale. He sells and trades all the time. He'll be willing to sell you a few," Jilla said.

"Oh, that will be perfect," Haya said. "We'll have a nice little homestead when we get our cattle and our furniture."

"I can ride with you all back up the road. His place is along a side road not too far from you. I can walk back. It will do me good to get out." Jilla smiled.

Haya nodded to her.

Bradford stood and raised his cup. "I'd like to thank you all for helping make our day so special. I can't imagine being any happier than I am right now." He turned to Haya. "I have never loved so deeply."

Haya took his hand and squeezed it tightly.

Alahandra knew she would remember this moment forever.

As they finished their cake, Alahandra took the plates to the kitchen.

Jilla followed her. "Thanks for helping. Your family is so wonderful."

"Oh, they're not my family. Just friends," Alahandra said.

"Friends, family. Seems the same to me," Jilla said.

"It really is," Alahandra said.

Sero shook Bradford's hand. "Take a week or so to settle in and then come by when you're ready to start work."

"Thank you, Sero. I'll see you soon."

Rylic carried the basket of puppies to the wagon. Alahandra walked beside him. "Thank you."

"Anything for you, Alahandra," Rylic said, turning to her. "I'll see you soon."

"See you soon, my pirate," Alahandra said.

"Your pirate," Rylic smiled.

"You belong to no one," Alahandra said. "But you are always

welcome by my fire."

"Are you inviting me to your house?" Rylic said.

"You should go," Alahandra laughed.

"Now you want me to leave," Rylic said, stepping close to her.

"You're impossible," Alahandra said.

"You're stunning. You're amazing. You have taken my every thought captive," he whispered.

"You're too close," Alahandra whispered.

"I could be closer," he whispered and kissed her gently. "I'll come back soon."

Alahandra stepped back from him and climbed into the wagon. She watched him as they drove away. He stood still in the middle of the street and watched until he could no longer see their wagon.

"She is a good match for you," the minister said, passing him in the street.

"She is too good for me," Rylic said quietly. He turned to walk back to the pier. He knew Alahandra's life would move forward here while his was at sea. There was no room for him in her life. She needed to find someone that would give her the life she wanted.

Rylic boarded the ship without talking to anyone. He walked to the edge and looked out over the sea.

Joab came to stand beside him. "I love Trobornia. I want to live there one day."

Rylic turned to him. "How would you like to live with Haya and Bradford? I could ask if you could stay with them. Or with Alahandra? They could really use your strength and know how."

"I could really stay? I could really have a home?" Joab said.

"Yes, my friend. I think it's time you retire from the sea and be a part of a family."

"Are you going to be there too?" Joab asked.

"No. Not yet. I've got some things to do first," Rylic said.

"I thought you liked Alahandra?" Joab said.

"I do, but for now, I have to let her live her life. You'll learn about girls soon enough. For now, how about you just help take care of the women in our lives."

"I can do that," Joab said.

"The next time we make port, we'll set you up in Haya's house. Bradford can teach you a lot of things that I can't. And Alahandra can teach you how to shoot with a bow."

"A bow, really?" Joab asked.

"And so much more. Now, let's get this ship cleaned up," Rylic said.

"Aye, aye, Captain," Joab shouted and ran from him.

Rylic watched as Trobornia got smaller and smaller. His heart ached. He wanted to turn the Silver Phoenix around, race to Alahandra, and ask her to be his forever.

He looked up and sighed. "Take care of her for me."

Alahandra's thoughts were jumbled with the want for Rylic to stay and the joy of going back to the first home of her own.

Bradford turned the wagon down the side road as Jilla instructed. Alahandra was amazed at the land that stretched out before her. A modest house and barn with a fence encompassing many cattle. There was a sense of peace about the place. A sense of home.

A man came out of the barn and waved his hat as he approached the wagon. "Hello, Jilla, how are you?"

Jilla hopped out of the wagon. "Hello, Mr. Troy. I have a new family here wanting to purchase a few head of cattle."

"You know I've always got a few to sell," the man smiled.

Bradford got out of the wagon. "Could you spare six?" He extended his hand to Mr. Troy.

Mr. Troy shook his hand. "I'm Bradford, this is Haya, my wife, and Alahandra."

Two boys walked out of the barn and approached the wagon. "These are my sons…"

"Alexander!" Alahandra smiled and ran to hug the older boy.

"Alahandra! How are you here?"

"We live here now," she smiled at him.

Mr. Troy smiled, "How do you two know each other?"

"Pardon me, sir, I met Alexander at the festival."

"Ah, the festival. It is a grand event. It would seem you are not attached?" Mr. Troy smiled at her.

Alahandra looked at Jilla.

"She's spoken for, I assure you," Jilla laughed. "You'll have to excuse Mr. Troy. He is forever in search of a wife."

"I've been widowed for several years. I need a mother for my sons, a wife for my house, and a good woman to work alongside me. If you're looking for a good home, I would be glad to take you on here. In truth, it wouldn't matter if all you did was smile at me and hold my hand."

"Mr. Troy, I appreciate your offer, but I'm just getting used to being on my own, and I can't wait to have these cattle to look after." She smiled at the boys. "If you two would ever want to work for extra money, I'll have plenty of work for hired hands in a couple of weeks."

Alexander smiled, "You just let me know when you need me and I'll be there." He blushed and looked down. He cleared his throat. "This is Eddie. He doesn't talk much, but he works hard."

Mr. Troy looked down as he spoke, "He hasn't talked much since his mother passed."

Alahandra knelt in front of Eddie. "I have a friend named Joab, and when he comes to visit, maybe you can visit our farm to play with him."

Eddie smiled and nodded.

"We'll bring the cattle on a bit later."

"Thank you. We sure appreciate it," Bradford said as the three returned to the wagon.

Jilla started walking toward town. "See you all soon!" She turned and waved to them as their wagon pulled away.

As the day passed Alahandra busied herself in her house. She sat on the floor and cuddled the puppies in her lap. "What shall I name you? Something regal. Royal. Hmm, something royal. She picked one up and looked into his little face. Niklas?" she laughed. "No. That won't do. What are you up to now, Niklas? Do you even think about me?"

Alahandra sighed. "Time to let go of all the things in my past and move on. There are hills that I'll explore one day. Places I'll travel. People I'll meet. Men I will love." She picked up the other puppy. "Let's concentrate on you. What do you want your name to be?"

The puppy licked her nose. "We'll think of a wonderful name for both of you. For now, it's time for cleaning. I'm ready to make this place my home."

Alahandra took the puppies outside and they followed her around. She fed the chickens and gathered the eggs she found in the barn.

She watched as a wagon came up the road toward her home. Behind the wagon six cows were being pulled. Alahandra ran out to meet the wagon waving to Mr. Troy and his sons.

"Oh, my goodness, I'm so excited!" she said.

Mr. Troy nodded. "Do you want me to put them in the fence for you?"

"Yes, please," Alahandra said.

"Will you be taking care of these?" he asked.

"Yes. I'll be the main person caring for these. I really don't know exactly what I'm doing, but I'm going to try," Alahandra said.

"Just make sure they have enough to eat and drink. Do you know how to milk them?"

"Yes, sir. That's the one thing I know."

Alexander put the cattle in the fence. "Have a good day, Miss Alahandra."

"Thank you so much," Alahnadra said. "I am quite serious about needing help if you and your brother would like the work."

Alexander's face reddened. "We'll be glad to help." He closed the gate and smiled.

Eddie followed Alexander to the wagon and turned to Alahandra. "Bye!" he shouted and waved.

Mr. Troy put his hand over his mouth and his eyes instantly filled with tears. He knelt in front of Eddie and hugged him. Alexander hugged them both, and they all turned to wave again at Alahandra. Alahandra felt her own tears threaten to spill onto her cheeks.

She watched as the three climbed into the wagon and it moved down the road around the bend. She looked at the cows in the fence, the chickens in the yard, and her puppies running around her feet.

"This is the life," Alahandra whispered.

As time began to move on and the weeks began to find their routine, the furniture arrived for Alahandra and Haya. Once the wagons left and everything was arranged Haya knocked on Alahanadra's door. There was no answer.

"Alahandra?"

"Yes, come in."

Haya entered to find Alahandra sitting in the middle of the floor with her legs pulled in tight to her and tears streaming down her cheeks.

"Oh, my dear, what's wrong?"

"I was overwhelmed with everything. With the house, the new things, myself, and no one to share it with." Alahandra wiped her eyes.

Haya came to sit beside her on the floor. "You deserve this life and so much more. It's no wonder you're overwhelmed. You've also never spent this much time alone. So let's do some decorating. What do you say? I've got some fabric out to make some beautiful aprons for us both and a vest for Bradford."

"Haya," she paused, "thank you."

Haya hugged her. "I love you, my dear."

Alahandra nodded and hugged Haya tightly. She was loved.

On the seas The Silver Phoenix overtook a merchant ship. The captain was on his knees. "Please spare the lives of my crew."

"I don't kill for fun, good man. Now, let's see what goods you have for me today."

Rylic watched his crew take all the merchant ship had. He watched the other crew cower in fear. He stood by the other captain with his sword drawn.

"Tell me your name," Rylic spoke loudly.

"Barnis," the captain said, holding his head up.

Rylic lowered his sword. "Let's talk." Rylic paused and looked at the crew. "I want to make you a deal, Barnis. I want your ship to sail under my authority."

Barnis laughed. "You think me a fool? I'll not traverse these waters as a pirate. I live a life of integrity. If you wish to run me through, good sir, then do so, but I'll not succumb to a life of piracy."

Rylic laughed. "You have the tongue of the educated, and my deepest respect. I'm offering you a life of luxury to travel as a merchant ship under my rule."

"You take my haul and expect me to be under your authority?" Barnis asked.

"Yes, actually. I want to give up this life. I want to start running merchant ships, but I need someone to head up my business." Rylic said, offering his hand.

The other captain got to his feet. "I work for someone else, and I'm completely happy."

"But, you aren't protected. I can guarantee protection, and a monthly payment that no man can match," Rylic said.

Barnis watched the pirates raid his ship.

"I'm keeping what I take from you today, and then we'll make port in Trobonia. I'll base our shipping company from there," Rylic said.

"Trobonia? My crew will be delighted," Barnis said.

Rylic turned to him. "So, it's a deal?" he extended his hand.

"I can do this. What kind of money are you talking?" Barnis said.

155

"Enough to keep you and your crew happy for a long time," Rylic said. "Take your ship and port in Trobonia. I'll return by the end of the week. I have one more ship to take."

"Why not stop now?" Barnis said.

"I've been waiting on this ship." Rylic said. "We'll be set after this."

Barnis shook his head. "Perhaps you'll never be happy then."

"There's only one thing that can make me happy," Rylic said.

"Oh, is there now? What's her name?" Barnis laughed.

Rylic laughed and clapped Barnis on the back.

"She's tamed the sea in me, my friend, and I'll never be good enough for her."

"Good enough? That's not a thing. You only have to love her, and let her love you in return," Barnis said.

"How do you know so much about love?" Rylic said.

"Easy. I love all the women I meet," Barnis said laughing. He turned to his men when the last of the haul was complete. "Men, we are off to Trobornia. Meet the new owner of the Seafairer, Captain Rylic of the Silver Phoenix and The Lady Amore. We are now shipping for his company, and we'll make port in Trobonia. You have the opportunity to stay with us, or make your own way."

Rylic turned to him. "How did you know about The Lady Amore?"

"You overtook one of the merchant ships I was on years ago. I was so impressed that no one was hurt, you took all of our haul, and you didn't burn our ship. I've been on ships before that were plundered and people were killed. Piracy can be ugly, and you, sir, are a gentleman. I appreciate you, and I look forward to working with you."

Rylic shook his hand and yelled out to his crew, "James, come over here!"

James made his way to Rylic. "Yes sir."

"Meet Barnis. He'll be working with us on our merchant ships. We'll be sailing throughout the ports within a day's travel to acquire new business. James, will be in charge. He could persuade the color from a rainbow," Rylic laughed. "Barnis, you answer only to James and myself. If you prove yourself loyal we will become the largest merchant trader in the region."

After the raid was over, Barnis took his ship away. Rylic knew the next ship would be in route soon. It would be one of the biggest he would take, and he was ready. One more raid and he would go back to Trobornia to surprise Alahandra. One more raid and they would never have to think about piracy again.

Joab and James came to stand beside Rylic. Rylic spoke quietly, "One more raid."

James whispered, "The Temptress."

"The Temptress," Rylic smiled. "Joab, you'll stay below for this one."

"I can do my part," Joab said.

"Not this time. The Temptress has a crew that doesn't mind a kill. They are the largest merchant ship that comes from the East. When the sun breaks the horizon, we'll be upon them. Have the crew get some rest. We'll need it."

"Yes, sir," James said. He walked away. Joab stayed near Rylic.

"Are you worried?" Joab asked.

"I never worry, but I am cautious," Rylic said. "Promise you'll stay below."

"I promise," Joab said, turning to go. "And thank you, Rylic. Thank you for telling me I can go to Trobornia."

"Thank me after you clean out the barn a time or two," Rylic laughed.

Joab laughed and went below.

As the sun rose Rylic could see the ship coming across the horizon. "Men, ready your arms."

The crew looked out across the sea. They positioned themselves as The Silver Phoenix came close to The Temptress. At Rylic's command, the crew began to overtake the Temptress sword for sword. With the constant clink of metal surrounding him, Rylic knew something was wrong. The Temptress crew were barbaric and ready to fight. He watched as men fell around him. His sword swung true and took down man after man. The fight grew thicker, and Rylick heard a yell from behind him. Joab had been injured. As he was running to help he felt a burning sensation in the back of his leg. He turned, swinging his blade, and a sharp pain seared his head. Everything went black.

Rylic woke with his head pounding with pain.

"Don't move. You're losing a lot of blood," James said.

"Where's Joab?" Rylic tried to raise up and winced in pain.

"He's okay. He's cut pretty bad, but Trek sewed him up. I gave him some whiskey, and he's sleeping."

Rylic nodded. "What about the take?"

"It's all done. The Temptress was stripped of her cargo. We lost crew members this time, Rylic. Their crew was ready and they were violent. That was not a merchant trader crew. They were pirates. I remember some of them from earlier times. They were prepared. Morik led them. He knew you wanted the Temptress, and he was prepared to take the Phoenix. He meant to kill you."

"Morik. I was right to turn him out, but I should have killed him when I had the chance. He was the most evil pirate that ever sailed with me. Is he dead? How many crew members did we lose?" Rylic said through clenched teeth.

"He's dead. I killed him when he went for you. We lost seven in total. One just died with injuries I couldn't fix," James said quietly.

"And what of The Temptress? What of their crew?" Rylic said.

"We took her for you. She trails us now with our crew on board. We put all that was left of the cut throats in the dingy and sent them on their way. If they make it, they make it. If they don't, then may they go straight to Davy Jones's locker," James said, getting up.

"What of the merchant crew?" Rylic said.

"They were being held down below the deck of the Temptress. I offered them jobs aboard The Silver Phoenix. They agreed. They wanted to live. The pirates were going to slaughter them once we were overtaken, but they did not anticipate the crew of the Phoenix. The merchant crew are on board."

"It's time," Rylic whispered, "to go home." His eyes closed and darkness settled over him.

His mind wandered to Alahandra. Pirates surrounded her, and she was screaming his name.

"No!" he yelled in his sleep.

"Rylic, it's Joab. You're on the ship."

Sleep overcame him again. Time slipped by him. Someone would wake him to drink or eat something small and then he would sleep again.

"Rylic, we have to get you off this ship. Can you walk?" James asked.

Rylic opened his eyes. His throat felt dry, and he coughed as he tried to sit up. "My leg." He grabbed at his leg as he raised from the bed.

"It looks to be infected. We are going to have to get you to the doctor. I'll take you into Trobornia and get you to your family. We'll send for the doctor once you're home with your mum."

Rylic winced. "How long have I been in this bed?"

"Days sir. We've had enough time to travel all the way back to port. We've already anchored," James said.

"How is Joab? Where is he?" Rylic asked.

"He is fine, Sir. He is walking with a limp now, but he is working as hard as ever," James laughed. "He'll be glad to know you're getting up. He hasn't left your side."

"I'm glad I'm taking him to my mother's house. He'll be a nice addition to their family," Rylic said.

As James, Joab, and Rylice made their way off the ship, Rylic collapsed onto the pier.

Several of the crew picked up Rylic and found a man with a wagon willing to transport him to the homestead.

James took hold of Rylic's hand. "We'll get you well."

Rylic nodded, breathing heavily through the pain.

CHAPTER
Twelve

Alahandra saw a wagon coming toward Haya's house. She ran outside to see who it was. Haya and Bradford came out of their home.

Joab saw Alahandra and waved. Alahandra waved to him and approached the wagon to find Rylic lying in the back with his shirt soaked in sweat.

"What happened?" Alahandra said as he raised up. Haya and Bradford came running to the wagon.

"I was injured," he looked toward the driver of the wagon, "at sea. I'll tell you more inside."

Bradford and the driver helped him up.

"Wait, take him into my house. I'll care for him," Alahandra said.

"I don't want to do that to you," Rylic said.

The driver moved the wagon slowly to Alahandra's door. They all helped Rylic out of the wagon and into the house.

"My room is off to the left," she said.

Once Rylic was put in the bed, there was a knock at the door. The doctor came into the bedroom.

"Everyone leave us for a moment and allow me to examine his leg."

"I'm not leaving him," Joab said, limping toward the bed.

"Seems you need some looking after too," the doctor said. "You can stay and we'll check out your leg."

Joab nodded.

Everyone left the room, and Alahandra pulled the curtain to her room.

Everyone stood silently and waited. Rylic yelled out in pain.

Time passed slowly. Alahandra held her hands tightly together.

The doctor came out of the room. "It's a lot worse than I expected. He's lost a lot of blood. There is infection in the wound that's causing him to be in so much pain and accounts for the fever. I've cleaned the wound and gave him medication so he can sleep. The boy appears to have injured a muscle and he should heal in a few weeks."

"How long will it take my son to heal?" Haya said.

"He will have to be watched closely. That fever has to stay down, and if that infection gets worse someone needs to come get me. I'll be back to see him in a couple of days," the doctor said.

"Thank you doctor," Bradford said, shaking his hand.

Joab came out of the room. He had tears running down his cheeks. "He just can't die, miss," he said, hugging Alahandra. "He's the only family I've got."

Haya stood and came to Joab. "He's going to be fine, Joab. He's going to have to rest for now, and I bet you could use some food."

Joab nodded.

"I've got dinner cooking, and we always have more than enough. Doctor, would you please join us too?" Haya asked.

"Perhaps next time. I've got dinner waiting on me at Sero's," the doctor said, moving toward the door.

"Doctor, how much do we owe you?" Haya asked.

"No charge," he said, and winked at Joab.

Joab nodded.

When the doctor was gone, Haya asked. "Joab, what was that all about?"

"The doctor said I could come to his office and clean up three times a week to pay my debt and Rylic's. I do for myself. He said once the debt is paid I am welcome to keep working with him. I asked him if I could be a doctor like him, and he said he would train me if I was serious, and then help me go to school. I told him I would be glad to work, and then I could go to school here in Trobornia. Rylic said once we came here I could stay. He can't talk right now, Miss Haya, but he said I could help around here if you would let me stay."

Haya took Joab's hand. "Well, you can only stay if you'll consider yourself family."

Joab hugged her and smiled. "Let's go eat. I'm starving."

Haya laughed. She looked to Alahandra. "I'll bring you dinner, dear. Are you sure you're okay taking care of him?"

"I promise, I'm fine. I'll go in and sit with him," Alahandra said. She shut the door as the others left. Turning toward her bedroom, she paused. "Please, Lord, don't let him die."

She pulled the curtain back and slowly walked toward the bed. Rylic was motionless and his breathing was ragged because of fever. She knelt beside the bed and touched his forehead and moved her fingers down the side of his face.

He moaned in pain and opened his eyes. "Alahandra," he said softly.

"Don't try to talk. Just rest," Alahandra said, taking a damp cloth and wiping his face.

Rylic took her hand. "Thank you, my beautiful Alahandra." His eyes closed and he continued holding her hand.

Alahandra sat beside him staring at his face and wondering how long it would be before he got killed out at sea. How long before that ship sailed into port without him. Her heart ached.

Haya pulled back the curtain and whispered. "I've got your dinner, dear."

"You can leave it on the table." Alahandra said, not looking away from Rylic.

"Come," Haya whispered. "I'll sit with you while you eat."

Alahandra stood up and walked quietly out of the room. She didn't want to talk to Haya about Rylic. She had warned her long ago to not let her heart get involved with a man who loved the sea.

"He'll be fine. It will just take time," Haya said.

"I know. I believe he will," Alahandra said.

"And then he'll leave again," Haya said.

Alahandra looked away from her.

"Unless you ask him to stay," Haya said, taking her hand.

"I would never ask him to stay, Haya. If he wants to stay, he would stay. His heart would never be happy here," Alahandra said.

"His heart would be happy with you," Haya said.

"That would be a choice for him," Alahandra said. "My choice is to let him go."

"Sometimes the heart changes when we don't even know it. Look at me. Do you think I thought I would marry again? Do you think I ever thought I could love again? Dear, don't lose sight of your heart. If not Rylic, then be open to love that will come," Haya said.

"Perhaps, dear friend. Perhaps." Alahandra finished her meal, and Haya left quietly.

Rylic moaned loudly. Alahandra ran to him.

"Water," he whispered.

She picked up the bucket and dipped a cup of water. She leaned a cup to his lips, and he sipped it slowly. He lay his head slowly back on the pillow.

"Thank you," Rylic whispered. "I don't know what I would do without you."

"Well, thankfully you won't have to find out right now," Alahandra said. "I won't leave. I promise."

Alahandra took his hand. She could see the pain and worry move across his face.

Her eyes felt heavy. She sat on the floor and continued to hold his hand. She leaned against the bedding and closed her eyes. Sleep came quickly.

Rylic turned his head and looked at Alahandra. She was beautiful, so amazing, and he wondered if someone like her could ever really love him knowing all he has done. She deserved better than him, but he would give all he had to make sure she never wanted for anything.

Time passed quietly through the night. Alahandra drifted in and out of sleep still holding onto Rylic's hand.

"Alahandra," Rylic whispered. His voice shook.

She stood up beside the bed and allowed her eyes time to adjust. "You're chilled. Your fever must be higher. I have to get help."

"Don't leave me," Rylic squeezed her hand.

She knelt beside him. "I'll be back." She kissed his cheek and ran out of the room. There was no time to hitch the wagon. Running to Haya's, she fell and scraped her arm on a rock. Blood poured quickly from the wound, but she couldn't think about it. She pounded on the front door, and Bradford opened it quickly.

"It's Rylic. He's burning up with fever. I need to take a horse to get the doctor."

Bradford nodded. "I'll get it." He disappeared into the house as Haya came out.

"Dear, have you ever ridden a horse?"

"No, but I will. Whatever I need to do to help." Alahandra could feel tears threatening to spill over.

Bradford came out of the house dressed and took hold of Alahandra's arms. "I'm going. I can ride fast. Wet a lot of towels and lay them on Rylic. Keep them rotating to cool him off. I'll be back as soon as I can."

Haya, Joab, and Alahandra worked quickly to wet the cloth and drape over Rylic. His breathing was ragged and forced.

"I'm… sorry… to burden… you all," he spoke with his voice still shaking.

Alahandra knelt beside him, took his hand in hers, and pressed it to her face. "You could never be a burden. Aggravating, yes, but never a burden." She kissed his cheek and adjusted the towel around him.

Bradford arrived soon with the doctor, and they both entered the room quickly.

The doctor pulled back the sheet to look at Rylic's leg. He turned to Bradford.

"Heat a knife in the fire. The wound has to be opened to release the infection so I can treat it." He looked at Haya. He's going to need some soup and a lot of water to drink to give him strength. He is severely dehydrated." He looked at Joab. "Keep rotating the wet cloth on him. As soon as you put one on, replace another with a fresh one." He looked at Alahandra. "Can you assist me, and keep everything clean? I will need you to hold the lantern, help wash his leg, and replace anything that gets soiled. Then you'll need to keep a wet cloth with you to keep dabbing on him the rest of the night to keep water on him. Can you do this?"

Alahandra nodded. Fear gripped her quickly. What if she couldn't follow through? What if what they did wasn't enough? What if she lost the only man she had ever loved? She looked at Rylic and knew love was more true in that moment than she had ever felt.

Everyone began to work quickly around the room. Alahandra brought two more lanterns in the room. The doctor nodded to her.

"It's time. Hold the lantern close. Bradford, Haya, Joab. We are going to need everyone to hold him down. He's going to scream, and I need him steady so that the knife doesn't injure him more."

Bradford gave the doctor the knife he had placed over the flames in the fire. He had been instructed to hold it while it cooled. His hand shook as he passed the knife to the doctor.

"Rylic, do you hear me?" The doctor touched his arm.

"Yes," Rylic whispered.

"Do you understand what I'm about to do? I have to cut open the infected area on your leg. I have to pour water over it, and I'm going to clean it. Do you understand?"

Rylic shook and put his arms down at his sides. "I understand. I know you have to hold me down. I'm ready."

The doctor looked at the others. "Hold his arms, feet, and chest."

No one spoke but took hold of Rylic.

The doctor took the knife and slid it over the infected area. Rylic screamed out in pain. He tilted his head back and clenched the sheet beneath him. Tears rolled down the sides of his face. The doctor cut once more, and Rylic screamed louder. His breath was rapid, and he looked at Alahandra. Tears welled in her eyes seeing him in pain. He closed his eyes and tried to keep still.

Alahandra wiped all the infection away as it ran from the wound. The doctor began cleaning the area to remove as much infection as possible. Rylic screamed out once more, and tried to breathe deeply.

As the procedure continued the doctor told Joab and Haya they could release Rylic and asked if they could bring more water to him. Haya nodded. Joab ran out and returned quickly with a bucket of water.

The doctor smiled at him. He looked at everyone. "Once the bandage is on, he should be able to rest. Alahandra, remember, you'll need to stay and keep cool water on him throughout the night and day. Try to get him to drink as much water as possible. He'll sleep a lot, and that's normal. Rest will help. Someone needs to stay with him at all times. Keep his leg uncovered, and check the wound every hour. If the swelling gets worse, he may lose his leg. I can't let the infection grow or it will start going throughout his body."

Rylic whispered, "Water."

"That's good, son. It's good that you're awake and thirsty," the doctor paused. "Drink as much as you can."

After the bandages were in place and the doctor had cleaned up, he looked at Alahandra. "He's lucky to have you. I've never had anyone stay strong during that kind of procedure. Most people end up fainting."

"I thought I was going a couple of times, but I would do anything for Rylic," she said, looking at him.

Rylic smiled, "You're a witness, doc. You heard her confess that. Anything. I'm going to remember that." He winced and breathed deeply.

"Humor in place. That's a good sign. Time for you to rest," the doctor smiled at him.

"What's your name, doc?" Rylic asked.

"Wilford Troborn."

Alahandra looked at him and started to speak.

"Yes, like Trobornia. My family had one of the founding fathers of this town. You can call me Wilford, or Doc. I answer to both."

"Doc, we appreciate your help. I know you're tired, and we've got a bed over there if you'd like to rest before you go home." Bradford shook his hand.

"I've got my horse, and a slow ride home as the sun rises sounds like a good cleansing for my mind. I'm going to go home, wash off, and rest. Thank you for your offer though."

Haya hugged him. "Thank you for…everything." Tears ran down her cheeks.

"I think he'll be okay now. He's got the love of a strong woman to live for." He winked at Alahandra.

"Oh, we're not… I'm not…" She didn't know what to say to the Doc.

He nodded and walked out the door. Haya stood in the doorway.

"We'll have you back for dinner soon."

"I look forward to it." The doctor got on his horse and rode away.

Bradford hugged Haya as she started to cry. "He's going to be okay. I know it."

Haya nodded.

Joab came up and hugged them both. "That was the scariest thing I've ever seen, and I'm a pirate."

"You're not a pirate anymore," Bradford knelt in front of him, "you're family."

Joab began to cry too, and Bradford put his arms around him in a tight hug. Haya hugged them both.

Alahandra watched the three from the doorway of the bedroom. "You all are going to make me cry," she said, wiping her eyes. "I think we'll be okay now if you want to go rest."

"I don't want to leave you here to do everything," Haya said.

"How about you bring me a hot breakfast when you wake up. I'll stay up for now, and when you all get up, I'll rest."

Bradford put his hand on Haya's shoulder and nodded.

Haya wiped her eyes and nodded to them both.

Once the house was quiet, Alahandra brought fresh water into the bedroom to start dabbing the cloth over Rylic. As she started he winced in pain as he moved his leg.

"I forgot for a moment," he whispered.

She wiped his arms and across his neck and didn't respond. He sighed and slightly opened his eyes to watch her. She continued to move the wet cloth over him.

"Alahandra, are you okay?" his voice came out in a low whisper, and he coughed.

"I'll get you some water." She stopped and moved to the table to dip out water in a cup.

As she brought it to his lips he leaned his head up to drink. As he finished he smiled.

"Thank you," he sighed.

She nodded.

"Are you not going to talk?" he asked.

She stopped wiping his arm and looked at him. "What if I had lost you?"

"You didn't. You won't."

Rylic took her hand in his and kissed it gently. She leaned over him and kissed his forehead.

"Rest," she whispered.

He nodded and closed his eyes once more. Exhaustion was overwhelming, but she stayed close to him.

After the sun rose, Haya, Bradford, and Joab each came in at different times to take turns sitting with Rylic as he slept throughout the day. Wet towels were kept on him to help keep the fever down. Doc came by to check the bandages and clean the wound.

"You should be able to leave the wound bound for a day now before you check it," he said Haya. "Make sure Alahandra knows. She's doing a wonderful job taking care of him."

When the doc left, Bradford came in to take the next shift.

"Is he going to get better?" Joab asked.

"He'll get better. Like the good doctor said, he's got love to keep him fighting."

"I hope someday someone loves me as much as Alahandra loves

Rylic," Joab said quietly.

Alahandra came in the front door and overheard the conversation. She put her hand over her mouth trying not to make noise. Joab came from the bedroom and his eyes widened.

"Meaning no disrespect to you," he said quietly. "You love like my mum loved my dad."

Alahandra nodded and smiled as she hugged Joab. He left smiling, and Alahandra entered the bedroom.

"I think I've rested enough. The day has almost ended. You can go, Bradford. I had dinner with Haya, and she has a plate waiting for you. I'll come get you if I need you, but I think the worst is over. Don't you?"

Bradford nodded. "I do believe he's going to be okay. I'll come back or Haya will at first light."

Alahandra nodded.

Bradford patted her on the arm as he left, and Alahandra was left alone with her thoughts. Everyone was noticing her caring for Rylic. Would he see it? Would it matter? Who was she to have the heart of a man so driven by the sea? She shook her head and didn't want to think about him leaving again.

Moving to the bed she wiped a wet cloth over his face. He opened his eyes and smiled at her.

"Are you still in a lot of pain?"

"It comes and goes. Thank you for taking care of me," he whispered. "Will you sit with me? I think a wet cloth on my forehead is all I need now, and I finally get to cover up."

Alahandra nodded and sat down on the side of the bed. She moved up beside him and leaned on the headboard.

"You could stretch out here beside me and rest." He looked up at her.

"I'll fall asleep for sure. I would feel better if I just watched you for tonight." She placed the wet cloth across his head.

"Would you hold my hand while I fall asleep? I would feel better knowing you're near."

Alahandra took his hand in hers and took a deep breath in.

He closed his eyes and squeezed her hand holding it close to his face. He fell asleep quickly, and she leaned over to kiss his hand.

The sun broke through the horizon and Haya walked quietly in the morning air. She entered Alahandra's house and put two plates of food on the table. She moved the curtain back and walked into the bedroom. Alahandra was asleep, still leaning against the headboard. Rylic smiled at Haya. As Rylic sat up, Alahandra woke.

"Good morning Haya. Good morning Rylic. Are you feeling better?" Alahandra asked.

Haya moved closer to the bed as Alahandra stood. Rylic smiled at Haya.

"I am doing better. I can focus better, and the pain isn't searing," Rylic said.

"That doctor knows what he's doing. You gave us all a good scare," Haya said.

"I'm still weak, but I'd like to sit up," Rylic said.

"I'll help!" Joab said, running through the door.

The three of them helped him to sit.

"You were right, Rylic. I can stay!" Joab said. "Glad you're better. Glad we're brothers!" He ran back out of the house to go help in the barn.

"Thank you for taking him in. It was time he left the Phoenix. He needs family," Rylic said, trying to pull his leg over in the bed.

"Time to eat you two. I've got breakfast waiting. I'll bring it in," Haya said. "James left your clothes so after you eat, you can wash off and change." She brought their plates in the bedroom.

"Thank you, Mum," Rylic said.

"Thank you, Haya," Alahandra said.

"I'll go draw the water while you two eat."

Rylic ate slowly. He took deep breaths and didn't look up at

Alahandra.

"You're in more pain than you're saying."

"I'll be fine. I just can't believe this happened. They knew we were coming, Alahandra. Men were killed. This was my last raid, and I had to do one more haul. One more ship. We lost a lot of good men, and so did they. The merchant ship had been boarded by cut throats. Some of their crew had already been slaughtered. We overtook them, and now the Temptress is mine along with the last ship I took before her. I'll have four ships now running for me."

"Running for you. So four pirate ships?" Alahandra said.

"No, not pirate ships. Not anymore," Rylic said. "I'm going to have a fleet of merchant ships. I've made enough on the last three hauls that we'll never have to worry about money again."

"Money, is that all you care about?" Alahandra said.

Rylic took hold of her arm. "It's time for a change. You showed me that. Look at me. I almost died. It was always just one more haul. When I was knocked out, all I could see before I closed my eyes was Joab lying on the deck holding his leg crying. Because of me. My greed got those men killed. I will not apologize for the life I've led or the money I have. I'll still sail the seas, but with the merchant fleet. I know enough people that I will never be without a port to deliver in. I care about money, yes, but I care about you. I care about my mum and Bradford, about Joab. So before you judge me, remember where you came from Alahandra, and if it wasn't for me, you'd either be stealing bread from the back of the baker's stand or married to the Prince."

Alahandra started to get up. Rylic still had hold of her arm.

Haya walked back in with the water. "Alahandra, can you help Rylic or would you like me to do it?"

"No, of course I will help. You made breakfast. Anything I can do to help, you know I will."

"When he changes clothes, bring them to me and I'll wash them," Haya said.

Alahandra nodded.

She took their plates and left them alone. They sat in silence for a moment.

"Let's just get this over with and you don't have to deal with me for the rest of the day or night," Rylic said.

Alahandra didn't respond. She pulled the blanket back and gasped. Where the doctor had cut open the leg of his pants to dress the wound was saturated with blood, and it had dried on his skin. Blood had covered the cloth under him so as not to spoil her bed. The dressing on the wound had to be changed. They both stared at the horrific mess.

"I thought the doctor said it was going to be okay," Alahandra couldn't take her eyes from the wound.

"The wound is draining. It feels better. Sore, but better. I'm so sorry. I had no idea it was this bad. If you'll leave the bucket, I will take care of this."

"You need help. I can do this," Alahandra took a deep breath and took the wet cloth in her hands.

"Wait, turn around, and I'll take these soiled trousers off. I'll stay covered, mind you. I'll let you know when I'm ready.

Alahandra turned her back to him. He slid his trousers and undergarments down to his hips and screamed out in pain.

"What's happening?" she asked.

"Moving hurts," he gasped as he spoke through clenched teeth. "It will take me a little longer." He slid the clothes off slower until he had moved them down to his thighs. His shirt was covered with blood where he had held his leg and wiped his hands. He removed it and tossed it to the edge of the bed. He pulled the blanket up to cover himself.

"Okay, you may turn around."

Alahandra tried not to look at him with his chest bare. She moved close to him to help finish removing his trousers and undergarments. "I'll move them down side to side so they will come off easier without having to move you."

Her fingers moved inside the top of his pants and moved them down slowly. His skin was warm and he breathed deeply. When she moved his trousers down to his knees she stopped. "I'll remove your leg that isn't injured first. If you can move your leg out gently."

He winced.

"I'm sorry. Let's do this slower," she said.

"I'm fine. Let's finish."

She held his ankle up and pulled his clothes off slowly keeping them from touching his wound. She placed the ripped pants and undergarments on the stained shirt and became aware that he was near her without clothing.

"Haya heated some of the water so it wouldn't be as cold. I'll go retrieve it from the stove top."

Alahandra left the bedroom and took a deep breath. She took the kettle to the room and added the boiling water to the bucket. She then poured the warmed water into her wash bowl. Dipping the cloth in, the water warmed her hands and she thought how pleasant the feel of the warmth on her skin. Taking a deep breath, she began cleaning his wound.

He gripped the bed covers and she stopped.

"It's okay. Keep going," Rylic winced.

Alahandra took her time and cleaned him gently. She moved the cloth around the wound and didn't notice she had placed her hand on his other leg. She moved with precision around the wound and cleaned the dried blood away, intermittently emptying the bowl out the window and then bringing in more water from the kettle. She would go pump more water for the kettle and have to heat it again.

Without thinking she placed the warm cloth on his chest and began wiping away the blood that had dried through his shirt. He drew in his breath.

"Oh, forgive me. I just got caught up in taking care of this," Alahandra said softly.

Rylic held her arm as she pulled away. "Thank you for taking care of me." He raised up close to her. She sat gently on the bed.

"I did what I had to do. No need to thank me," She whispered.

Cleaning all the blood from him took all of the morning. Haya brought them both lunch. Alahandra came out of the bedroom, her face covered in sweat.

"Are you okay?" Haya asked.

"It's almost cleaned." Alahandra breathed deeply. "The wound had drained, and it all had to be cleaned."

"Why don't you go outside, and I'll finish."

"No, I promise I'm fine. I appreciate the food." Alahandra poured hot water into the basin and rinsed her hands to eat.

"I'll bring you both dinner. I'll cook early and leave it in here so you can eat whenever you want."

Alahandra nodded, and Haya left the house.

"Time for lunch," Alahandra announced, coming through the curtain.

"I don't think I can eat yet," Rylic winced, moving his leg over slightly.

"Just a bite or two and we'll try again later." She offered him a plate of food. He took a small bite of bread and closed his eyes. He set the plate on the side table.

"Let's get more of this cleaned up." She took the plate into the kitchen and returned with a fresh basin of water. She sat on the bed and moved the wet cloth over his leg gently.

He took hold of her arm and pulled her closer. She moved her hand up his arm.

"You're nervous around me," Rylic said, leaning near her.

"We are different people than we were when we first met. However, I still enjoy being near you. I still enjoy touching you."

"Would you enjoy kissing me?" Rylic said, moving his hands to her face.

She leaned into him moving her mouth to his. His lips parted, inviting her. Kissing him deeply, the only thing that mattered was being near him.

She moved slightly away from him and moved her lips to his cheek. Her hand slid down his chest. He breathed in deeply and closed his eyes.

"Time to finish cleaning this up."

He smiled and moved the hair from her cheek. She looked up and smiled at him. "It's going to be closer to the wound this time."

"Just do it. I'm going to lay back and breathe through it." Rylic lay back on the bed and put his arm up over his face.

Alahandra paused for a moment admiring Rylic's body. He was such a beautiful man, and all she wanted to do was love him completely and be loved by him. She moved closer and washed his blood stained leg slowly. His muscles tightened and he inhaled deeply. If she was going to do this, she couldn't keep thinking about how much pain he was in. She had to finish. Slowly she removed the dressing on the wound and he screamed out.

"Oh, Rylic, I'm sorry."

His breath was quick and he winced as he spoke. "I'm okay. The dressing had stuck to one side. It's okay now. Do all you need to do and don't stop. Even if I make noise. Just keep going."

Alahandra took a long deep breath. "Okay," she whispered and started cleaning the wound to dress once again. The doctor had given her instructions on what to do, so she did all she had to do without stopping.

Rylic squeezed the bed in his grip and groaned loudly, but Alahandra didn't stop until Rylic was covered up and comfortable once again.

"I'll be right back. I have to go empty all of the water and wash out all the cloth."

Rylic nodded. She knew the pain was too much to talk through at the moment by the look on his face.

As she moved the cloth aside to walk through Haya came through the front door with food.

Alahandra looked confused. "It's dinner time already? I just got finished with everything in there helping to clean and dress his wound."

"No, not quite dinner time. Remember I was bringing food early so you two could eat when you wanted?"

"Oh, that's right. I'm so tired I forgot we had that conversation.

Haya placed the plates on the table and put her arm around Alahandra. "Give me all the cloth and the basin. I'll clean those. Joab can help. You rest and eat something."

"On any other day I would protest, but not this day. I'll gladly go rest. Exhaustion from worry is one of the worst kinds of tired," Alahandra yawned.

"Especially when you care so deeply for the person you worry over." Haya hugged her tightly.

There was no cause to argue with Haya about her feelings tonight.

Haya left and Alahandra lifted the cloth covering the food. She was too tired to eat and lunch had been so filling. Moving the cloth aside she entered the bedroom, and Rylic was staring at the ceiling. She had expected him to be asleep.

"Thank you for helping me," he said quietly.

"I'll do all I can to help you get better."

"I know something that would help," he smiled.

"Do you now?" she smirked and sat on the side of the bed to lean over him.

His hand moved to the top of her dress, and he slowly united the front. The cloth gave way and opened slightly.

"Rest with me," he whispered.

She stood and slid the dress from her shoulders and moved it slowly down her body. Her undergarment clung to her in the oil light.

"You are a beautiful woman, Alahandra." he said, extending his hand. He moved over slightly in the bed trying to control the pain as he lifted his leg to move it over and he held the covering over his hips.

Alahandra hesitated. He smiled at her, and she moved to lie beside him.

"Will you be comfortable with me beside you?" she whispered.

"I would be miserable without you beside me."

He moved his hand to the small of her back and held her close. He slid it slowly up her arm as she moaned softly.

"You overwhelm me," he said.

"You make my body want all of you," she said.

He brought his face to hers quickly, and she moved her mouth with an urgency to satisfy the longing in her.

He leaned slightly from her. "When I am well, I shall do all I can give you all you want of me. But, for tonight, share your bed with me, and allow me to hold you in my arms. Give me the joy of being near you while we rest."

"Then let us rest," she said, taking the blanket that covered his hips and raising it to cover them both. She moved her arm over him, and he pulled her close. Her thoughts ran wild with him so near.

He moved his arm around her and slowly slid her undergarment down her shoulder. She pulled the tie of her undergarment in the front and it gave way so that more of her was exposed to him. He sighed heavily, pulled her close, and closed his eyes.

Sleep overcame them both in the security of one another's arms.

CHAPTER
Thirteen

As the sun rose, the rooster crowing startled Alahandra awake. She got up from the bed quickly.

"Are you alright?" Rylic asked, not moving.

"There is much to do when the sun rises," she said, picking up her dress from the floor.

"Stay with me throughout this day. Let the others tend to the chores. Please, stay with me," he said.

Alahandra sat down on the bed beside him. He raised to her and held her in a tight embrace, kissing her deeply.

"I will do the chores, but I'll be back to check on you every chance I can." She tied her undergarment and put her dress on quickly.

"Check on me, and make sure no one else is in the house," he said, kissing her hand as she got up from the bed.

"I can tell you're better," she laughed.

"I'll make it," he said. "I'm going to go back to sleep if that's okay."

"Yes, please rest. Get well," she laughed while securing her dress.

"So you can get rid of me?" he smiled.

She laughed and then stopped to look at him. "You can always come home."

She left the room not wanting to hear his response. She couldn't let her feelings show and then watch him leave again. She would never be enough for him.

As the days passed Rylic regained his strength. He would do exercises the doctor showed him to make sure he could use his leg properly again. He slept most of the day trying to allow his body to heal. One morning Alahandra called from the main room. "I'll bring breakfast in just a moment."

"No need, I can make it to the table," Rylic said, limping out of the bedroom.

"Oh, my goodness, you're walking!" Alahandra said.

"It still hurts a little, but I'm ready to move around more. Doc said as soon as I felt like I could, that I should try. I guess you'll be rid of me soon," he laughed.

"Well, you've been intolerable," she laughed. "I'll make us some coffee."

"I like the new clothes Haya brought for me from the mercantile. Rugged."

"You look like a farmer and less like a pirate," Alahandra said, bringing their cups to the table.

"I'll always be your pirate," Rylic smiled over the rim of his cup. "Looks like you'll be getting your bed back after all. Sooner than we thought."

"I never said you had to leave my bed, Pirate King," she laughed.

"Aye, my wench, come kiss me," Rylic said, swiping at her, and she twirled away from him.

Alahandra laughed. "I have an idea. Let's get you stronger without telling the others and surprise them. We need you walking. Here. Let me help you, and let's do a few laps around the table."

"Before long I'll be chasing you," Rylic said, draping his arm around her shoulders.

"Let's concentrate before I get distracted," Alahandra said, looking up at him.

They stopped walking and he turned to her. "Alahandra…"

"Walk, pirate," she laughed. She didn't want to hear his goodbyes right now.

After a week of strengthening and walking, Alahandra found Bradford in the barn before he left for the dinner.

"Do you think we could have a fire outside tonight? I think Rylic would love it. He needs to get outside for some fresh air."

"I think that's a great idea." Bradford said, putting the feed bucket down. "Well, I'll build a fire only if I get to play the violin."

"The violin?" Alahandra laughed. "Since when do you play the violin?"

"I've played forever but just got so busy that I stopped. Haya makes me want to play again."

"Well then tune those strings, and let's have a beautiful night," Alahandra said.

She hurried back in the house. "We'll have our fire tonight!"

"Won't Mum be surprised?" Rylic laughed.

"Oh, and Bradford is going to play the violin. Haya will love this night!" Alahandra said, rushing over to kiss Rylic on the cheek.

"Happy looks good on you, Alahandra."

"Happy feels good in me," she said.

They went about their day doing all the necessary chores for the homestead. "We could bring food out to the fire, and eat outside tonight. I'll have Joab help carry the chairs out."

"He loves it here. Thank you for taking so much time with him," Rylic said.

"Like Haya said, we're his family now," she smiled.

The sun began to set, and Joab moved all the chairs needed for dinner by the fire. He helped Bradford bring out the table so Haya could set food out to eat as they enjoyed the evening.

The fire began to roar, and Haya brought out stew and bread to join Bradford and Joab. Alahandra opened the door and came out with

Rylic. He was leaning on her and trying to hobble along.

Haya came to him. "Are you sure you should be up. It looks like you are struggling too much. Are you in pain?"

"No, I'm doing fine," Rylic said and sat down in a chair near the table.

Bradford went inside and brought out his violin. He stood by the fire and began to play.

Haya put a hand over her mouth and tears escaped her eyes, sparkling on her cheeks in the firelight.

"I love you, dear man," Haya said softly.

"I love you," he whispered.

Rylic stood and offered his hand to Alahandra. Haya looked at them and waited.

Alahandra took his hand and stood. She placed her hand on his arm and one in his hand. He slid his hand behind her and they began to dance slowly.

Haya allowed the tears to flow freely. "My son. What a surprise!"

"We thought you would like this," he said, moving by her.

Joab walked over to Haya and extended his hand. "My lady."

"Yes, kind sir," Haya laughed and began to dance around with Joab.

She danced by Bradford, stopped and kissed him, and said, "This will be a night I will never forget."

Rylic danced again with Alahandra and then with Haya. When they were on the opposite side of the fire, Haya hugged him tightly.

"She would love you forever," she whispered.

"She sees me as a pirate," he whispered back.

"She sees you as a man."

"A man that will never be good enough for her," he said.

"Why don't you let her decide that?" Haya said.

"What if she decides to leave? I'm not going to have my heart broken. I can't," he said.

"You can't keep that heart of yours closed up forever," Haya said, patting him on the back. "You are stumbling. Let's not overwork that

181

leg."

"Agreed," Rylic said.

Haya raised an eyebrow.

He laughed, "About my leg and nothing more."

Rylic limped over to the chair and sat sighing. "That was the most fun I've had in a long time."

"Me too," said Alahandra, sitting near him.

"Can we eat now, I'm so hungry!" Joab said.

"Let us feast!" Haya laughed. She took Bradford's hand and smiled at him.

Alahandra wondered if she would ever know the depth of love they shared, and who would love her in such a way?

As they cleaned up from the fun, Rylic hugged Haya. "You have a grand life now, Mum."

She nodded.

"Bradford," Rylic said, "can you take me to town tomorrow? I need to check on my ships and have James ready the cargo for sail. I'm leaving this port an honest man."

Bradford laughed, "Pirate gone businessman. I've seen it all."

"You haven't seen anything yet," Rylic laughed.

As everyone retired for the evening, Haya watched Rylic go with Alahandra without question. She smiled and took Joab's hand. "I think tomorrow, we shall plant a garden."

"I would like that. May I have a little piece of land all my own to plant? I could sell in the market."

"My boy, you can have anything your heart desires," Haya said, sighing. She did have a grand life.

Rylic entered Alahandra's house behind her. She was quiet as she placed the chairs under the table.

"I think we surprised them for sure," Rylic said.

"I think so," Alahandra said. "I'm going to go get ready for bed. I'll heat some water for you if you'd like a bath. I can bring the tub in and build a fire."

"I would like that. A hot bath would do these aching muscles good. I didn't know I would be this tired just from that little bit of fun."

"You'll get your strength back," she said, putting water on the stovetop. "I'll be back."

When the bath was full, Alahandra left the room while Rylic got undressed and got in.

"You can come back," Rylic said.

He sat back in the water and closed his eyes.

"Thank you for this. I needed it more than I thought," he said.

"I'm glad you are enjoying it. I've set the cloth and soap on the bench beside the tub. Oh, and a hot cup of coffee too."

"You spoil me," Rylic said.

"I actually enjoy it," Alahnadra said. "I've always had to take care of my father and whoever we were staying with, but I've never done this because I wanted to. I enjoy getting things ready, getting things done. I like seeing my accomplishments," she said, moving to be near him.

He reached from the water and took her hand. "You, my wild maiden, will accomplish great things."

"We shall see," Alahandra said, kissing him on the cheek. "I'm going to get ready for bed."

She walked away from him wanting nothing more than for him to say he would stay, but she knew the sea called to him.

In her dressing gown, she returned with a towel and placed it near him. "When you're out of the tub, let me know and I'll empty the water."

"How about instead of me getting out, you join me!" He laughed, pulling her arm toward him, causing her to fall and splash into the tub, catching her in his lap.

"Oh, you! Look at us!" Alahandra said, trying to pull herself up.

"I'm sorry," he laughed. "I couldn't resist!"

Her hand slipped and she splashed into the water again. Her face was close to his.

"You are beautiful in the firelight," he whispered, kissing her gently.

She breathed deeply and turned to position herself to get out of the tub.

She stood up and he exhaled slowly trying not to think of the man sitting in the tub at her feet. She pulled her hem up and stepped out of the tub. The wet fabric clung to her every curve. She knew her body was tempting him, and she enjoyed his eyes on her. She knew if she didn't walk away that he would possess her heart forever.

"Since you're soaked, you might as well get back in," he said. We can both enjoy the warm water."

Without speaking she stepped back in the tub, sat down with her back to him, leaned onto his chest, and closed her eyes. He wrapped his arms around her and held tight. Softly his lips met the side of her face and her neck. His hands moved down into the water to the side of her night gown. He gathered the garment in his hands until her legs were exposed. His hand moved along her thigh as his breath warmed her neck.

"Your hands on me make my heart race," she whispered.

"Can I touch more of you?" he whispered against her ear.

Alahandra raised her hands and stretched them to clasp behind his neck. She sighed and kept her eyes closed. "Touch all of me."

Rylic breathed deeply, moving his hands slowly up her sides. She arched slightly and moved her hands into the water placing them on his legs. His hands moved across her stomach. She turned her head slightly to brush her lips to his.

Turning again from him she brought her hands up to the top of her gown and unlaced the top. Pulling the edges open, she laid back on him and waited.

Rylic moved his hands from the water and pulled the top of her gown open to expose the fullness of her chest in the firelight. He traced the rim of her gown, caressing her skin.

"You're shaking. Do you want me to stop?" he asked.

"I'm enjoying your touch," she whispered.

Rylic's hands moved to cup the fullness of her. She gasped. He kissed her cheek.

She raised up slowly and turned around, propping herself up with her hands on the side of the tub.

Rylic sat up sliding his arms around her and pulling her close. He lowered himself back into the tub and pulled her down to him.

He kissed her gently as his hands moved to her hips.

"You stir fire within me," she whispered.

"I want you to feel everything," he whispered, kissing her with urgency.

She whispered as she kissed him. "This gown is in the way."

"Let's take care of that." He said, pushing the gown down her arms. "If you stand, I can pull the gown from you," he said softly.

Holding the side of the tub, she lifted herself up and stood before him in the light of the fire. He raised up and pulled the sides of the gown to help it slide down her body. She smiled down at him as she helped push the wet garment from her.

He held the side of the tub and raised himself up to stand before her. Neither spoke or moved for a moment. He reached out to take her hand and stepped out of the tub. She smiled and stepped out beside him. The firelight illuminated the room as they stood together motionless. He turned and took her hand to lead her to her room. She followed and still neither spoke.

As they stood by her bed she kissed him gently and sat down pulling him down with her. He moved to lay beside her.

"I want to make love to you," he whispered.

She kissed him and pulled him close, pressing herself to him.

"I can't imagine being anywhere else but in your arms," he said.

She wanted to get lost in him, but something inside stopped her. She stopped kissing him. "You're leaving. I can't do this."

"I will always come back to you," Rylic said, kissing her cheek.

"But how many women will you have until you are here with me? Forgive me. What you do is none of my business. My thoughts have gotten the best of me."

Rylic pulled her close and touched her face. "I know you have a

185

hard time trusting me. Know this if nothing else, my heart belongs to you, and perhaps someday you will see me as more than a pirate."

"My dear Rylic," she whispered, leaning her forehead to his, "I fear I'll never be enough to hold your heart."

He searched her eyes and saw the loneliness there. "I know you have doubt of tomorrow, the fear of love, the hate of the past. I wanted to wipe away all the scars of our yesterdays and start anew."

She looked at him as a tear escaped her eye.

"Alahandra," he said softly. Their eyes locked in a gaze as he pulled her quickly to him.

Her lips met his with a fierce passion as her arms encircled him. She moaned, rolling to her back and pulling him to her. She moved her body against his igniting passion within them both.

Rylic took a deep breath and looked at her. "I want all of you. I want to kiss all of you. I want to pleasure you in all the ways we can make love. I will wait until you are ready. Until we are ready. Your body is flawless and fair. One day. One day I hope to know the feel of your body wrapped around mine."

She kissed him and breathed slowly. "I want you now, and I don't want to think about tomorrow. Only you. Only now. Only us."

Her lips met his slowly. He lowered himself to her until the full length of his body pressed to hers. His hand moved down her side, squeezed her hip, and moved lower to her leg. He slid his hand slowly under her thigh for a moment and then pulled her leg up tight against his hip. Her breath quickened as she moved her other leg to the side, inviting him.

His lips hovered above hers, and he moved to gently kiss her chin, and then lower to her neck. He brushed his lips along her shoulder. She exhaled quietly.

"Your lips sent a pulse of desire through me," she whispered.

"Your body has me ravaged. I need all of you."

His lips met hers as he moved his body over her and moved slowly within her. She moaned and gasped as she moved with him. Her body answered his and he deepened his kiss as her lips parted. Her hands moved down his back and pulled him tight against her. Their bodies moved in rhythmic silence as hands explored and lips caressed.

He raised his face above hers. "Look into my eyes, Alahandra. I want to see you when pleasure overtakes us."

She arched her back as waves of pleasure pulsed through her. He continued to move until his body riveted with pleasure above her.

She started to release him, but he bent to kiss her with urgency and a passion she could not have fathomed.

Another wave of pleasure exploded through her.

He kissed her slowly as their breathing slowed.

"Perhaps you can make love to me through the night to stay the sun from breaking through the horizon," she whispered.

"We can try." he smiled, meeting her lips with a soft kiss. "Let's move to the fire."

They both stood, taking blankets with them to the floor in front of the fireplace. The soft light of the dying fire warmed them.

"You are incredibly beautiful, Alahandra," he whispered as they sat down together on the floor.

She smiled and kissed him deeply, pulling him to her and laying back on the blanket.

She gave her body to him as the fire warmed their skin, and he looked into her eyes as their bodies moved slowly together. Her hands moved to his hips to pull him tight against her as they were both consumed in pleasure.

He raised himself above her and smiled. "Let's go outside. I want to see your body bathed in the light of the full moon." he whispered.

They made their way to the backyard, and Alahandra spread her blanket on the ground. She sat down and he joined her quickly, wrapping his blanket around them both.

"You are enchanting under the stars." he said quietly, kissing her neck.

She leaned her head back, inviting. With one swift motion he pulled her to his lap. She smiled and kissed him with a slow wanting as her lips played along his.

Their bodies moved in rhythm until Alahandra could barely breathe. Waves of pleasure washed over her. Rylic smiled as he held her tight against him and continued to move with her. Another explosive wave moved through her as his body shook with hers. He lay his head against her chest and she wrapped her arms around him leaning her head to his, both enjoying the moment of quiet warmth between them.

He raised his head, smiled, and kissed her gently. "Let's go get inside."

They entered the house wrapped in blankets, and Alahandra whispered. "We should empty the tub."

"Let's get dressed, empty the tub, and have some fresh bread. I'm starving," he said, wrapping the blanket tight around him.

"We've worked up quite an appetite. I'm starving too," she said, blushing.

After working together for some time the water was out of the tub and it was taken back outside. Rylic sat at the table. Alahandra put bread on a plate and they ate quickly.

Rylic looked down at his hands. "I'll be gone for a long while this first run. I have to go to different ports and establish who I am with the different businesses. I think I'll bring back new gowns for you and Mum. Perhaps some fine dishes. Would you like those?"

"I'll like anything you bring us, but you don't have to do all of that. I'm happy with all that I have," Alahandra said.

"I want you to have the world," Rylic said, looking up at her.

"Then all I need is for you to return," Alahandra whispered, kissing him on the cheek.

"You are the only woman that has ever taken all my thoughts and scrambled them so that I forget what I was saying," Rylic laughed.

"We've had a full day. If you are leaving tomorrow, let's go rest. You can hold me all night long, and we won't think about anything else."

"In your arms is the best way to spend all of my time," he said.

They both got in bed, and Rylic placed his arms around her,

holding her close. She draped an arm over him, moving to fit her body next to his.

"You need a bigger bed," he laughed.

"Perhaps you need a bed of your own," she smiled, moving her hand across his stomach.

"I'll be cold in my bed on that ship soon enough," Rylic said. Neither spoke for a moment. He did not want to leave, but he knew she would never ask him to stay. He knew she would never make him choose between her and the sea. Would he stay? Could he make a life with her? Would she have him? Did she not know how much he cared for her? The fear of opening his heart to her kept him silent.

"Tell me about your father," she said.

"There's not that much to tell. He was a pirate through and through. He did love Mum though. She always loved the sea. She is good on a boat. He taught her well."

"Pirate? Haya said he went out on a merchant ship and didn't return," Alahandra said.

Rylic sighed. "She doesn't like to talk about the truth of him, and I know it's why her heart has broken so long over me. She has worried for too long." He paused and breathed in deeply. "I often wonder what life would have been like if my father was normal like Bradford. Bradford. What a character. I'm so happy for my mum."

"They really do love each other," Alahandra said.

Neither spoke for a while. They enjoyed the warmth of each other and the knowing that someone cared. He kissed her softly. She moved her hands along his face and his arms. His fingertips moved over her and graced her chest. She inhaled quickly..

"If you keep touching me like that, I'll have to strip you down and make love to you again," she smiled.

"You and your wild heart," he smiled. "Promise me you will never change."

She kissed him gently and smiled, taking his hand in hers.

"I enjoyed learning what my body can feel with you," she said.

"I want to always be the one to give you all your body needs," he smiled, taking her hand and brushing his lips over her fingers.

She sighed and smiled.

The sun broke through the window with the rooster announcing the day. Rylic sat up and looked at her.

"Well, I know Bradford will want to leave out soon." He leaned to her, kissing her with a desire that made him want to stay. "Would you like to ride into town and have breakfast with me? I want Haya and Joab to go too."

"Yes, of course. I'll go tell them before Haya starts cooking."

Alahandra dressed quickly and left the house. Rylic sat on the edge of the bed and looked around. Would he be happy in one place? He closed his eyes and thought of dancing with Alahandra while Bradford played the violin. He had never felt such happiness before. His heart had never felt so full. So in love. He stood up. Did he love her? Was this love? Could he win her heart and have her love him in return? Could she ever love someone like him?

Rylic dressed quickly and knew he had to leave. He would go and take the memory of her body against his.

Before long, the five set out on the wagon toward town.

Breakfast at Sero's was somber. Haya took Rylic's hand. "Why don't you put James in charge of your ships? He's a good man."

"He was a good pirate. I need to see if he'll be a fair business man. Then perhaps I can relinquish some of the responsibility to him. I have to make a strong start. I'll return and settle someday," he winked at Haya.

As they said their goodbyes Haya and Joab got into the wagon and Bradford went back to the restaurant. Alahandra stood with Rylic. They didn't say anything.

"Haya, I think I'll walk Rylic to the pier," Alahandra said.

"I'll see you back at home," Haya nodded.

Alahandra walked along with Rylic. He took her hand.

"I'll miss you beautiful woman," Rylic said.

"Then hurry back," Alahandra whispered.

"I will think about you in my arms until I return," he whispered.

190

He kissed her cheek, and turned to go.

Alahandra watched him walk onto the ship. He turned one last time to smile at her. All the men cheered to see him come aboard. He was loved by all, most of all her. Did she love him? She loved him! Should she run to him and just tell him? Would he care? Would he laugh? Would he leave and never return? Why would any man accept her love? Just another emotion she would push down below the hate and anger that kept her alive and moving forward.

CHAPTER
Fourteen

Alahandra walked slowly through the town looking at all the stores, and watching the people. She wanted to get to know them. She wanted to make this her home. She wanted people to see her in the street and say hello.

The small church where Haya was married also served as the town school. As she walked by she could hear the teacher ask a question about something and the students responded. How wonderful it would be to know the things in books. Perhaps the teacher could help her learn to read. Maybe she would allow her to help around the school to trade for that kind of help. She stopped and turned toward the school.

She walked slowly up the stairs and into the building trying not to make a lot of noise so as not to disturb the instruction. The teacher noticed her, and Alahandra smiled at her.

"May I help you?" the woman asked.

The class turned toward the back of the room to see who had entered. Alahandra recognized Alexander. He sat closer to the back with the older boys. She nodded to him and smiled. One of his friends nudged him and the others around him laughed. Alexander nodded back to her and turned a bright red.

Alahandra addressed the teacher, "I would like to talk to you for a moment if you have time. I just needed to ask you something."

"Class, I'll be just outside the door. Continue your reading aloud, and we'll answer questions when I return." She walked toward

Alahandra and motioned her out the door. "Now, what is it you wish to ask me, dear?"

Alahandra smiled at her, noticing her features for the first time. How her glasses propped on her nose and her hair was pulled tightly behind her head.

She cleared her throat. "I want to learn. I mean, I want to read. I, well you see…"

"Do you want me to teach you to read?" the teacher asked.

"I can read a lot of things, like things in the market, but I want to learn about things I've never known. I want to learn about other places, and how other people think," Alahandra said excitedly.

"Slow down dear. I usually don't tutor individual adults. I have adult classes once a week if you'd like to attend."

"Oh, no thank you. I don't want to be a part of any class like that. I'd rather sit in with the little ones who don't know to hate you," Alahandra said. "I'm sorry to waste your time." She turned to go.

"I'm Mrs. Martin, by the way. And you are?"

"My name is Alahandra."

"Alahandra, would you be able to come maybe twice a week around noon? I can teach you some things during my lunch break while the children eat their lunch and play."

"You can help me?" Alahandra asked.

"I can try," Mrs. Martin said.

"I also know a little boy that needs to start school here. I think he must have been in school before… I mean he's old enough to… I guess…"

"How about you have him come to school tomorrow, and we'll get him started. How does that sound?" Mrs. Martin smiled.

"He'll be delighted, I'm sure. He'll be working for the doc three times a week after school lets out, so how about I come in after school three times a week to clean? I can walk him home after that. I can clean the schoolhouse for you in return for helping me. I'll do whatever you need me to do to help out around here," Alahandra said.

"I would like that, Alahandra. I don't have many women around here that I talk to and you will be welcome company. You see, my husband died three years ago, and there isn't a lot for me to do here. Oh, I have my school and the children. I've sold my home and moved to a little place here in town. I just couldn't keep up with everything there and here, so my little house here is just perfect. Now, I've rattled on and on. How about you drop in tomorrow and we can begin. Then you can fill me in on you."

"I look forward to seeing you tomorrow, Mrs. Martin. And, I'm glad to have you as a new friend," Alahandra said.

Mrs. Martin took her hands. "My new friend. Yes, I like that. See you tomorrow, Alahandra. And thank you."

"For what?"

"For coming in here today," Mrs. Martin smiled and turned to go back into class.

"Okay, class. Let's see, how would you like an extra long lunch and playtime tomorrow?" The class cheered. "I'll be meeting with Miss Alahandra." Mrs. Martin turned and smiled at her.

Alahandra nodded to her and turned to go as she walked down the stairs smiling. Just like that she met someone new and made a friend. She couldn't wait to come back and learn something. Anything. Most of all she wanted to know the story of Mrs. Martin. Perhaps she should bring her something. Something for her class perhaps.

She walked to the mercantile and went inside. Dedria and Morris were talking behind the counter.

"Hello, Alahandra," Dedria said. "How are those chickens working out for you?"

"You remembered my name?" Alahandra.

"Of course," Dedria said. "I just love new people in town. Forgive me for not coming out for a visit to see if you needed anything. We are doing inventory this whole month, and I work all day then take care of things in our home at night. It's all I can do..."

"To keep your head on straight. Yes, we know," Morris said.

Dedria bumped him on the arm. "You just keep your words, Mister."

Morris turned to Alandra. "Did the furniture all work out for your two houses? If there's anything you aren't pleased with, we can send it back."

"Oh, no sir, everything is wonderful," Alahandra said. She turned to Dedria. "Can I have your help with something? It's personal."

Morris smiled. "I'll be in the kitchen where the pie is cooling." He laughed and walked out the side door.

"That man," Dedria laughed. "Now, what is it that you need, dear?"

"I wanted to buy a gift for a friend," Alahandra said.

"That man friend of yours that you were in the store with? My, he was handsome."

Alahandra laughed. "No. I mean yes, he's handsome, but no, not a gift for him. This is for a friend of mine. Mrs. Martin. She is doing a favor for me, and I wanted to show my gratitude."

"Did you have anything in mind?"

"Can I tell you a secret?" Alahandra said.

"Of course you can," Dedria said.

"I've never really bought a gift for a friend before. I've bought lunch for someone, but never a gift."

Dedria took hold of her arm. "My dear, I won't ask about your past but know if you ever need a friend to talk to, I'm here, and you are welcome anytime. I'm always looking for a reason to have tea and cake in the back," she laughed. "Now, let's think together. Mrs. Martin is a teacher. So do you want something for her desk or something for her home?"

"I'm not sure. I don't even really know her yet. What do women like?" Alahandra asked, looking at the things on the table in front of her.

"You're a woman. What do you like?" Dedria asked.

Alahandra laughed. "I'm not like other women. I don't like a lot of things other women like or like to do. I like swimming in the sea, hunting with a bow, watching the sun rise in the arms of a beautiful man," Alahandra coughed and turned to go. "I'm sorry. I don't belong here."

"Dear, wait," Dedria walked close to her. "I don't judge people for who they are or what they've done. I don't look at you and see someone who doesn't belong. I look at you and think perhaps we could become friends."

"I would like that, Dedria. I don't make friends easily, but I like that you do," Alahandra laughed.

She bumped a table, and a teacup turned over.

"How about a teacup?" Alahandra asked. "You said you like tea. Do you think she would like it?"

"Oh, it's a perfect gift for her. I know she likes tea because she buys it from me! She will adore this!"

Alahandra sighed in relief.

"Do you want me to put this on your credit?"

"No, I'll pay now. If my father taught me anything, it's pay as you go. I don't like to owe anyone anything."

"That's smart business," Dedria said. She took Alahandra's money and gave her the change. "Would you like me to wrap it?"

"Oh, yes! I would love that!" Alahandra said. "Can I watch you? I've never wrapped a present."

"Would you like for me to teach you?" Dedria said.

"Oh my, yes, I would," Alahandra said.

"Come behind here with me so you can have all the supplies on hand. Take the paper and pull it out gently."

Alahandra did as she was told, and little by little she followed the instructions until the gift was wrapped.

"See, you can do anything," Dedria said. "And now let's have tea and whatever pie is left. Morris can watch the front."

"I would like that," Alahandra said.

"Well, you might have to tell me more about that beautiful man," Dedria winked.

Alahandra laughed and followed her new friend into her tea room. Alahandra wasn't expecting the room they entered. The floor was covered with a beautiful rug, Delicate lamps adorned each small table.

A beautiful round table sat in the middle of the room with a glass vase filled with flowers in the center. Lace covered the top of the table. Two place settings were prepared and on each plate was a piece of pie. Morris came from the kitchen.

"Your tea, my ladies. Please be seated," Morris said.

"How did you know I would invite Alahandra for pie?" Dedira asked, kissing his cheek.

"How did I know? My dear, I know you better than I know myself."

"And I'm still the luckiest woman alive," Dedria said.

"Let's count the dead ones too, and say of all time," Morris said laughing and kissing his wife's hand.

"Go mind the store, and I'll keep this seat warm a while," Dedria laughed.

"Take your time. Enjoy yourselves ladies. My customers await!" Morris leaped away and ran out the door.

"I do love that man," Dedria laughed. "He is usually all business around customers. But there's something about you that just brings joy out. You are full of secrets, I think, Alahandra. I do love secrets," she laughed.

"Some secrets are too hard to share," Alahandra said, picking up her tea.

"Some secrets are the keys to our hearts and some secrets are meant to be forgotten so you can simply live and love," Dedria said.

"You talk as if you have a secret," Alahandra said.

"Oh, I have many. One of which I will share now, and one I will share the next time you come have tea," Dedria took a deep breath. "I was not exactly the kind of woman who sat in church on Sundays before I met Morris."

Alahandra raised her eyebrow. "Do tell."

Dedria laughed and leaned forward. "I was a lady of the night. Do you know what that means?"

Alahandra thought about the women she saw through the tavern window hanging on the men with little clothing to cover them. "I think

197

I know."

"I sold my time, and I sold my body to men," Dedria paused as if the words were stuck in her mouth. "And, I did this for years. I was alone, and had to make my own way. I cried every time."

Alahandra reached out and put her hand on Dedria's arm. "I'm sorry. I know what it's like to do things you don't want to do for money."

"One night," Dedria smiled, "Morris was walking down the street and bumped into me. He smiled and I saw forever in those eyes. I said, 'Excuse me.' He looked around and asked how much I charged to spend time with him. He wasn't like other men; I could see that. I lowered my price because something was different about him and I wanted to know what. He took my hand and said he would pay for the whole night with me. All he did was walk around the street and hold my hand. We walked out to a pond and sat on the banks talking about what we wanted in life. When that sun rose, my heart sank. My time was up. He stood up, took my hand, and told me his wagon was sitting just on the edge of town if I would like a ride to Trobornia. He said he just opened a little store there and could use some help. No one knew me here, so I said sure. I sold what little I had to buy a dress proper to wear while working in a store. Modest and boring, but necessary. We pulled up to the store that day and he said, 'I don't have anywhere for you to sleep.' I didn't know what to do then, let me tell you. I was scared to death. He took my hands again and told me if we were married I could just be his wife and I would have a place to call my own.

"Let me say, I was overwhelmed by him. I stepped close to him, kissed him and said yes. We were married that day, and have been completely happy ever since."

Alahandra was smiling. "That was beautiful, Dedria. I do love seeing people in love."

"Well, what of this man you speak of? Beautiful was he?" Dedria laughed.

"More than that. He's stunning and amazing. He makes me feel like I can do anything, and he makes me feel beautiful. I've never known a man like that," Alahanadra said.

"Oh, a man that can make you believe in yourself is a rare find indeed. Most men are quite stupid and love the drink more than the woman they're with. Mind you a drunk man is a poor man," she winked at Alahandra. They both laughed.

"Is there room for him in your future?" Dedria asked.

"Perhaps not room for me in his," Alahandra said, sipping her tea.

"He can widen the dream of what he wants to include you, or you can find someone who will. No need to be second to anything in a man's life. No need to feel like you don't measure up or aren't good enough. I know that feeling and it's lonely. Leave it behind you, and move on."

"I don't know how to not feel lonely," Alahandra said.

"You don't have to feel lonely anymore. You have a home here and now you have friends," Dedria said.

"What kind of place is beyond the hills that I've heard mention?" she asked Dedria.

Dedria smiled and put her cup down. "Oh, the usual tales of fairies and elves, but in truth there are a few towns that have developed over that road. Hill country is different from a coastal town. Places are harder to get to, but I hear it's beautiful. There is a vast kingdom farther beyond the hill country with a new king that adores women. He's a sight to see. Beautiful, but arrogant."

"He sure knows a woman's body." Alahandra sighed and smiled.

"It would seem you know said King?" Dedria raised her eyebrow.

"A bit of history there, but no fear of repeating. He just needs someone to entertain him."

"And you have a beautiful man to love."

"I'm just going to sip my tea." Alahandra laughed.

Dedria laughed loudly. "I would like to travel inland in the summer to visit new places and see what the towns are like. Morris said we could go this year."

"Oh, that's thrilling!" Alahandra said. "I think I would like to go

199

on an adventure through the hills one day. Just take off and see what I could see."

"Would you invite your beautiful man?" Dedria said.

"Perhaps. Nothing like a warm bed at night," Alahandra winked.

Dedria laughed again. "You sure don't talk like the other women here either. It's nice to laugh with someone not so formal."

"Can I ask you something personal?" Alahandra whispered.

"You can ask me anything dear."

"Is it wrong to ask a man if… if he… if we could…" Alahandra stammered.

"I think if you asked that of a man that he would be so overwhelmed with excitement that he might just fall right out of bed!" The two laughed loudly again.

"Most men do want to be married before they enjoy your bed, though Alahandra. It's just the way of most. However, there are those that just live so passionately that being with a woman is natural and beautiful for them. That's a decision you two would have to make."

"We've already… I just…" Alahandra looked down at her plate.

"Oh, I think I understand," Dedria said quietly. "For the next time you see him."

Alahandra nodded and smiled. "Perhaps I'll know what to say, or how to ask if the time presents itself, or perhaps I'll pack my bags and hike those hills. Freedom is a precious gift."

Dedria took her hand. "You are so right, dear friend."

They finished their tea and made their way back to the front of the store.

Morris put his hands on his hips. "Well, something was sure funny in that room," he said, kissing Dedria on the cheek.

"The most fun I've had in a long while," Dedria said. "Alahandra, you are welcome to visit me anytime."

"I will come back soon. I've enjoyed today more than you can ever know," Alahandra smiled and walked out of the store.

"Seems like a good fit for you. Instant friends," Morris said.

"Yes, my love. She is quite something, and I think we'll be great friends."

Alahandra walked back to the homestead smiling and humming. She felt different. More at peace. More like the person she wanted to be and less like the thief she had been.

Haya saw her coming around the bend of the road. Alahandra twirled as she sang, not knowing she was being watched. Haya hoped her happiness had to do with Rylic, but she doubted he was seeing what was happening before him. Alahandra was changing, and if he didn't act quickly, that girl would be gone.

CHAPTER
Fifteen

Alahandra worked the homestead sewing curtains for her windows and making pillows for their beds. With the cloth from Rylic she made a couple of new dresses for herself and a few things for Joab. She and Joab cleaned the barn and worked the small field to prepare it for a garden.

Days were long but wonderfully spent. She went to the school twice a week during lunch and worked with Mrs. Martin. She was learning to read more and more, and enjoying all the things Mrs. Martin told her. The day Alahandra finished her first reader, Mrs. Martin hugged her.

"How about we celebrate tonight, and I'll make us a fine dinner?"

Alahandra nodded trying to control the tears that wanted to overflow. "I would love that!"

"Then drop by around five, or you can come a little earlier if you'd like. We can talk while I cook."

"I'll see you later this afternoon then," Alahandra said, getting up, "and, thank you for all you've done for me."

"It's been exciting to watch you learn, and I look forward to many more days teaching you."

Alahandra hurried home and rushed through all of her afternoon chores. She smiled as her puppies bounced around her because she was walking so fast. She stopped and looked out over her property, wiping the sweat from her brow.

She looked up. "God, I don't know if you can hear me, but thank you for my home."

Simply saying those words made her stomach knot. Her home. In all her life she could have never imagined having a real home. She wiped the tear from the corner of her eye and went inside to wash up for dinner with Mrs. Martin.

Haya told her to drive the wagon into town since it would be darker coming back. The full moon would guide her if she stayed too long.

Pulling up to Mrs. Martin's, she hopped out of the wagon and smoothed her dress. When Mrs. Martin opened the door, Alahandra stopped smiling.

"Dear, are you okay?" Mrs. Martin took her by the arm and led her inside. "Here, sit at the table."

"Oh, I'm okay. I just realized this is the first time anyone has ever invited me to have dinner. I guess my nerves just got the best of me."

Mrs. Martin gave her a cup of water. "If you want to talk about anything, I'm a good listener."

"I've never had nice things, or a home until now. I'm new to all of this."

"Well, do you know how to make a pie crust?" Mrs. Martin smiled.

"Not yet." Alahandra felt more at ease knowing she was accepted at Mrs. Martin's table.

"Then it's time you learn. Let's work on this pie together. I should have made it already, but it's going to be cooling while we eat, and there's nothing like a warm pie."

The two cooked together until dinner was ready and the pie was cooling. Alahandra laughed and told Mrs. Martin about swimming in her lagoon, coming to Trobornia once before for the festival where she danced in the street, and how she longed to sail to far off places.

Mrs. Martin took their empty plates to the sink. "Do you know what I miss? Holding someone's hand. Just the simple touch of a man that loves you."

"Do you think you'll ever marry again?"

"Most men want a woman who will either stay at home or work alongside him on a farm. I'm not interested in either of those."

"I know someone who would love to hold your hand." Alahandra smiled and sipped her coffee.

Mrs. Martin laughed, "Oh, do you?"

"Mr. Troy, Alexander's father. He wants a wife."

"He is a very nice looking man. Why don't you pursue him?" Mrs. Martin said, smiling.

"I'm completely happy with my pirate."

Mrs. Martin raised an eyebrow. "Pirate?"

"It's a long story for another time. But let's talk about you and Mr. Troy."

"I don't think he would be the kind to like me working, and I'll not give up teaching for any man."

"Well, don't disregard him yet." Alahandra smiled. "You never know."

"You never know," Mrs. Martin laughed.

Life developed into a happy routing for Alahandra as she continued to learn. Joab worked three days a week for the doctor, and on those days Alahandra cleaned the school and then would stop by the mercantile and visit with Dedria while she waited on Joab.

She shared stories with Dedria of hiking through the woods to hunt for her food and swimming in the ocean while the waves graced the shore. Of bathing in creeks and learning to sew. How her first kiss was not so long ago, and all she could think about was kissing her beautiful man once again.

One afternoon Dedria sat out on the front steps with Alahandra. Dedria smiled. "You know, I owe you one more secret."

"That's right, you do."

"It's how I came to be alone and do what I did to survive."

Alahandra nodded. Dedria continued.

"I was a lot like you. My father died when my mom was still pregnant with me. I watched her struggle through life having to take care of me. She sold herself. It's how I knew that I could do that too. Then she became pregnant with my brother. I had to work in the market long hours to help buy food. When he was born, he was sick all of the time. We couldn't afford a doctor, and we had no help. He died while my mother rocked him to sleep. I could see that he was not breathing, but she kept singing over him and rocking him. I was so scared of her that night. She wouldn't listen to me, like I wasn't even there. I stayed with her and tried my best to stay in school while I worked in the market. She was always with one man after another trying to keep food on the table."

"I came home late one night from the market and she was sitting in her rocking chair in her robe. I knew some man must have just left her. Her eyes were closed, so I got ready for bed quietly and fell asleep. It wasn't until the next morning when I woke up and realized she hadn't moved that I knew she had died. The doctor said her heart just gave out. I knew it was because it was broken so many times over and over and over. She finally just gave up. I was put into a home for girls and ran away. I worked in the markets and would sleep anywhere I could.

"When I got old enough that I knew men were looking at me as a woman and not a child, I began selling myself like my mom. Until one night. One man was just terrible. He was trying to kill me and laughing about it. I took a gun from my bag and shot him right on the side of the head. I put the gun in his hand like he had done it to himself and left town. Killing that man left me with such a horrible feeling inside. It was as if being a real person just stopped. My heart felt hollow from selling myself, and it was like that was the end of who I was. The next place I stopped was where I stayed until I met my sweet husband. That night we met and all he wanted to do was talk to me seemed to breathe life back into me. Life has a funny way of working itself out." Dedria sipped her tea and looked out over the street.

"Thank you for trusting me with your secret," Alahandra said quietly.

Dedria nodded. "I knew you wouldn't judge me, and I feel like if you know more of the real me, then my heart can release some of that burden and perhaps heal a little more."

"The man that my father and I stayed with offered me a chance to sell myself to men that would make port. He said I would make a lot of money, and after we talked I considered trying that for myself except I wasn't sure how to do anything." Alahandra laughed.

"Well, maybe your beautiful man can teach you a thing or two."

"I've learned quite a lot from him already." Alahandra winked at Dedria.

Dedria laughed and held up her teacup. "Here's to extra study!"

Alahandra clinked her teacup to Dedria's and they both laughed loudly.

Morris came out of the front of the mercantile. "Laughter is always loud with you two." He smiled at his wife.

"The sign of true friendship." Dedria hugged Alahandra's shoulders.

"Or the topic being some poor bloke that's not here to defend himself." Morris winked and nudged Alahandra with the broom and then turned to go back inside laughing.

Loneliness began to fade for Alahandra. She was learning to cook better on her stove. She stopped by Sero's one day and asked if she could watch them cook so she could learn more. She enjoyed spending time with people and learning their stories. Bradford taught her many things about cooking and gardening as the days passed, but her thoughts were always filled with Rylic. She wanted to make a life here all her own, but he was always going to come back. He was always going to leave. The friendships that were taking root in her heart made her feel this could be her home, but the thoughts of Rylic pushed her to think perhaps there was an adventure for her over the hill.

With all the good in her life she constantly wondered if Rylic even thought of her while on that open sea.

As the days moved on a stranger wandered into Sero's restaurant.

"My good man, may I ask of you, have you met anyone here by the name of Alahandra?"

"No, sir. That's a quite unusual name, and I would have remembered that name," Sero said.

Bradford continued to cook and didn't hear the exchange.

"I'll keep looking and asking around. Thank you for your help," the man said and walked out the door.

Bradford came out of the kitchen drying his hands "Who was that?"

Sero looked out the window at the stranger talking to people on the street with his back to the restaurant. He knew he had to act fast. "Bradford, take my wagon from the back and go warn Alahandra that someone is looking for her."

Bradford nodded and ran out the back. He hurried home and found Alahandra hanging clothes on the line to dry. The happiness in her face would fade quickly with his news.

"Alahandra, come here, child," Bradford yelled.

Alahandra dropped the basket and ran to him. Haya came out of the house.

"What is it, Bradford?" Alahandra asked.

"There's a strange man in town asking about you. He came into Sero's, but I was in the back room and didn't see him. We watched him walk down the street and he stopped everyone to ask about you. It won't be long before someone points him this way."

"Then take me back to town. I can lie in the wagon and find out who this is being so inquisitive about me."

Once Bradford had parked the wagon behind the restaurant once more, Alahandra raised up slowly.

"You go back inside, and I'll take care of this," she said.

"I'll stay and protect you," Bradford said.

"Dear Bradford, I don't need protecting. I've been a shadow in the markets for years. I know how to go unseen," she affirmed. "I'll let you know back at home."

He nodded and she was on her way, moving along the sides of buildings and trying to catch a glimpse of this stranger.

She made her passage safely by the land office, the school and was nearing the mercantile when she saw Sero's stranger. Straightening her dress and hair she stepped out of the shadow of the building and spoke loudly.

"I don't believe my eyes. Prince Niklas."

He turned and smiled at her. She had seen him smile that way at her before down by the creek. She shook the thought from her head.

He ran to her. "My dearest Alahandra. I have looked everywhere for you. It is good to see your face." He stepped closer. "Your beautiful face."

She didn't move. He stepped close. "I have thought of little else except our time together."

"You and Algoron," she said.

"What?" he asked.

"Algoron was here not long ago. He propositioned me. He wanted me to be his queen, and he sought me out to have me. He did what he could to try to convince me, but I could not follow through. He is not for me. Not his kind. He was enjoyable with you that day at the creek and nothing more. I was shocked to see him and for him to come such a long way to have his way with me," she said.

"I will kill him. I should have never allowed him to be so forward with you," Niklas said, seething. "His kingdom is beyond the hill country, and he would do anything if he thought he could have a woman."

"He is nothing. Do not confront him. I do not carry him in my thoughts," she said. "Why were you looking for me?" Alahandra said.

"The King and Queen have declared that I marry, so they arranged a marriage to a princess from a neighboring kingdom. I have told you that before, I know. We are to wed, and my family is pushing that it be soon," he sighed.

"I'm so sorry, Niklas," she said.

"I told them I didn't want to marry for convenience's sake, that I wanted it to be for love. My father sat back on his throne and asked, 'Who would you love, my son?'

"I stepped forward with thunder in my words and told him that it was the thief that stole me away in the night would forever have my heart, and I would search until I found you again."

"He and my mother sat in silence and then he took her hand. He looked at me and said, 'Find her, but if you don't return with her then you will wed within the week.'

"My heart raced with the anticipation of seeing you again. I have taken every ship I could find to every port looking for you."

"We could never work, Niklas. We discussed this, and you know your family would always see me as a thief."

"I talked to my father in length about your situation. You are no longer wanted in connection with my kidnapping, and all of your connection with Jazier has been pardoned. Speaking of Jazier. You won't ever have to think of him again. He's been sent to a prison far away and his crimes will keep him there for life."

"Niklas, was my father punished with him?" Alahandra asked, afraid to know the answer.

Someone cleared his throat behind her. She turned around to see her father.

"I can't believe it." Alahandra began to cry as she ran to him and threw her arms around him. "What happened that you are here?" she asked.

"When Jazier was taken from the forest, I went to the Prince and told him you never had a choice in your part of Jazier's plan, and I did what I did to keep a roof over your head. I begged for your pardon. He gave me one also. Prince Niklas also offered me a job as a groundskeeper for the castle grounds. I get to stay in a workhouse with some of the other caretakers."

She turned to Niklas. "You saved him. I will forever be grateful to you."

"Come back with me, Alahandra," Niklas said.

"Niklas, I can't."

"You could. You could be with me, be my wife. I want to give you everything your heart desires."

Mikal took her hand. "My child, come back with us. You deserve so much more than the life you've had to live."

"I have a good life here," Alahandra said.

Mikal looked to the ground. "I'm going to allow you two some privacy. My dear, I love you, and I wish you would come with us."

"Father," she hugged him, "I want you to have a good life. This is your time. Make a life for yourself and come visit me when you can. You are always welcome in my home."

Mikal hugged her tight and turned to Niklas. "I'll be waiting at the pier."

Niklas nodded.

When they were alone he took her hand and stepped near the side of the mercantile so they would have more privacy.

"Alahandra, marry me. You will one day reign with me and be queen of all the lands."

"I simply can't. I know your family will only see me as the thief that stole your heart and ruined their plans," she said. "I don't think I could ever feel at home in the palace. I can never repay you for all you've done for my father, but even being around him would be more than I could bear. I love him, but I don't think I could ever trust him again.

"Niklas, I'm happy here, for the first time in my life. I don't have to worry about others. My entire life has been focused on taking care of Mikal and making sure we had food on the table. I don't have to answer to anyone or be on anyone's schedule."

"I'm not just saying come be my queen and rule, Alahandra," he stepped closer. "Being with you, and being free was the happiest I've ever been. I'm in love with you." He stepped closer and took both of her hands. "I want the opportunity to love you forever and do all that I can to make you happy. I made you something," he reached inside the pouch around his shoulder. "I found the wood on our beach."

"Our beach. That was a wonderful day with you," She turned the piece of wood over and saw what he had done. On the side was a heart carved into the wood with her name engraved. She looked up at him.

"You did this?" she asked.

"I go to that beach and stand in the water thinking of you. This wood washed up at my feet and I knew I wanted to make something for you."

"The carving is intricate and the lettering is beautiful. This is amazing."

"You make me feel like I can do anything. My heart felt something for the first time when I was with you. I want you with me, always."

Alahandra looked up at him. "You are an amazingly wonderful man. The palace life just isn't for me."

"Then I shall denounce the crown. If that's what it takes to have you love me. I will stay here with you."

Alahandra put her hand on his cheek. He pressed his hand to the back of hers and sighed. "I have missed your touch."

Alahandra closed her eyes and enjoyed his closeness. Here he was, standing in front of her wanting to love her forever.

He stepped closer and slid his arms around her, pulling her close. She stepped into his embrace, enjoying the feel of his arms.

"May I kiss you?" Niklas whispered.

She looked up at him and smiled softly. He lowered his face to hers and their lips met gently. She moved her arms around him and pulled herself close to him. He moved his lips over hers, and she felt a deep passion rise in her. The knowing someone could love her made her feel free in his arms. She didn't want to think about anything but being in the moment with Niklas.

He leaned his head back slightly from her. "I promise I would fill our lives with passion and love if you would but honor me with the gift of your love."

Alahandra sighed. "My beautiful prince. You cannot denounce your crown. You were meant to rule."

"Rule by my side. You would bring such life to the crown."

"Dear man, what have I done to deserve your love?" She kissed him once more. "But loving you would mean becoming something that I'm not."

He leaned his forehead to hers. "How can I go on without you with me?" he whispered.

"You tell your family you will not marry someone you do not love. Find someone that you want in your life. Someone you can love forever, and that will love a life with you."

"If you thought you would change your mind, I would wait on you forever," Niklas said quietly.

"You will forever be in my heart, sweet man. Knowing someone could love me is the most amazing gift I have ever received."

"One last kiss from you, beautiful woman, and I shall go," he said.

She kissed him with great passion, as he held her tight. A tear escaped her eye as he held her. He leaned back and looked at her. Gently he wiped her tear away.

"Why do you cry?" he asked.

"I've just never had to say goodbye to anyone that I care about," she said.

He kissed her forehead. "You never have to say goodbye to me. My heart will always be open for you."

He stepped back from her and let her go. "I'll always love you, and I can never repay the love of life you have given me."

She nodded, unable to speak. He turned to walk away from her, and she knew she would never see him again.

She wondered if she should run after him and be his queen. He loved her, and it was more than she could ever hope for with Rylic. A wonderful man loved her, but her heart belonged to a man that would never tell her. She crumpled to the ground by the mercantile and began to cry. How could her life be so messed up? Why couldn't she just go with Niklas? She turned the wood over in her hands and touched her name. He cared for her so. She hung her head and cried quietly.

Across the street in the shadow of the restaurant, Rylic had watched her in the arms of the Prince, and he watched her crying over him. He couldn't stand seeing her suffer even if her tears were for another. As he started toward her, he stopped abruptly. He knew what he had to do. It was time for him to leave Trobornia.

Rylic arrived at the homestead and walked into Haya's house. She wasn't in there so he went back outside. "Haya! Are you here?" he called.

She came from behind the house with a basket of eggs. "Son of mine! You have been gone a long time."

"I've come to say goodbye. I'm going to sail full time with my merchant ships. I'll come around and say hello every now and then like I used to do."

Haya's smile faded. "I thought you were happy here."

"I thought I could be, but it's time for me to go," Rylic said.

Alahandra walked up to the house wiping her eyes. She heard Rylic's voice beyond the house and stopped to listen.

"I wanted to make this my home, but things have changed. This isn't the life for me. There's nothing left for me here," Rylic said.

"How can you say that?" Haya said.

"I've come to say goodbye," Rylic said

Alahandra walked to the back of the house. "So this is goodbye? Where are you going?"

Rylic turned abruptly. "I'm sailing full time with the merchant ships."

Alahandra didn't respond.

Haya watched the two. "Well, you can't leave until we have a proper meal together. I need you two to go into town, fetch Bradford, and pick up some bread from the market. We'll have a grand feast. Go get your things and stay the night. Have your crew enjoy Trobornia for the evening."

"It's best if I stay on the ship."

"It's best if you do as your old mum says. Now go on you two. I'll

213

start cooking and we'll eat when you return. Well, go."

Alahandra turned to start walking and Rylic began walking to catch up.

"You said you were going to be gone a long time. Where will you be sailing?"

"Away," Rylic said. "I'll find new ports along the way."

"I must have just missed you in town," Alahandra said.

"I didn't miss a thing," Rylic said, walking faster.

Alahandra stopped and she took hold of his arm. "You saw me."

"With the Prince," Rylic added.

"He came to see me and brought my father," Alahandra said dryly. "Why is it that you are not coming back? You know your mother will miss you?"

"Like you would miss your life with the Prince?" Rylic said sternly.

"You have no idea what I feel or what I'm thinking," Alahandra said.

"You're right, I don't. That's why I'm leaving. You deserve a life with Prince Niklas."

"Did you ever think I have dreams of my own? Deserve? You don't know what I deserve. I don't deserve anything I have, but I am thankful for every happy moment I have had. I love my home, but it still feels like a dream. I love being a part of Haya's family, but it's not my family. It's yours."

"Why didn't you go with him? I saw you crying in the street. Weeping over him," Rylic said.

"You could never imagine the pain I felt in that moment. My father is finally free. He has a job, a place to live, and he's happy. Yet, I didn't want to be with him. It's something I've wanted for him my entire life, and he's lost to me forever because in my heart I don't think I can ever trust him.

"And, someone actually loves me. Someone actually said he loves me. Me. Someone loves me, and I don't want a life with him because I would never be seen as his equal. His family will never see me as good

214

enough.

"Do you want to know the real reason for my tears? The one thing that broke my heart? No matter how much I love you, you will never love me. You can never love me. You will never settle here. Don't you understand? My entire life has been about never being good enough, never having enough, and never feeling like I could be enough for any man to love.

"You know, you're right, you should go away. That's what you're good for. Leaving." She turned to walk back to the homestead.

He didn't say anything as he watched her walking away from him.

Walking slowly to the market he thought about all the things she had said to him. He bought all Haya had asked for, and went to retrieve Bradford.

"If you can wait for just a moment, I can leave with you and I'll drive us home. I need a few things from the mercantile before we go." Bradford said.

"I'll wait for you. I'll be outside. Haya wants this to be a grand feast since I've decided to leave." Rylic said, walking out of Sero's and breathing in deeply. Alahandra's words had pierced his heart.

She loved him, and she had no idea how he felt about her. He never had the courage to tell her.

On the ride home, Bradford spoke quietly. "It's not my place to say so, but you have a lot to stay for around here. It would be a shame to leave so much behind."

Rylic nodded and remained silent. He knew after the speech she gave him he should leave her to find real love, and not settle with love from him. Did he know how to love? His way of life was bigger than him. He had a crew that depended on him for their livelihood. How could he possibly leave with his fleet of merchant ships taking to the water? His crew. His ships.

He thought about all the wealth he had obtained on his last raid. Even Haya had no idea how much he still had on board the Silver Phoenix. But with all he had, he knew it would mean nothing if he lost Alahandra.

"Bradford, stop the wagon." Rylic said. He turned to him. "I have an idea. I know Haya is expecting us. You go ahead. I need to go to the pier. Tell Haya I'll be there shortly."

Bradford nodded. "See you there."

Rylic jumped from the wagon and made his way quickly to the pier. He stood there looking at the Silver Phoenix, and knew what he must do.

CHAPTER

As Rylic boarded his ship, James came to stand beside him. "You have done a good thing making these fine vessels into merchant ships. We've picked up quite a few new ports. We'll all be taken care of nicely for years to come."

Rylic took a deep breath. Alahandra was worth giving all of this up, but her anger ran deep. Could she truly learn to love him with his past? Could she really see him as more than a pirate? It was a chance he was willing to take.

"James, I have a proposition for you. You've been my second in command for a long time, and I know you can handle anything. I want you to captain the ships and oversee all our business. I will keep our ships supplied and take care of all the needs of our crew, and you give me a cut of the profits when you port in Trobornia."

"So you want to make an honest man out of me after all," James laughed.

"Somebody had to try," Rylic said, extending his hand.

James gripped his hand and they shook on their agreement.

"Now, can you get some of your crew to help me unload my belongings? I'm going to go buy a wagon to haul it in."

Chest after chest was brought off the ships and placed on the pier. Rylic pulled up with a wagon, and James laughed.

"That was quick."

"It is amazing what a few gold pieces will do for a man riding

217

down the road. He was quite eager to hand over his team and wagon." Rylic laughed. "Now let's get this all loaded."

Rylice went into a closet in his quarters and asked James to help him because the trunk was so heavy.

"Do you think I could be see what's inside such a heavy chest?" James asked as they loaded it onto the wagon.

Rylic opened the chest and they both stood there speechless.

Rylic spoke low. "I actually had to dig this one up on an island. The pirate who put it there would come back someday for it, and I wish I could see his face."

"How did you learn of such a treasure?" James asked.

Rylic laughed, "A fairy told me."

James nodded, "Aye, she did well."

Rylic took a handful of gold pieces from the chest and held them out to James. James nodded and took the bounty.

"Thank you, my friend," James said.

"Take care of my ships and my crew. When you need more, come see me. I'm going home."

"It is time," James waved to him and boarded the ship.

Rylic sat in the wagon alone with all his belongings. His wagon. His belongings. All he had to his name. And all he wanted lay before him.

What would Alahandra say? Would she still have him? He rode slowly wondering if he was making the right decision.

"Now there's a man lost in thought. Going so slow that he's almost going backwards," Dedria said to Morris and Rylic passed in front of the mercantile.

"Hello!" Rylic yelled.

"Hello!" Morris waved. "How are you?"

"I'm finally going home. Wish me luck!" Rylic smiled.

"She'll be happy to have you there," Dedria said, smiling back at him.

Rylic and Morris looked at her with eyebrows raised.

Dedria waved him on and hugged her husband.

Rylic rode on thinking about what he would say to Alahandra. When he arrived at Haya's, he jumped from the wagon and ran inside. Haya was sitting by the fire. Bradford was still at the table.

"Do you think you could possibly spare enough food to take in a weary sea dog?" Rylic laughed.

"There's always enough for you, my dear," Haya said. "Get a plate. All the dinner is on the table."

"Any room here for a weary sea dog in need of a place to live?" he said walking over to her.

"What are you saying?" Haya asked.

"I'm saying. I'm here," he laughed. "I'm here to stay."

Haya stood up and hugged him. "Oh son, you made me the happiest mum in the world," she patted him on the back and sighed.

"You don't sound like the happiest. What's wrong?" Rylic asked.

"It's Alahandra, Rylic. She's gone. She left."

"What do you mean, she left?" Rylic asked.

"She said she couldn't live here anymore. She was crying so much when she came in to help with dinner. We sat down and she told me everything. The Prince, her dad. Your argument. My heart broke for that sweet child, and I begged her to stay. I told her she is my family. She just stood there with tears streaming down her cheeks. She said she would come get her things when she found a place to stay. She just didn't want to be here anymore because seeing you would be too painful. Her freedom was the one thing she had, and she had to go. She said she would see me soon and left. I begged her to wait until morning. She said the night would be easier to travel and the moon was full. She mumbled something about a prince that would take her in. The morning would find her in a new place. She took as much gold as she could carry with her clothes and food in her bag."

Rylic hugged her. "I'll find her. Bradford I need a horse. Can you help me?"

"I'll get one quickly." Bradford said.

"Mum, can you get Joab to start unloading the wagon? The little containers he can handle."

Bradford returned. "The horse is ready."

Rylic walked out quickly and looked back at them. "I'll find her."

He set out on the road that traveled inland to the other villages. He hoped she had not gone too far. The dark had settled in and it became harder to see so he was moving slower than he had hoped. As he moved over a hill he noticed a dark figure ahead of him. He rode harder to catch up. It had to be her.

She moved over to the edge of the road when she heard the sound of hooves coming up fast behind her.

"You've covered a lot of ground in a short time," Rylic said.

Alahandra stopped and put down the heavy bag. "Why are you here?"

"To bring you home," he said.

"I don't have a home," she said, picking her bag up and turning to go.

"You do."

"No, Rylic, I don't. I want my own life away from the memories of you. Prince Algoron has offered me a place to stay if I ever needed it. I'm going to find a new place to live. A place where I belong." She continued to walk away.

Rylic slid from his horse and ran out in front of her. "Well, I'll never escape the memories of you no matter where I go, and you sure don't need to go stay with Prince Algoron. I know the stories of Algoron."

"Then I'll travel alone and see all the world. Just go. Sail the seas and stay away from me," Alahandra said. "I'm leaving for good so you can forget me."

"I don't want to stay away from you. The memories of the curve of your face fill my mind. The memories of your lips on mine when I close my eyes. The memories of your laughter, your smile, your strength. You invade my every waking moment, and I never want to be without you," Rylic said, moving closer to her.

"I don't want to wonder when I'll see you again. I don't want to wait for you to decide to make port. I don't want to fear for you.

Please, Rylic. Please just go," Alahandra said.

"The only place I want to go is home. Home with you. I want to make a home with you. I don't want to leave you. Ever. I want to wake up each day and know I have your love. I want to go to sleep each night with you by my side. I want to kiss you whenever I want, and I want to make love to you for the rest of our lives. I want our children to have your smile. I want to know that from this moment forward, I can call you mine, and I'll be yours forever." He stepped closer and took her hands. "I want you to love me and tell me you love me all the time."

He slid his arms around her, and she began to cry. "I want to wipe away all the tears when you are sad, and find thousands of ways to make you happy. Please stay with me. Be my wife. Be the joy in my every day, and I will always love you."

"I feel that you'll regret being with me," she said.

"How could I regret anything when I'm in love with you."

"You love me?" She asked.

"Yes, woman!" Rylic said, and hugged her tightly.

Alahandra threw her arms around him. "Then, yes, I'll be your wife. Let's go home."

The light of the moon cloaked them in a quiet moment of love that Alahandra knew she would never forget.

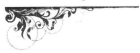

They arrived at Haya's and she quickly ran out of the door.

Alahandra ran to Haya and hugged her. "It seems that now we can really be family."

Haya looked at Rylic.

"My future wife," he said, motioning to Alahandra.

"So we can plan a wedding!" Haya clapped her hands.

Alahandra took Rylic's hand. "We were thinking about tomorrow. Maybe at sundown so we have time to do a few things to make it special."

Haya hugged them both. "Now, let's get Rylic moved in."

All five of them began taking Rylic's crates that Joab had unloaded on into Alahandra's house. Crates of clothes, treasure, and items Rylic had collected along the way. Hours passed, but just before midnight they were finished. Haya, Joab, and Bradford went to rest while Rylic and Alahandra sorted things.

"We might need a bigger house," Alahandra laughs.

"Can I help if I have so much gold?" Rylic smiled at her. He stood up and looked around. "I think I can store some of this in the barn until I can sort through it all."

"I think we could order a couple of extra chests and dressers. We can hang a lot of things on the walls, and put shelves up along that wall," Alahandra said, spinning around.

"I like that you're excited about this," Rylic said, standing up and taking her in his arms.

"I like being excited about us," Alahandra kissed him softly.

"Let's get up with the sun and go to town. We can ask around for decorations and see if all our friends would like to attend the wedding," Rylic said. "I'll go to Sero's and see if we can borrow the tables for our reception. Bradford is going to make our cake, and why are you staring at me?"

"I just can't believe you love me. We're getting married. Tomorrow," Alahandra laughed.

"We could go wake the minister if you'd like and go ahead," Rylic laughed.

"Oh, I'll wait." She kissed him gently. "I'll wait and have everyone see how wonderful you are."

He stopped smiling.

"What?" she asked.

"I want to make you happy, Alahandra."

"I have all I could ever dream," she whispered. "Let's rest and wake up on our wedding day."

She took his hand and led him to the bedroom. "Just think," she said, untying her dress, "one more night and you won't have to turn around or go into the other room when I change clothes."

"After making love to you all night, you still want me to turn away from you?" he asked.

"That didn't even feel real," she whispered.

"I can make you feel everything. We could practice right now," Rylic said, pulling her dress slowly from her shoulder and gently kissing her exposed skin.

She turned to him. "Tomorrow." She said louder and pushed him away. "I want to wait to have you again when you are my husband."

"Your husband," he smiled. "I've moved up in the ranking from pirate to husband."

"You'll always be my pirate." she said, kissing him gently.

"And I want you with all that I am," he said, kissing her on the neck.

She sighed heavily.

Once in bed Alahandra faced the window and watched the full moon. Rylic fell asleep quickly with his arm draped over her. What a turn the day took. He loved her. The only man that had ever truly seen her for who she really was. Someone wanting to be loved.

The sun rose and Rylic stretched. "Time to get up," he said, opening his eyes.

Alahandra raised up and turned to him. "Kiss me."

Rylic got out of bed quickly pulling her to her feet. "I will kiss you all day, all night, forever." He brushed his lips against hers.

After they were dressed they took the wagon into town to tell their friends about the wedding. They stopped at the mercantile, and ran to the door holding hands. "Derdria, Morris!" They yelled knocking on the door.

Dedria came to the front and unlocked the door. "Is everything okay?" She asked, looking at their hands clasped together.

"I'm marrying my beautiful man," Alahandra said.

"Oh my dear, that's wonderful! When is the big day?" Dedria asked.

Rylic and Alahandra looked at each other. "Today!" Alahandra said loudly.

"Today? Well, then we have work to do! I'll help spread the word," Dedria said.

Rylic took her hand and they went across the street to Sero's. Bradford was there making the cake. Sero's wife saw them coming and ran out to meet them.

"We'll bring the tables out in the afternoon along with all the chairs. I'm going to run to the dress shop and see if they can open early to get you a wedding dress," Jilla said.

"Oh, I haven't thought about a dress," Alahandra said.

"Tell the owner I'll pay her later, to give Alahandra whatever she wants," Rylic took her hand and kissed it as she started to walk away.

Alahandra slowly slid her hand from his and smiled as she left out of the door.

The street began to fill with people, and all who passed her told her happy wedding day. News was spreading fast about her happy day, and Rylic's crew helped all day wherever they were needed.

Mrs. Martin came running up to her. "Oh, Alahandra, is there anything I can do?"

"Do you think you could find flowers for me to hold? I forgot about flowers until I saw you," Alahandra said. "Oh, and would you save a dance for Mr. Troy, Alexander's father?"

"You know, I just might do that!" Mrs. Martin laughed. "Oh, sweet friend, I'll go get you lots of flowers! I'm so excited. Love you! Have fun! I'll see you soon!" Mrs. Martin said, walking away really fast.

Alahandra stopped abruptly as she took in the moment. Mrs. Martin said she loved her. She had real friends, and they cared about her. She looked around at the people moving along the street. People greeted her or smiled at her. For the first time home had meaning.

The day moved on and preparations were made, it seemed that everyone wanted to help. After leaving Rylic in Sero's, Alahandra had not seen him for most of the time in town. She came out of the mercantile and saw him talking with the minister. He waved to her and walked quickly to her.

"Hello, my bride to be. Your smile lights up this entire street."

Alahandra hugged him tightly and sighed happily. "Such a fun day. I'm going to head back home to bathe and get ready."

"I'll send Bradford to pick you up when it's time," he squeezed her hand.

"I'll be back soon. I can't wait," she said, kissing him gently.

The sun moved into the western sky and the light began to fade. Flowers and candles were placed on tables all around the center of town. The band was set up as they do for the town celebrations. The dance area was cleared. Lanterns were hung in the trees and placed all around the steps of the church where they were to stand.

Bradford and Haya arrive at the homestead to pick up Alahandra. She walked out the door and Haya gasped.

"Oh, Alahandra, you are stunning."

"I feel beautiful, and I can't wait to marry your son," Alahandra said.

"You'll officially be my daughter," Haya said. Her eyes began to tear up.

"Stop. You're going to make me cry," she said, climbing in the wagon.

Haya hugged her and they both shed a tear.

"You two save your tears for later, we have a wedding party to get to," Bradford said.

As they rode into the opening at the end of town, Alahandra noticed all the lights. The band began to play and all their friends began to line the street. The wagon pulled through slowly and everyone waved at her. Rylic was waiting for her on the steps of the church, and Bradford pulled up close beside him.

Rylic extended his hand to help her from the wagon. As she climbed down he saw the tears in her eyes. He kissed her on the cheek. "I'm terrified," he said.

"Of what?" she asked.

"Waking up," he said, wiping the tear from under her eye.

She kissed him on the cheek.

Mrs. Martin walked up to her and handed her a bouquet of flowers.

"Are all these flowers from your home?" Alahandra asked.

"Yes, from my garden, and everyone has helped to make your day special. We love you. We love your friendship, and we couldn't be happier," She kissed Alahandra on the cheek.

Haya, Bradford, and Joab came to stand at the bottom of the stairs.

Rylic offered his arm to Alahandra. "Shall we?"

She took his arm and they walked up the stairs. The lanterns that hung around the entrance illuminated them.

"I feel like I'm in a dream," Rylic said.

"Then let's not wake up," Alahandra said.

The minister began to speak and Alahandra was lost in the words staring at Rylic. When the minister completed the ceremony, Rylic turned and took Alahandra in his arms and kissed her gently. She put her arms around his neck and pulled him close.

Everyone cheered and clapped, as the couple made their way into the crowd. The band began to play softly, and everyone parted. Rylic took Alahandra's hand and spun her out away from him. Everyone cheered again. She twirled back in and he caught her, dipping her low, and he kissed her gently.

The songs continued as everyone joined in. Haya and Bradford twirled by them. She noticed Mr. Troy with Mrs. Martin. They both looked at her and smiled. She nodded to them. Joab and Eddie ran by laughing. Dedria and Morris danced and smiled at each other. Sero kissed Jilla on the cheek as he served food on the table in front of his restaurant. Alahandra looked around at all the people who cared for them. Cared for her. Joy overwhelmed her in that moment. Her life once filled with so much tragedy was more beautiful than she could have ever imagined.

"I have a surprise for you," Rylic said. "We'll have to walk to the pier."

"What did you do?" she said, taking his hand.

They walked along closely. He whispered. "Just a little more. Close your eyes."

Alahandra could hear the waves on the docks.

"We're here. You can look."

Anchored by the docks was a small ship with the name The Alahandra painted on the side.

"Your very own. Time to teach you to sail," he whispered.

She turned to him, "I love you."

He turned to hold her. "And that's what makes this our happy ending. I love you, my bride."

"And that," she smiled and kissed him gently, "is what makes this our happy beginning."

Made in the USA
Columbia, SC
22 November 2024

47329939R00136